SAFE HARBOR

a novel

PAMELA CARRINGTON REID

Covenant Communications, Inc.

Covenant®

Cover image by Tyler Moulton

Cover design copyrighted 2004 by Covenant Communications, Inc.

Published by Covenant Communications, Inc.
American Fork, Utah

Printed in Canada
First Printing: July 2004

11 10 09 08 07 06 05 04   10 9 8 7 6 5 4 3 2 1

ISBN 1-59156-538-3

Dedication

To my husband Paul, who constantly inspires me.
To Tina, who makes me feel I can achieve anything.
To my children and granddaughter, Olivia,
who make all the effort worthwhile.

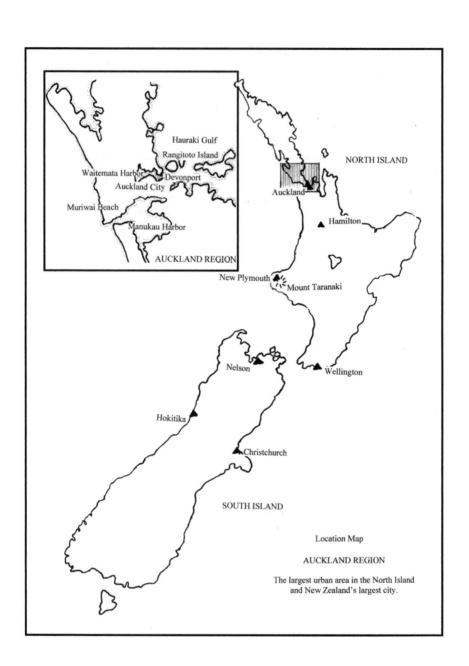

Hauraki Gulf

Rangitoto Island

Waitemata Harbor

Devonport

Auckland City

Muriwai Beach

Manukau Harbor

AUCKLAND REGION

NORTH ISLAND

Auckland

▲ Hamilton

New Plymouth

Mount Taranaki

Nelson

▲ Wellington

Hokitika

▲ Christchurch

SOUTH ISLAND

Location Map

AUCKLAND REGION

The largest urban area in the North Island
and New Zealand's largest city.

CHAPTER 1

"Still an hour to go. Good timing." As she glanced at her wristwatch, Meredith congratulated herself on having enough time for a run before her shift. She reached into the backseat of her car for the silver sun-protector mat. She unrolled it and spread it across the front windshield of the VW, taking another quick look at the sky as she tucked the mat firmly in at the corners. "Not that there's going to be much sun today," she said to herself.

With a few deft movements, she'd fixed the screen in place, picked up her backpack, locked the car, and was heading across the rough, sandy parking area toward the Muriwai Beach lifeguard clubhouse. She noted the old, red jeep parked at an erratic angle to the wooden barrier bars and smiled.

"Good old Mitch. At least duty won't be boring."

It always made a difference to be on surf patrol with someone you enjoyed being with, especially in these last days of summer when there were usually only a few swimmers and the patrol hours seemed to last longer.

"Hey, Meredith! You're early!" Mitch Savage called as he strolled out of the clubhouse with a piece of toast in each hand. "Couldn't wait to see me, eh?"

He settled himself on a wooden bench with one piece of toast on his knee while he sunk his teeth into the other—a thick layer of bread, butter, and slices of tomato.

"Absolutely," Meredith grinned as she crossed the grassed clearing and stopped beside the bench. "It just makes my day to know you're my patrol buddy."

"Ah, I knew it was a wise move switching with Terry." Mitch licked his fingers. "It was even worth doing a double shift yesterday and today."

"You're just a glutton for punishment," Meredith laughed. "Did anyone else stay?"

"Nope . . . just me. I should've called you. It gets pretty lonely down here." Mitch raised a hopeful eyebrow, but Meredith just laughed.

"Oh, you're a big boy." She rested her backpack on the bench and patted the tight, sandy-colored curls on his head. "Besides, I was fast asleep. I worked all day at the bakery, and I crashed as soon as I got to the cottage."

"Well, at least if you fail as a lawyer, you could start your own bakery. You spend enough time there," Mitch joked as he stood up, but then stopped smiling as Meredith faced him, eyebrow raised, and poked a straight finger at his chest.

"I am not going to fail as a lawyer, Mitch Savage. I know you guys think it's a bit of a laugh, but I am going to be a really good lawyer, and one day you'll come begging me for help."

She poked his chest once more for emphasis as Mitch raised his hands in mock surrender, but his tone was serious as he studied her face.

"Hey, I believe you, Meredith. Honest . . . and if I should ever need a lawyer, you'd be the first person I'd choose. You Mormons are as honest as the day is long."

Meredith smiled her forgiveness and folded her arms. "Well, at least I'll have one client. Now, tell me what's been happening up here. And do I need to do anything before I go for a run? I want to do a couple of lengths of the beach before we start duty, and you can probably devour another loaf of bread with tomatoes. Yuck." She pulled a face.

"Yep, I should just about be finished in time for patrol at ten." Mitch patted his stomach, then glanced up at the dark clouds gathering. "You'd better hurry with the run before the weather sets in."

Meredith nodded. "I'll run a few lengths, then I can swim later. I need to get ready for the final beach carnival next week." She turned toward the clubhouse with her gear. "I'll be starving when I'm done. Try to save me some toast."

"Oh, that's right! I nearly forgot." Mitch smacked his forehead with the palm of his hand. "Speaking of saving . . . you missed the drama up here yesterday."

She was immediately concerned. "What drama? Was someone hurt?"

"Not hurt, but we almost lost a couple of people." Mitch shook his head, remembering. "I was up on tower duty with Dave and there was hardly anyone on the beach. Then all at once, Robyn rushes up to say that a young boy had gotten swept off the rocks over by the Gannet Colony. We rushed off to that and managed to get him in. Then, after we'd just got back to the tower, some girl runs up and reckons a guy is trying to drown himself down the other end of the beach, by the old tree—she saw him go in fully clothed and he'd just kept on swimming."

"And was she right?" Meredith frowned, thinking about the merciless riptide that often developed at that part of the beach. It could pull even the strongest surfer and his board out to sea very quickly.

Mitch nodded. "Apparently. We checked with the binoculars and we could just see a body floating way out down by the old tree root. We couldn't tell what state he was in, so Dave ran down with the tube and I got the surf ski." He shook his head. "It's amazing how the adrenaline gets you going. We got out there pretty fast."

"You got him in time?" Meredith frowned. "You said you nearly lost them."

Mitch nodded. "Dave had got to him, but apparently he gave Dave a bit of a struggle. I don't know what Dave did, but the guy was out cold when I got there, and then I brought him in on the ski."

"Did he take long to come 'round?"

"No, just a few minutes." Mitch frowned. "But I'll tell you what . . . he sure wasn't grateful when he did come to. I helped him up to the dry sand and tried to ask him a few questions, but he wasn't responding at all. Then I suggested we go over to the clubhouse so I could check for shock, and he just looked at me really hard. Then he told me that I'd 'done quite enough, thank you.' He sat for a while, then went off to his car."

"And then he just left?"

"No, I followed a bit behind him and saw which car he was in, and I checked on him a few times before he drove away a while later." Mitch drew a deep breath. "So . . . you missed quite a session."

Meredith nodded slowly. "Isn't it weird how we keep training and being here in case something happens, and it's almost exciting when something does happen, but at the same time it's terrible to actually use our training because it means someone could be injured or dying." She shivered slightly and rubbed the sudden goose bumps on her arms. "I'm so glad the little boy was all right . . . and the man as well. I just hope he doesn't try anything else when someone isn't there to help him."

Mitch leaned over and gave her a hug as she shivered again. "I know what you mean. It was amazing to help those people, especially the boy and his folks. They were so grateful. It made everything feel really worthwhile."

They were both silent for a moment, then Meredith leaned her head on Mitch's shoulder. "I'm glad you were there for them. You're a good man, Mitch." She took a deep breath and straightened up. "Now I need to go run and think about everything. See you soon, buddy."

Mitch watched as she made her way over the sandy ridge in front of the surf club. Even in her baggy red nylon jacket and shorts with her cap pulled down firmly over her thick brown hair, she looked trim and vital, her tanned legs sporting well-defined muscles from long hours of swimming and training in the summer sun. He shook his head as he wandered inside.

"Meredith's patrol buddy. Ah well, I can think of worse things to be."

Pausing by the patrol tower at the top of the black sand dune, Meredith stood with her hands on her hips, doing her customary sweeping inspection of the wide expanse of black-iron sand, dunes, and rugged surf that made up Muriwai Beach. The beach was relatively deserted, since school holidays had finished a few days before; now, the chatter of people and random music of portable players were replaced by the occasional strident call of a seagull. Even the regular sound of the surf was diminished because the tide was only cresting halfway up the beach.

The wind blowing from offshore whipped her shoulder-length hair around and swirled it under her chin. She quickly used a hair tie from her wrist to twist it up into a ponytail, then pulled her cap down even more firmly over her forehead. Still, the wind tugged at her, so she pushed her sunglasses back onto the bridge of her nose and bent her head into the wind as she began to jog along the sand that had been left wet and packed hard by the earlier high tide.

As always when she ran, Meredith began to feel a sense of exhilaration as the fresh air rejuvenated her lungs and mind. She passed the familiar red-and-yellow patrol flag that Mitch would have put out earlier and felt once again a sense of gratitude at being involved in the Surf Life-Saving Program. *No deaths between the flags since the association started,* she thought. It was good to know that her hobby actually helped save lives—and then there was the additional sheer enjoyment of surf, sand, and open spaces. She breathed in again deeply. It was good. Life was good.

A few minutes along the beach, she drew near the twisted black-and-gray skeleton of a large tree root that years before had been left high on the beach by a turbulent tide. The sand at this part of the beach was just drying out from the rain a couple of days ago, and in the still-damp sand she could just make out a single set of footprints leading down to the tree from the dune and then continuing toward the surf. They were suddenly obliterated where the high tide had washed the impression away, and there was no returning set. *Of course. They must have pulled him out closer to the surf club,* Meredith reasoned. But that such evidence of yesterday's drama was so starkly preserved somehow chilled her—though her thoughts remained positive, if more contemplative.

She slowed and studied the prints, then stopped and pressed her foot into the sand beside one of them. *Yesterday that footprint was made by a man who wanted to give up his life, and yet I can stand in the same spot today and feel that life is really good.*

She took a deep breath and stared out to the ocean. The waves were fairly small and even, rolling in a continuous flow along the expanse of the beach, the deep green of the waves interspersed with moving swaths of white froth. She stared a while longer at the horizon where the deep, dark green of the ocean created a flawless line against the pale gray-blue of the sky. At times like this, when she stopped to notice the vastness of the world, she could really appreciate the creation and the gospel concept of a plan for mankind. *Heavenly Father really is amazing . . . His creations are amazing. If only everybody in the world could appreciate them . . . and the lives they've been given.* But her mood changed slightly as she thought about the things that didn't make sense with God's plan—and why people maybe didn't feel peace. She thought for a moment about some cases she had studied—cases of parents abusing their children, cases of rape, fraud, and divorce.

All her life she had lived with parents who loved each other and their family, and stressed the importance of integrity. Most of the people they associated with had lived the same way. It had been a shock to move to the city, where she realized things weren't always so easy with families. And when Meredith started to study law, she read about terrible things people did to each other, seemingly without conscience, things she had difficulty reconciling with the protective care of a loving God. She'd found herself beginning to scrutinize people at church and the university, and she began to doubt that the gospel could really change people . . . that law and order and punishment were probably more effective.

With a final glance at the twisted tree and the footprints, Meredith began to run again.

* * *

"That's what . . . I needed," Meredith panted as she kicked hard at the punching bag, then spun and kicked with the other foot. Mitch stood behind the bag, keeping it straight. "A really good workout gets . . . rid of so . . . much anxiety."

"And what are you anxious about? Your dough not rising at the bakery?"

Meredith grinned, then punched hard with her left fist. "Actually . . . it's starting school again. This is for that professor who gave me a C last year," she said as she punched again.

Mitch peered around the bag. "You're a funny girl. You always seem an unlikely person to be doing all this martial arts and fitness stuff. You're way too . . . feminine."

"I'll take that as . . . a compliment," she puffed as she ran through another kicking sequence.

"But it's a bit deceptive for unsuspecting guys."

"Meaning?"

"Well, take poor Barry the other night. He didn't know what hit him."

Meredith stopped and dropped her hands to her sides. "That man is a leech. He deserved what he got."

"He was drunk!"

"Exactly!" Meredith shook her head vehemently. "He shouldn't have been."

"But we don't all have the same standards as you, Meredith. You were the only one in the whole place that wasn't drinking, and he was just being . . . friendly."

"Friendly? He attacked me!" She punched at the bag indignantly.

"And you flattened him."

"The only thing that kept him on the ground was his pride, Mitch. The longer he stayed down, the more sympathy he got. I barely touched him."

"So you could've hurt him more?"

"Much more." She bit her lip. "I didn't want to hurt him, but my memories are still vivid. And when I feel a man touch me like that . . ." She shuddered. "Never again, Mitch."

"I understand that, Meredith," Mitch answered quietly and swung the bag to the side. "But no one else does. To them, you're just an uptight Mormon."

"Well, let them think what they like." Meredith shrugged her shoulders. "Maybe I can't break the 'immoral surf lifeguard' image, but I don't intend to be part of it."

"Ouch, I'd take that as an insult . . . if I had half the chance." Mitch laughed but Meredith knew he wasn't being unkind. In fact, of all the people at the surf club, Mitch was the one who had proved to be a true friend since she had ventured on the scene last year after moving up from Taranaki.

"Now, I reckon that's enough practice at man-flattening for one day." He pointed to the clock on the wall. "We need to get out on patrol."

Meredith slipped on the red-and-yellow patrol cap, tying the strings under her chin, then letting the cap hang around her neck. The sun was actually making a valiant effort to shine and the wind had dropped, but she kept her shorts on over her red swimsuit as she went down to the beach again. A few more people, mainly teenagers, had appeared with the sunshine.

It only took a minute to wave some swimmers inside the flagged area and to ensure they were keeping clear of the tidal rip that had developed. Then she walked back up to the wooden patrol tower where Mitch was settling down for a few hours of watching.

"So, what are you going to do this year?" Meredith sat down beside him on the seat running along the edge of the balcony. "Any more building projects lined up?"

"Not really." Mitch shook his head. "Actually, I was thinking I might do the big 'OE.' Dad's got some more houses ready to start, but I'm getting a bit tired of building. It's all I've done since I left school, and I want to take some time out and go overseas."

"The great Kiwi overseas experience." Meredith nodded. "I loved my year away in Europe. I did so many different things that I'd never have thought of doing here . . . but it was still good to get back home again. Being away helped me realize how much I love it in New Zealand."

"But see, you've had the opportunity. I want to go now, before I get too old and settled."

"Well, it certainly helped give me a different perspective." Meredith picked up the binoculars. "I always knew I wanted to be a lawyer, but somehow the thought of going straight to university after high school just didn't appeal. When I came back from Europe I was so much more inclined to work and study . . . so much more focused."

She put the binoculars up to her eyes and scanned the beach, unaware of Mitch studying her carefully.

"Meredith . . . would you ever seriously consider dating anyone who didn't go to your church?"

Mitch's question was quietly spoken and completely unexpected, and as Meredith slowly lowered the binoculars, she didn't look at him but fixed her gaze on the blackness of the sand dune that rose beside the tower. Finally she turned and spoke thoughtfully.

"I guess I might . . . if they really seriously considered finding out more about my beliefs first."

"So that's the prerequisite?" Mitch gave a short laugh. "No trial runs?"

She shrugged and smiled shyly. "I've never really met anybody that has made me want to question my decision . . . or consider any trial runs."

"Nobody . . . ?" Mitch raised one sandy-colored eyebrow and pretended to look crestfallen. "Not even a good friend?"

Meredith smiled. Mitch was a good friend and one of the kindest men she had ever met, in or out of the Church. Her eyes glistened warmly as she laid a hand on his arm. "Well, maybe a really, really good friend."

* * *

"Oh, my goodness, what did he say next? Did anything happen?"

"Nothing really," Meredith shook her head at the expectant expression on her friend Telesia's face. "He just gave me a hug and said we'd better clean up the patrol room. Although we did go out to dinner and a movie after we'd finished duty." *And he kissed me good night . . . and I really liked it,* she added silently.

The two girls sat in silence, enjoying the last few minutes of lunchtime sunshine before going back to afternoon lectures. The carefully manicured grass areas of Albert Park were dotted with students lying down or sitting alone and in groups. It was only their second day back at Auckland University after the summer vacation and many students had opted to spend their time outside rather than in the library or the student café.

Meredith sat cross-legged, playing with the blades of bright green grass that tickled at her legs. She began to visualize Mitch's face and his strong body that had saved two lives that weekend.

"Would you go out with him?" Telesia frowned. "I mean, he sounds like a very nice person, but . . ."

"But he's not a member of the Church. Its okay, Sia . . ." Meredith picked up the morning newspaper that lay between them. "I'm not about to compromise my ideals . . . it's just that . . ." She hesitated and Telesia looked at her quickly.

"Just what, Mele?"

Meredith smiled absently at the easy way Telesia used the Samoan form of her name. She'd known Telesia Leota for over a year now, and they had become firm friends while studying law together. Telesia had moved to Auckland with her family from Samoa when she was twelve and, like Meredith, she was determined to become a successful lawyer. The girls had quickly found out that they were both members of the Church, and although they didn't belong to the same ward, they had attended off-campus institute classes and activities together.

"It's just that . . . sometimes I sit at church and I don't really see anyone there that I want to date, either. In fact, Mitch appeals much more." She gave a short laugh and pointed at the front page of the paper. "Anyway, enough of that stuff . . . Did you see this picture? It's the little boy that Mitch and Dave rescued at Muriwai, with his parents. They look so happy, don't they?"

"Wouldn't you be? After almost losing someone so close." Telesia shuddered. "I don't even want to think about losing someone I loved like that."

Meredith nodded as she quickly perused the remaining pages of the front section.

"What are you looking for?" Telesia began to pack her books into her bag.

"Um . . . just looking in case there's a mention of the other guy they pulled out of the water. He didn't want to be saved, and I keep thinking he might have tried something else . . . dangerous." She frowned. "It's funny . . . ever since Mitch told me about him . . . I've just found myself hoping that he's all right."

"Well, it's not like you can do anything now." Telesia brought both hands up to the sides of her head and pulled her perennially springy black hair up into a knot, twisted it several times, and left it, its curliness forming its own locking device. "Now, you need to put these thoughts behind you and get on with your studies, my friend."

"I guess so," Meredith sighed and began to gather up her books. "I wonder why professors don't get a bit smarter and put Criminal Law after lunch, instead of Legal Research. At least we'd stay awake a bit longer."

Telesia laughed as she stood up and offered her hand to help Meredith to her feet.

"I agree, but you know what's really sad? It's only the second day of the year and we're already complaining."

They laughed together as they walked out of the park and made their way past the ornate Victorian Clock Tower and down Waterloo Quadrant.

"I wonder why they built the law buildings so far off campus." Meredith glanced both ways as they crossed to Parliament Street.

"It's so we can be continually motivated by the awe-inspiring presence of the High Court," Telesia dropped her voice to a droll tone and waved her arm toward the vintage building beside them.

"Amazing to think we might even work there one day."

Meredith glanced up at the intricate cornices and high, vaulted doors.

"Not *might*, my girl. We *will!*"

"What if it were against each other?" Meredith's eyes widened.

"Oh, I'll take it easy on you," Telesia giggled. "Until I become a judge, then I'll have you begging for mercy."

"Oh, you snob!"

"No, I'm a prophetess," Telesia retorted loftily as they pushed open the door of the Davis Building and made their way upstairs to the lecture room. "And speaking of prophets . . . are you coming to the CES fireside on Sunday night? I think it's one with the First Presidency on the video."

Meredith hesitated before she shook her head. "You know . . . I think I'll pass on this one."

"But it's the first one for the year." Telesia frowned. "You don't want to get into bad habits straight off, and you already missed a few at the end of last year."

"I know. And I won't get into bad habits." Meredith shrugged. "I just want to get myself organized, and I have a photo album project that I need to finish, and a skirt to finish sewing before I get into studying." *And Mitch said he was going to call around eight o'clock.*

"Aah . . . you mean you're going to let worldly things interfere with your spiritual growth?" Telesia rolled her eyes ominously and laughed, but there was a concerned undertone as she watched her friend.

"No," Meredith shook her head. "I just don't feel like going right now while I'm getting organized. I really want to focus this year . . . I'm not going to settle for any more C grades."

Her friend stopped by the lecture room door.

"Mele, have you been to church much over the vacation?"

"Yes, I went with my parents at Christmas," Meredith started defensively, then shrugged. "But I guess I haven't been much since I got back. It's just that . . . at home, I know everybody and was totally involved but, up here . . . I've been here a year and I've only had an assignment to teach in Primary while a teacher was away for four weeks. I don't feel like there's much point in turning up every week."

Telesia regarded her kindly. "Maybe they're trying to give you more time for your studies. They don't have many lawyers or even would-be lawyers in your ward." She pushed the door open.

"But I'm so much better with having something to do . . . especially teaching since it helps me read the scriptures more." Meredith shook her head. "Okay, I'll be straight with you. I never used to have a problem with my testimony, but . . . I'm starting to really doubt some things. Not Heavenly Father's love or the gospel plan in general—just what I'm supposed to be doing with my own life."

Telesia nodded quietly and said, "Well, let's talk about it after class."

CHAPTER 2

"Son, where are you? Are you downstairs?"

Grant Bascombe turned his head slightly as his father called from upstairs, then he pressed his fingertips together, leaned his head back against the oxblood leather armchair, and ignored the question.

"Grant?" The voice sounded more urgent, and he could hear his father's footsteps on the wooden staircase. "Where are you, son?"

"I'm in here, Dad." He closed his eyes. Just as much as he wanted solitude, his father seemed to need company.

The study door opened and Frank Bascombe stood with his hand on the doorknob. "Ah, there you are. I was just wondering."

"I'm right here, Dad, with no place else to go, and no one to go with."

There was one of the long silences that had become so common of late as both men struggled to find something to say. Frank walked across to the bay window that faced the open expanse of ocean and Rangitoto Island. He stood with his hands behind his back, watching tiny yachts dance their way across a deep, green-blue harbor, nimble white triangles against the dark conical dome of the island.

"I've been thinking, son." He spoke directly to the window pane and Grant waited. "It's time we got back to work. Our clients need us." He waited for a response but there wasn't one. "It's been nearly two months now . . ."

Grant slowly stood up as his father's emotions got the better of him.

"And what good are we going to do our clients if we can't even speak to each other without breaking down. I'm sorry, Dad, I just don't know that I'm ready yet."

Frank turned and watched his son walk to the desk. They weren't really alike physically, as Grant had inherited his mother's slim build and dark hair compared to Frank's stockiness and his once-sandy hair now turned a thick, silvery gray, but their personalities were similar enough for Frank to understand his son's way of coping with distress.

Grant picked up a silver diptych photo frame from the desk and stared at it for a long time. One side held an image of a slender, older woman whose faint wrinkles were mostly laugh lines and whose tanned face was framed by silvery hair cut into a neat bob. On the other side of the frame, a young mother with wavy, shoulder-length red hair proudly held a very young baby. The child was dressed in a pink, ruffled dress and had a tiny pink bow stuck to her almost-bald head.

"It was bad enough losing Mum. After all those months when she was so sick, I was almost prepared for it." He stopped and looked straight at his father, then his voice became a ragged choke. "But I can't get Hannah and Emily off my mind. I killed them, Dad. I killed my wife and my baby girl, and I can't just forget that."

Frank watched his son's shoulders droop, and his first instinct was to try to comfort him again; then he remembered Barbara's words just before she'd lost her long-fought battle with the cancer. *Be tough, Frank. You've got to keep going. There's so much to do and I'll always be there with you and the boys, even if you can't see me. I just know it.*

"Grant, that's enough." He was surprised at the firmness of his own voice. "Do you think Hannah would want you moping around like this? I don't think so, and your mother certainly wouldn't let you if she were here."

The determined tone took his son by surprise and Frank watched as Grant blinked away tears, then put the frame down.

"Your mother made me promise that I would keep going, son, and I have to keep that promise. We can pull each other down with our grief, or we can save each other from drowning in it."

He waited for a reaction, and Grant's slow answer surprised him.

"I nearly did that, too, Dad," he responded flatly.

"Pardon?"

"Drowned." Grant's voice was monotone. "I tried that, too."

Frank felt a coldness grip his chest as he tried to comprehend his son's words.

"I'm sorry? You mean . . ."

"I tried to drown. I swam until I couldn't swim anymore." His voice dropped. "I just wanted to be with them so much, with Hannah and Emily. And I nearly made it."

Frank licked his lips and tried to swallow the lump in his throat. "What happened? When was this?"

Grant ran his finger back and forth around the edge of the frame. "About three weeks ago. I drove out to Muriwai . . . I don't know why . . . to just relive the times Hannah and I had there together, I guess. But when I got there, I felt so empty. I sat for ages and all I could feel was . . . how much I wanted to hold my wife and my baby again." He turned the frame away. "So, I just swam until I was exhausted, and then I just let go. I nearly made it. I remember . . . a warm feeling of peace . . . but then I was being pulled back by a lifeguard."

Frank waited, chilled by the cold flatness of his son's words.

"I tried to fight. I really didn't want to come back . . ."

"You fought?" Frank couldn't keep the disbelief out of his voice.

"I really don't know. I just remember not wanting to leave that . . . that light, and then struggling, and then . . . darkness." He shook his head. "I was so angry when I came to."

"What did the lifeguard do?"

"He tried to talk to me but I just took off." Grant looked despairingly at his father. "I've been frustrated ever since. Why didn't he just leave me?"

His father waited as he digested the new information, then he reached out and rested his hand on Grant's shoulder. "I wonder what Grant Bascombe would do if he saw someone drowning . . . with no time to ask questions. Whatever you might feel, son, I'll always be grateful to that lifeguard. I don't know if I could have coped with losing you as well."

There was another long silence, and Frank dropped his hand to his side.

Grant stared at the desk, then turned and, without speaking, the two men embraced. Finally, Frank drew back and cleared his throat.

"You know, your mother was always more . . . religious than me. She seemed to have so much faith that everything would be all right . . . after she'd gone. She told me she'd always be here for us, and I've always believed her. I can't help thinking that Hannah and Emily are here too, and they'd want you to have a second chance."

Grant nodded and looked slowly around the room as if absorbing the reality of it all. His father was right. His mother had always taught him that God would look after him, and even when he had rebelled against the concept as a teenager, she had continued to reassure him of her prayers for him. Marrying Hannah and witnessing the birth of their daughter had brought about a sudden return to his mother's faith, but now . . . his gaze rested once more on the photo frame. They were all gone . . .

"I'll try to believe that, Dad." Grant tapped his finger on the desk. "I'm not sure I can anymore . . . but I'll try." He looked up. "And . . . thanks for letting me stay here . . . it really has helped. Those first days at the apartment were just so empty. I kept waiting to hear Emily laugh or Hannah talking to her—" He broke off.

"I know what you mean." Frank took a deep breath. "I hated the hollowness . . ."

His son was silent, so Frank finished, "It's a huge house, Grant . . . you can stay as long as you want." He was about to leave, but then cleared his throat. "And Grant . . . maybe we should talk to somebody . . . professionally . . . to help us through all this."

Grant continued to stare at the desk, then he slowly nodded.

"Maybe we should."

CHAPTER 3

Meredith pulled at the metal stand until the wet sand loosened its grip and relinquished the patrol flag. She carried it up the beach, the wind still tugging at the flag so that the stand bucked in her hands. Typically, the Auckland weather had changed abruptly from brilliant sunshine to heavily overcast and windy. Surfers and swimmers were beginning to make their way out of the water, and she knew from experience that the beach would be nearly deserted within the hour.

She reached the clubhouse and stowed the flag in the side room, then quickly checked that all the equipment was there. On a Sunday afternoon, she knew there was more chance of things being left out after the weekend's activity.

Sunday afternoon. She glanced at her watch—4:15. Her ward would just have finished their three-hour block. A few brief images came to mind of sacrament meeting and Relief Society. *I wonder if they miss me at all?* The young adults group might. *No, they'll notice I'm not there, but they won't really miss me. And I don't really miss them. If I were back at home it'd be different.*

But she wasn't home in Taranaki, and when Rob had called her about the emergency replacement of an injured lifeguard on the Sunday shift, she'd only hesitated briefly. *Besides, I do more good out here at the beach than sitting in a classroom just talking about being of service.*

"Meredith!" She turned at the sound of Mitch's voice in the doorway behind her. "Did you hear about the letter?"

"What letter?"

"Obviously you didn't." Mitch folded his arms as he leaned against the doorjamb. "The club captain received a letter this week along with a check for several thousand dollars."

He nodded at her look of surprise. "The letter was expressing appreciation to the anonymous lifeguard who saved his son's life a few weeks ago."

"Was it your man?"

"It must've been. The man's parents knew who we were and we haven't had any other rescues lately."

Meredith was silent, then she frowned. "And it was the father that wrote it?"

Mitch nodded. "I guess the son must still be alive if the father has only just written the letter. At least he must have finally talked to his old man about it."

"But I wonder if he's still upset. It would be so horrible if he tried again."

"Well, we did what we could." Mitch shrugged as he walked into the room. "Haven't you nearly finished?"

"Mm-hmm." Meredith smiled, suddenly aware of how broad his shoulders were in the small room. "There's not much to do except make sure the seagulls don't collide."

"So would you like to go out for a hamburger?" Mitch wiggled one sandy eyebrow. "I'll pay so you don't have to buy anything on Sunday."

Meredith laughed self-consciously as she grasped a clipboard across her chest. There was another fireside on tonight, and she knew Telesia was expecting her to go. She looked at the clock. She'd probably be late at this point anyway.

"Okay . . . you've twisted my arm, Mr. Savage." She rested her chin on top of the board. "Let's celebrate the safety of our mystery man and the generous donation for your services rendered."

* * *

Meredith sighed and, leaning back in her chair, patted her stomach contentedly.

"That was good. I'm glad you suggested it."

"I'm glad you came with me," Mitch agreed, smiling as he finished off the last bite of his burger. "Oh." He swallowed before continuing. "You left your jacket in my car the other day when I gave you that ride home. For some reason I took it inside, and then I forgot to bring it with me to the club. Do you have time to follow me to my flat to retrieve it? The weather seems to be turning worse—you might need it before I see you again."

Meredith didn't even hesitate. She'd already blown off the fireside, and she liked spending time with Mitch. Especially lately, as they had become closer over the past few weeks. It only took a few minutes to reach Mitch's apartment, and Meredith followed him upstairs. They'd been there a number of times together with his flatmates, and she smiled as she glanced around the room at the piles of magazines and weight lifting gear.

"I think everything is exactly where it was when I was here last week." She smiled as he handed her the jacket.

"Probably." He grinned as he glanced around. "Including that game of chess we never finished. Do you still want to try and beat me?"

"Now?"

"Why not?" Mitch moved some books off the couch and cleared a magazine off the chessboard. "I'll get us some soda while you figure out your next move."

An hour later she'd won, but she wasn't sure if it was because he'd let her.

"You let me have that last move." She sat back against the cushions. "I could have beaten you fair and square."

"But then I would have felt beaten by a woman." He grinned as he laid his arm along the back of the couch behind her head and rested his hand on her shoulder. "This way I feel generous and you'll want a rematch."

Meredith smiled and leaned her head against his arm, enjoying his company and the fact that she didn't immediately stiffen at his touch. They sat quietly for a few moments, then Mitch pointed toward her jacket lying on a chair by the door.

"Well, there's your jacket." His voice had a regretful tone to it. "I suppose you'd better get home."

"I guess so," Meredith sighed and closed her eyes. "School tomorrow and another test. There's no rest for the wicked."

"I can't imagine anyone less wicked than you, Meredith Winstone." Mitch's voice was surprisingly gentle, and she opened her eyes to find him looking straight at her.

He hesitated at first, then took her hand as it lay on her lap.

"I'm going away soon." He didn't look at her. "I've bought my ticket."

"How soon?" She felt her heart beat faster.

"Two weeks."

"Oh, Mitch." She couldn't keep the dismay out of her voice and her fingers closed around his. "I'm going to miss you so much."

He pulled her against his shoulder and gave her a tight squeeze.

"Same here. I've learnt a lot about myself through our talks. You're a different girl, Meredith. A very good different."

She felt the tears coming as she turned her head and studied his face, the kind brown eyes and generous smattering of freckles. Her hand trembled slightly as she reached up and traced some of the freckles, then she pulled his head toward hers for a kiss.

CHAPTER 4

Mitch Savage. Meredith smiled reminiscently. It had been over two years now since he'd left New Zealand to travel overseas . . . since they'd agreed to go their separate ways. *Three years since I attended church.* She pursed her lips, remembering. They had been as close as friends could be, and Mitch had even attended functions at church with her. They'd laughed and joked and enjoyed lots of activities with Mitch's friends as well. She didn't blame Mitch, but their easy relationship had eventually just crumbled as a result of that fond goodnight kiss that had become more than they'd both intended. Meredith closed her eyes, replaying the imaginary interview she had often rehearsed since. *Not that anything major happened, Dad . . . just enough to make me feel a bit guilty about taking the sacrament. But it was the way people looked at me when I passed the sacrament tray on . . . like they were all seeing a different person . . . a corrupt person . . . and imagining what I'd been up to . . . even though some of them were probably doing things far worse,* she finished bitterly. She loosened her grip on the black robe where her hand had tightened. *I wonder where you're at, Mitch . . . because our friendship certainly changed my life.*

It was twelve thirty. She felt sudden panic as she fluffed out a clean, pale yellow sheet over the double bed, pulled the edges down at the end, and did a swift hospital tuck on each side as her mother had taught her to do years ago. The thought of her mother brought a smile to her face.

She'd been living away from home for four years, and now the thought of her parents' imminent arrival had her scurrying around the apartment tidying and retidying so they wouldn't worry that she wasn't fending properly for herself. The smile faded. Not that they'd be interested in all the temporal trappings—like the way she'd sewn a new duvet cover and coordinating cushions and curtains, or even that she'd saved up and bought a small sound system.

She knew that they would be pleased that she was comfortable, but they'd be waiting for the opportune moment to ask her about her activity at church.

Well, we should cover that topic pretty quickly. Meredith grimaced as she mentally rehearsed the inevitable conversation with her mother. *No, Mum, I still don't actually go to church . . . no, I don't really hang out with any young adults . . . well, I just get so busy studying and I don't really fit in with the group up here . . . I know, if I'd stayed in Taranaki I'd still be active . . . but I wanted to make a difference in the world . . . I wanted to be a lawyer, Mum—and I've done it.*

She bent and opened the bottom drawer of her dresser and sorted through some clothes before pulling out her dark blue leather-bound scriptures.

Maybe I should put these out on the table and just bluff my way through the visit. Pretend like I'm going to church.

An image of her father came to mind and she quickly dispelled that idea. Six years as a branch president and then as a bishop had made her father far too discerning for her to even try to trick him. Her mother might believe her just because she wanted to believe Meredith was attending church, but there would be no fooling her father. She pushed the scriptures back into the drawer and closed it.

Maybe I'll get back into the whole church thing later . . . after graduation.

The thought of graduation made her turn to the old free-standing oak wardrobe she'd bought at a secondhand shop four years ago when she'd first moved to Auckland. Today, the front of the wardrobe was obscured by the voluminous folds of a black graduation gown. The distinctive, pale blue satin hood of the law department draped over the shoulders. Meredith ran her hand lightly over the extra stripe of cold satin fabric on the edge of the hood. Four years of hard study and finally graduating with honors. She suddenly remembered that moment three years ago . . . prodding Mitch in the chest and telling him, vehemently, that she was going to be a great lawyer.

"And now you're Meredith Ann Winstone, twenty-five years old and L.L.B. Honors . . . and you are going to be a great lawyer." She picked up the black, tasseled cap with its distinctive square top and set it on her head before she turned to look in the full-length mirror on the wall. Her hair fell sleekly past her shoulders, medium brown hue and generously highlighted with lighter streaks. Her face was tanned and thin, with dark eyebrows and warm brown eyes. She sucked in her cheeks. "*Too thin. You're just too thin*"—she could almost hear her mother saying it, and she smiled. "Oh well, better to face all the music at once."

As if on cue, the apartment suddenly echoed with four loud knocks at the door.

Why don't they just come in? Meredith removed the mortarboard and placed it back on the dresser. *It's not like they're going to interrupt anything.*

She quickly ran her hands over her hips to make sure the new blue dress looked its best, then ran to open the door.

"Oh my goodness, it's practically everybody!" She cupped her hands to her mouth as her parents and two younger brothers began to file past her with their bags and cases.

"Hello, darling. We didn't want the boys to miss the great event." Her mother offered her cheek for a kiss, then moved straight through to the kitchen with the cake pan she was holding.

"Hey, Sis." She received a peck on the cheek from first Ryan and then Cam.

"And when did you boys grow again?" She peered up at their six-foot-plus lengths. "Or am I shrinking?"

"Bit of both, or at least I am." Her father struggled in last with a large suitcase. "I lost an inch or two just getting this thing up the stairs. I think your mother has one of the grandchildren stashed in here." Meredith laughed as Ryan dropped his bags and took the suitcase easily from his father with one hand. "Admit it, Dad. You only pretend to struggle so much to make us boys feel good."

Stewart Winstone raised his arm and pretended to wipe perspiration from his forehead. "You've got it, son. You see right through me." He turned to Meredith. "Now, how's my girl . . . my graduate?"

"Just fine, Dad." Meredith wrapped her arms around her father's neck and hugged him tightly, appreciating his familiar warmth. "I can't believe I'm finally graduating after four long years."

Cam grinned. "I'll say. I've nearly finished high school. Actually, I'm thinking I'll finish my year-twelve exams this year and go out to work."

"Cam!" Meredith's mother walked out of the kitchen with the customary tea towel in her hands. All her children held this classic image of Nan Winstone in their memories. "You're not leaving school and you were asked not to discuss it here. Not yet, anyway. We're here for Meredith's graduation." She raised a meaningful eyebrow. "All right?"

Meredith watched her younger brother closely as his cheeks reddened slightly and his shoulders drooped. At sixteen, he seemed to her to have grown overnight, but then Meredith realized it had been nearly nine months since she'd last seen him. She reached over and hugged him around the waist.

"C'mon, Cam. You have to at least pretend you're interested in going to university, or have I spent the last four years trying to be a good example for nothing?"

She caught the glance that passed quickly between her parents and knew immediately what they must be thinking. What was she a good example of—getting an education . . . or losing her way spiritually?

Ryan seemed to sense the tension and spread his arms wide as if to embrace the tiny apartment.

"So where are you going to sleep, Meredith? It looks like there's just enough floor space for us two, and Mum and Dad will have to have your bed."

The sound of his deep, mellow voice filled Meredith with a rush of affection for her gentle younger brother. She looked at him fondly, recognizing that he was trying to rescue a potentially awkward situation, and she pointed to the bathroom.

"Well, I've got the shower, and I'm not swapping for anybody," she joked.

She turned as the phone rang on the sideboard behind her.

"Has your family arrived yet?" As usual, Telesia started straight into conversation without saying who was speaking.

"Hi, Sia . . . Yes, they're all here." Meredith raised her eyebrows at her family. They had come to know Telesia reasonably well after she had visited Taranaki with Meredith a couple of times over the last four years.

"Hello, Sia," Nan and Stewart said in unison.

"She says, 'Hi.'" Meredith grinned, then frowned as she listened some more. "They're what? You're not serious? Oh, Sia. How can they do that to you?"

Her family waited silently as she continued to listen, then she ran her hand through her hair and spoke firmly into the phone.

"Look, Sia, aside from my sister Wendy, my whole family is here and we'll all be there for you," she listened again. "So he is coming? Well, at least that's one good thing. Good for him. Okay, so we'll meet at eleven o'clock, and Tavita can sit with my folks . . . and Sia, it'll be fine."

Meredith hung up the phone then turned to her father with tears in her eyes.

"Telesia's parents aren't coming to her graduation."

"Why ever not?" Stewart sounded surprised.

Meredith shrugged. "I really don't know . . . except that one of her aunties died, and her father wanted Sia to give him her government allowance money to help pay for the funeral. He already takes most of it as rent for her to stay in their home, but she'd used the bit she keeps to hire her graduation robes . . . so when she said she couldn't, her father got really mad with her, and now they're not coming as punishment." She shook her head. "He's got such a different view of things. He seems to think that since the government is giving Sia 'free money,' he doesn't even need to work."

"But how can he make her give up her money?" Cam frowned. "Why doesn't she just leave?"

"It's not as simple as that. Her father—actually he's her stepfather—he isn't educated at all, and he sort of rules them all by force. While she's at home she has to respect him, and because she's training and can't afford to stay anywhere else . . . she's trapped. It makes me so mad, because it's so different than what the Church teaches, but . . . he's been inactive for a long time. Her mum tries, but . . ." she trailed off.

Nan frowned. "But to think they won't even come to her graduation."

"I think her mother would, but she has to do what her husband says. It's so frustrating. Once he even told Sia that he can't understand why she doesn't just get a job at McDonald's or something and earn some 'real' money right now, instead of wasting her time at university." Meredith shook her head. "I don't know how Sia has maintained the courage to study law, but she says her own father wanted her to go to university and he made her promise before he died. She was only about twelve."

There was a long silence as each considered their own thoughts.

"Well, let's remember not to condemn her stepfather too harshly," Stewart suggested gently. "We can never be sure of exactly what his motivations are, even if we're sure we know all the circumstances. Different people have different priorities. McDonald's may not be our first choice . . ."

"Hey, let's go easy on McDonald's." Cam held up his hand and tried to laugh. "They're my employers, remember."

"And we're grateful someone will employ you." Ryan put his brother into a headlock. "But we're hoping you'll look a bit more long-term like Telesia. She's been working hard to make a career where she can earn far more, now that she's qualified." He released Cam's head and looked at Meredith. "Did you say Tavita was coming?"

Meredith's brother, Ryan, and Tavita, Telesia's boyfriend, had become good friends on Ryan's last visit to Auckland, and now Ryan had been called to serve in the same mission that Tavita had served in four years earlier, in Adelaide, Australia.

"Yes, at least he's supporting her. He's been wonderful and he tries to appreciate how she's feeling, but his parents are just the opposite. They came to New Zealand so their children could get educated, and all five of them are doing really well either at university or on missions."

"It's so frustrating when Church members don't understand what education can do, even when the prophet tells us all the time," Nan sighed and glanced at Cam. "Some just want to give up school as soon as they can. It's just such a shame that they can't see the bigger picture."

"It is a shame, but it's not surprising." Meredith shrugged and shook her head. "As I've said before, Mum, you meet all types of people in the big city." She turned to her brothers. "Look, let's forget about this for now. I believe I have a graduation to attend. Anyone want to come with me?"

* * *

As Meredith and Telesia walked together toward the town hall, where the conferment of their degrees would take place, Meredith reached for her friend's hand.

"We made it, Sia," she breathed. Her friend's chin lifted, and she saw a smile touch Sia's lips.

"We have, haven't we?" Telesia nodded. "You've been a wonderful friend, Mele. You've helped me get through."

"Not as much as you've helped me." Meredith's appreciation was genuine, and she felt tears gather in her eyes. "And now we're ready to take on the world, aren't we?"

There was the slightest pause before Telesia nodded. "Yes, we are." She managed a faint grin. "Do you think the world is ready for us?"

Meredith grinned and squeezed her friend's hand tightly. "It had better be."

As she took her allotted seat in the town hall, Meredith felt her heart pounding with anticipation. She let out a long breath, nervously blowing her hair off her forehead, and adjusted the thick black academic robes. "*Just think cold thoughts*"—she smiled as she remembered her father's advice for keeping cool under pressure, and she settled back against the seat, searching for her family among the rows of people in the balcony. As she twisted around in her seat, she saw Ryan's long arm reaching out above the crowd and waving in her direction. She quickly waved back, keeping her hand low but smiling widely.

Her brothers were sitting on either side of her parents, and Tavita was beside Ryan, his round, brown face a contrast to Ryan's paler complexion. Meredith glanced ahead three rows to see if Telesia had seen them, but she was scanning the balcony on the other side of the hall.

"Sia!" She leaned forward and hissed her friend's name. "Sia!"

There was no response. She recognized the man just in front of her, so she tapped his shoulder and pointed at Telesia's back. He nodded and spoke to the girl in front of him, who then got Telesia's attention and pointed back to Meredith.

"Up there," Meredith mouthed, pointing up to the right, enjoying the sparkle that lit up Telesia's dark brown eyes as she saw Tavita wave at her. For a second Meredith felt a twinge of envy at the feeling that seemed to radiate between them, but she quickly suppressed it and waved again as she saw her mother point the camera toward her.

* * *

"There he is." Frank Bascombe had settled himself in his seat and perused the rows of graduates below a few moments after they'd been seated. "About fifth in from the side and five . . . six . . . eight rows back." He pointed with his program so Grant could see. "It's hard to believe that's Charles down there. I didn't think he'd ever make it."

Grant nodded and smiled as his younger cousin suddenly caught sight of them. "I'm still not sure what kind of lawyer he's going to make. There're not many people who take six years full-time to complete a four-year degree."

"But at least he's done it now. He's finished something . . . despite his mother. She couldn't even make it to his graduation. Then again, maybe she didn't actually believe that he'd done it." Frank frowned, thinking about his kindly, but definitely eccentric, sister-in-law. "There really couldn't have been two more different sisters than your mother and your aunt."

Before Grant could acknowledge his father, he was distracted by the girl behind Charles reaching over to talk to him, then Charles in turn catching the attention of a Polynesian girl sitting in front. He watched the excitement and happiness on both girls' faces as they waved up to someone in the balcony, and glancing to his left he saw a whole family and a tall Polynesian man wave back. For a moment he felt a stab of jealousy as he remembered the last time he'd been here in the town hall . . . for his own graduation, with his mother holding the camera and his own fiancée waving back.

And now they're all gone. His hands tightened on the arms of the seat. *And nothing can bring them back.*

"I wonder who that girl is that Charles is talking to." Frank nudged Grant's arm. "He's obviously excited to talk to her."

Before Grant could respond, the procession of faculty began to file onto the stage, and the audience hushed. He watched the girl focus intently toward the front, her eyes direct, her head held high. She wasn't the type Charles would ignore—in fact, he thought wryly, she was probably one of the reasons his cousin had taken so long to grad-uate. He suppressed an inexplicable feeling of annoyance, but couldn't help his gaze traveling often in her direction throughout the ceremony.

"Charles Unsworth," the loudspeaker announced.

Grant watched as his cousin made his way across the stage and bent forward as the university chancellor touched the mortarboard ceremoniously on Charles's head. Then, as Charles stood up and placed his own mortarboard on his head and shifted the tassel to the left side with a flourish, a spontaneous cheer went up from the other graduates and Charles turned a laughing face to the audience in acknowledgement before he received his diploma.

"Young scoundrel." Frank couldn't help smiling, and Grant responded with a nod. As infuriating as Charles was, he still enjoyed his younger cousin, and the boy's fellow students obviously did as well.

"Sherilyn Waters . . . Amy Western . . . Meredith Winstone . . . Brianna Woods," the announcer continued.

Grant suddenly became aware of the girl standing with the next group, and he quickly scanned the program. *Waters, Western, Winstone, Woods* . . . He tried to calculate which she'd be, then put the program down impatiently. *What did it matter anyway?*

* * *

"Okay, okay . . . photo time. Please everybody . . . just for a moment," Nan Winstone said as she motioned desperately to get her family to stand in one place.

"Shall I take it, Sister Winstone?" Tavita asked quietly from behind her, and Nan glanced up gratefully.

"Oh thank you, dear. They'll probably listen to you better anyway, and you're less likely to cut their heads off in the photo. I'm famous for it." Nan handed him the camera and turned to her offspring. "Come on everybody . . . please."

Grant stood with his father in the shade of one of the trees outside the town hall and watched the group getting organized. The girls they'd seen with Charles stood close together in the middle of the group, their contrasting coloring united by the black robes and blue satin hoods they wore draped across their shoulders. They were laughing and looked completely relaxed.

"Seem like a happy family." His father nodded toward the group. "Reminds me of a few years ago."

Grant closed his eyes briefly as if to blot out the memory, then opened them as he heard the girl call out.

"One, two, three . . . go!" Both girls flung their mortarboards high in the air with arms extended as one of the brothers took a picture. Then they caught the hats and embraced again.

Let them enjoy it while it lasts. He thrust his hands into his pockets and turned the other way, shutting out the scene.

"Well, that's it, Uncle Frank! Charles Unsworth has finally graduated!"

He heard before he saw his cousin's exuberant approach. The cheerful voice and irrepressible laugh was followed by a pounding on his shoulder. "I'm one of you now, Cuz."

Grant turned and raised an eyebrow at his cousin. "Yes . . . well done, and at least you'll have a more mature perspective on things than some of these young ones. It's hard to imagine that they'll actually be representing people."

"Now who's sounding ancient?" Charles grinned. "Some of these girls leave me for dead in the courtroom procedures." He motioned with his head toward Meredith's family. "That one over there is a diligent type. She not only looks a treat, but she's really bright as well. So is her friend."

"The lighter-haired girl?" Frank looked back.

"Mm-hmm . . ." Charles nodded. "Name's Meredith. Tried asking her out a few times but always got rejected. Too busy studying. Then I found out they're both Mormons, so I figured it was a losing battle anyway. No drink, no drugs, no *nothing* . . . I mean, what's the point?" He laughed again. "She's a nice girl, though."

"Sounds like the sort of person you could do with." Frank put his arm around his nephew's shoulders. "She might keep you on the straight and narrow."

"Ha! I think not . . . she's definitely more Grant's type, and besides . . . that's not for me right now, Uncle Frank. I'm ready to see the world, now that all the studying is over."

"You mean you're not looking for a job?"

"No way! Not yet. I want to have some fun first. Get a bit of international experience under my belt before I settle down. I might even get a job overseas." Charles nodded as though that idea held the most appeal.

"So I guess you're not interested in working with us then?" Grant quietly studied his cousin's face, wondering suddenly if he wasn't actually pleased with Charles's decision.

"Well, no . . . not at the moment. I mean, Devonport is a nice place, but . . . there's so much more." Charles looked at his uncle. "You do understand, don't you? Really, you'd be better off with some diligent type like Mr. Kim over there or . . . or even young Meredith."

Meredith stood quietly as her parents discussed the final plans for their celebration dinner. The boys had wandered off for a few minutes to have a look around at the Aotea Center, and the girl's Samoan friends only had eyes for each other as they stood holding hands.

* * *

Meredith felt a bit deflated now that the excitement was suddenly over. She put the hat back on her head with a desultory tap and looked around, realizing that this was probably the last time she would see many of her fellow students who were gradually leaving Aotea Square in small family groups.

She raised a hand in brief acknowledgement as Charles Unsworth waved and smiled. He was with two other men . . . maybe his father and brother. The older man was comfortably clad in a tweed jacket and hat, and had his back to her, and the other, wearing dark glasses, seemed slighter and darker. They didn't look like Charles, but then again, no one was quite like Charles.

* * *

"So what are you going to do now?" Stewart Winstone set his glass down on the table and sat back in his chair. "Have you applied for any jobs?"

Meredith shook her head. "Not yet. I was thinking seriously all semester about applying down in Wellington, so I didn't really worry about the job possibilities up here. The really big firms did a recruiting drive up at the Sheraton Hotel a while ago, but I didn't feel impressed by any of them."

"So are you still going to try Wellington?" Nan sounded hopeful as she sat down on the arm of Stewart's chair. "Or what about coming back to Taranaki?"

Meredith smiled at her mother's quiet persistence and shook her head. "Not yet, Mum. I want to stay in the city for now. In fact, I've just been thinking in the last few days that I might stay here in Auckland and try a small firm. They say you get a wider variety of work, and much sooner. I think I'd find that a lot more interesting and challenging."

"Will you have time to go to church if you work with a smaller company?" Nan couldn't help asking the question even though it wasn't relevant to the topic and her husband was frowning at her.

"Oh, Mum, you deserve a medal for persistence." Meredith forced a smile this time and shrugged her shoulders. "I just don't know if I fit in there anymore. Maybe if Telesia and Tavita get married soon I'll be going to a chapel at least once . . ."

"Well, you'd better make that twice to a chapel." Ryan leaned back in his chair. "I've got my farewell in eight weeks."

"Oh, my goodness, Ry . . . so it is! I'd forgotten with all this graduation fuss going on. I'll definitely be there for that." She stared at her brother as if seeing him for the first time. "Elder Winstone. Who'd have thought? My little brother is going to be an actual missionary."

"Easy on the 'little.'" Cam slapped his brother's shoulder goodnaturedly and pulled himself to his full height beside him.

Meredith grimaced at her brothers. "If I don't use 'little,' you two will make me feel really old."

Her father snorted. "Make you feel old? How do you think your mother and I feel? We'll be starting to think about a mission of our own soon, and that's always seemed so far in the future. It makes me turn gray just thinking about it." He ran his hand through thick hair that was full of more silvery gray than Meredith remembered from her last visit. It was a shock to suddenly think of her parents as growing older and retiring, and she studied them both quietly. *I wonder how many of those gray hairs I caused.*

"Anyway . . ." Stewart coughed briefly as if to change the subject more than clear his throat. "Your mother has just been giving me the signal. Meredith . . ." He paused, then reached into the inside pocket of his jacket and withdrew a long, slim envelope. "We just wanted to recognize the great effort you've put into your studies. It isn't much . . . but your mother and I thought you might like a rest from all the study before you get a job."

Meredith frowned slightly and looked at her mother. She knew her parents had very little money to spare, but Nan Winstone nodded and moved toward her daughter, giving her a tight hug and a kiss on the cheek.

"We just thought a trip away would be nice, and your Auntie Tracy said you could stay there as long as you want."

"Australia? Broadbeach?" Meredith gasped as she opened the envelope and took out an airline ticket. "Oh, my heavens . . . this is wonderful!" She jumped up and embraced each of her parents in turn, then sat down and stared at the ticket. "I'll be able to visit Wendy, Jared, and the children up in Cairns . . . I haven't seen them for so long."

"We thought you might do that." Nan nodded. "And maybe even get your Aunt Tracy to go to church with you. I don't think she's been going for quite a while."

"And you think I might be a good example?" Meredith couldn't suppress a smile. "You're wonderful, Mum."

CHAPTER 5

For the third time, Meredith studied the address on the letterhead beside her briefcase, then turned her head toward the carefully restored Victorian building across the road. Even in the warm morning sunlight it seemed to have a cold, intimidating look to it. She shivered slightly and pulled nervously at the collar of her new beige suit as she glanced at her reflection in the rearview mirror.

Don't be silly. It's not that bad at all. You're just nervous because it's your first interview. Now calm down and think positively.

When she had returned from her holiday in Australia just a few days before, she'd felt the usual apprehension at the thought of actually entering the workforce, but, typically, she'd decided to attack the situation and organized her first interview immediately. Surprisingly, she'd been offered an appointment for two days later.

She looked at her watch and took a deep breath. Still another twenty minutes before she was due. She tapped her fingers pensively on the steering wheel, then reached down and turned the key in the ignition. No sense just waiting when she could go for a short drive and get an idea of whether she liked the area and what it offered.

The road ahead veered around to the right, passing the long building where the commuter ferry docked and the wharf extended out into the sea. Behind it, the city of Auckland formed a steel, concrete, and glass backdrop to the Sky Tower, a fantastical needle pointing its way to the clouds. Meredith smiled appreciatively. Although she had lived and studied in the city for all these years, she'd seldom taken the time to visit this part of North Shore in the daytime or to view the city from this angle. She sighed. It really was a pretty city, but she'd apparently been too busy to notice.

She drove on slowly, then turned around in front of the gates to the naval base. The austere outlines of the buildings and ships were a stark contrast to the friendly shops and cafés just down the road by the beach, or the rambling Victorian houses that graced the foreshore. She began to imagine the same road in a bygone era, with women in long gowns shading themselves with parasols, and men in three-quarter trousers and braces taking the ladies' arms as they walked. Devonport definitely had a peculiar charm, and she found herself nodding in pleasant anticipation of taking walks along King Edward Parade, then she shook her head as if to clear it.

My goodness, you haven't even been offered the job yet! Misters Bascombe and Bascombe might reject you on sight! They're probably very old and traditional, very set in their ways and only granting you an interview so they can tell their old cronies down at the club that they don't discriminate against women.

Meredith felt her jaw clenching at the thought, then just as quickly forced herself to relax. She smiled grimly as she slid the Volkswagen back into the same parking place. *Well, I'll just have to show them. I'll show them that they need this particular woman, and I'll be the best thing that ever happened to their lost-in-the-past practice.*

* * *

Frank Bascombe stood and held out his hand to the young man across the desk.

"Thank you for coming in, Mr. Connors. I have one more interview to conduct before I make a final choice, but I'll let you know our decision by Friday."

He remained standing until the door closed behind the man's back, then he shifted the resumé over to a pile of five or six other folders. He thoughtfully straightened them again and picked up the final curriculum vitae on the other side of the desk.

"Meredith Anne Winstone," he read aloud as he turned the front page to study the information once again.

"*She's a Mormon.*" He could hear Charles's voice sounding almost derogatory after graduation. "*Leaves me for dead in the courtroom procedures . . . too busy studying . . . a diligent type. Not only looks a treat, but she's really bright as well.*" Frank took off his glasses and tapped his chin with them. "Charles, you've probably given her a better reference than she could ever have given herself." He chuckled at the thought of his nephew gallivanting around Europe. "You might even have given her your own job."

He placed the CV back on the desk and went to stand over by the window overlooking King Edward Parade. The sun was putting the finishing touches to a perfect day on the Auckland Harbor, and he enviously watched some large yachts hauling past the ferry building under full sail. Maybe an early day at the office . . .

He shook his head at his own daydreaming, then looked across the road as a young woman unfolded herself from a well-preserved cream Volkswagen. He watched as she straightened the knee-length beige skirt at the sides, then fastened her jacket buttons before reaching back into the car for a burgundy leather briefcase that matched her shoes and shirt.

"Very well presented, Miss Winstone." He nodded his head approvingly and glanced at his gold wristwatch. "And punctual as well."

If Meredith had looked up toward the three windows that bore the etched "Bascombe and Bascombe" logo, she would have seen both father and son watching her from different windows, but whereas one was smiling, the other wore a frown that deepened as he watched her walk briskly toward the office doorway.

Despite Charles's open admiration for the woman's legal abilities, Grant Bascombe found himself resenting his father's premature preference for her among the list of new candidates for a place in the firm.

"Why would you take Charles's word—of all people—about her?" he had challenged his father as they'd discussed the resumés.

"Because Charles might be careless and a little reckless, but he's definitely not stupid. He was in awe of her."

"Because she ditched him," Grant had muttered.

"Then that surely is another credential in her favor." Frank refused to succumb to his son's abrupt dismissal of the girl. "It should make you feel even more comfortable. We'd have another 'Iron Maiden' to keep our noses to the grindstone."

Grant had reluctantly grinned at the Iron Maiden reference. It was the nickname he'd given his father's stalwart, legal executive secretary when he'd first crossed her as a brand new lawyer. Stella Osborne was still staunchly dedicated, loyal, and meticulous after seventeen years with the firm. She'd virtually carried the business for them both through many crises, including the deaths in their family. They appreciated her stability, and they both knew that any new recruit would have passed the ultimate test if Stella gave the nod.

Meredith paused to take a deep breath before pushing at the oak door with "Bascombe and Bascombe" etched on the glass inset panels. She almost wrinkled her nose in expectation of the smell of mothballs and musty furniture, so she was pleasantly surprised to find herself in a warmly decorated reception area. Rust-red walls offset a honey-beige Kauri reception desk and comfortable navy leather couches with red and beige cushions. Even the formidable-looking woman behind the desk was coordinated with the room in a neat, navy suit.

At least I complement the décor. Meredith straightened her beige skirt and said a silent thank you for the last-minute decision to go with deep red accessories rather than the bright green she'd chosen originally.

"Can I help you?" The woman had a firm but surprisingly mellow voice.

"Ah, yes. My name is Meredith Winstone. I have an appointment with Mr. Frank Bascombe."

"Yes, he's expecting you." There was almost a smile, but it was gone before Meredith could respond. "Would you please come through with me, Miss Winstone?"

She led the way through to the farthest office, and Meredith found herself shaking hands with a tall, distinguished man whose thick, silvery hair and tanned skin reminded her more of a sea captain than a lawyer. She found herself smiling at the instant image and realized that he was smiling in response.

"Good morning, Miss Winstone. I'm delighted to meet you at last." He shook her hand warmly and gestured to a comfortable leather armchair. Surprisingly, he then settled himself in another armchair beside hers rather than in his own behind the desk. Then he raised a fluffy silver eyebrow. "So, what would you like to know about us?"

"I . . ." Meredith stuttered at the unusual opening, still wondering what Frank Bascombe had meant by "meet you at last." She put her hand to her throat and coughed lightly, then she shook her head and laughed.

"Can we start this over again, please, Mr. Bascombe? I was getting all ready to tell you about me. Isn't that the usual procedure?"

Frank rested back with his elbows on the arms of the chair and pressed his fingertips together. "I've already received excellent references about you, as well as your CV, so I'm more interested in finding out if we're the sort of firm you'd feel comfortable representing. Employment is a two-way thing."

Meredith took a deep breath, crossed her ankles neatly, and glanced around. There really was nothing about the offices that was even remotely Victorian or musty, and she felt almost guilty at her preconceived notion of the firm.

"Well, I'd have to say that as far as first impressions go, I'm pleasantly surprised. I think your décor suits my wardrobe very well," she laughed awkwardly, then gained confidence as Frank nodded and smiled in return. "But obviously, you can't judge a book by its cover, and I would need to know that I was working for a company with integrity and compassion, as well as sound ethics. I guess one that believes in the spirit of the law, not just the letter of the law." She nodded her head as if confirming the statement to herself as well as to Frank. "Yes, that's where I'd feel comfortable and where I would give the best I was capable of."

"And do you think we might be that sort of company?" He leaned forward. "What's your gut feeling here, Miss Winstone? What might you think if you were a new client walking in off the street?"

"Honestly, Mr. Bascombe?" She found herself enjoying this man's approach and responded to it. "I'll have to admit I originally thought it might be too . . . traditional."

"As in old and stuffy?" Frank grunted as Meredith pursed her lips at his very accurate description of her feelings.

"But I did do some research before I applied, and I felt very comfortable applying for this job. Your firm has an excellent reputation."

There was a moment's silence before Frank rose and picked up her CV from off the desk. He flicked it open and skimmed it briefly.

"L.L.B. Honors?"

Meredith nodded.

"Professionals?"

"I did them in February." She nodded again

"Do you have any areas of preference?"

"I enjoyed family law, but commercial law was challenging."

"Did you like litigation?"

She smiled. "Not at first. It was a bit intimidating, but then I discovered that I actually enjoyed the challenge of defending and thinking fast."

"Well, we do everything here." His tone was suddenly more decisive. "A small practice takes on the whole gamut. Do you think you could handle it?"

"That's why I decided to go this way rather than a big firm," Meredith answered steadily. "I wanted a range of experiences."

"Well, we'd certainly see to that." Frank closed the file. "How did you happen to apply to us?"

She hesitated. "Actually, it was a very sudden thing. I was originally thinking about applying for work in Wellington because my family is in Taranaki, but then I started to think about Auckland again, and out of the blue, just hours after I arrived back here from overseas, a fellow student from law school called me just as *he* was going overseas and said that he'd been going to apply for this job and suggested that it might be a good choice for me."

Frank nodded slowly, remembering his conversation with Charles just before he had left, where he had extolled Meredith's virtues once more. He particularly remembered his last credential. *"She'll blow the cobwebs away, Uncle. She'll be good for you . . . and Grant."*

"Yes, he called to tell me." Frank smiled at the inquiring look on her face. "Charles Unsworth is my nephew."

Nephew! Meredith stared. *So that's why he said "at last."*

"You're Charles's uncle." It was a statement rather than a question. "But why didn't he say, and why . . . ?"

"Why didn't he want the job?" Frank tapped the CV on the desk, then sat back in his chair. "How well do you know Charles?"

"How well do I know Charles?" She considered for a moment and her immediate impressions were of always seeing him chatting with people (usually female) all over campus, but seldom actually at lectures. "I'd say I didn't know him as well as many people on campus, but that he's a very friendly person."

Frank smiled at her diplomacy. "He was far more outspoken about your skills and work ethic than you were about yourself."

"Charles was?" She looked genuinely surprised. "I didn't even realize he knew I existed." She thought of the two or three times she'd declined a date with him. "I mean, I knew he knew me . . . but not really. That's why it surprised me that he'd even think to call me about the job. The whole thing was a bit intriguing."

"Well, he said you were amazing and far more suited to our sort of business than he ever would be."

Meredith shifted uncomfortably in her chair at the direct compliment. "Goodness me, I'm flattered, Mr. Bascombe, and more than a little surprised, but . . ."

"But?" Frank nodded toward the closed door. "The only 'but' I could possibly foresee may come from my partner . . . my son."

"That sounds ominous." Meredith glanced at the door.

"Oh, I wouldn't be too concerned. He's a little outspoken, but my son generally trusts my judgment."

She remained silent, wondering what this son must be like. *Was he anything like Charles? No, that wasn't possible.*

As if in answer to her thoughts, Frank picked up the phone and pressed a button as he said, "Grant is nothing like Charles. They're like chalk and cheese, but I'll let you see for yourself."

Meredith felt a sudden prickling sensation run the length of her spine, and her silk top felt instantly cold against her shoulder blades as she gave an involuntary shudder. She adjusted her position on the chair and sat forward, turning her head to face out the window, her back toward the door.

In the reception area where the call rang through, Grant paused briefly beside Stella Osborne's desk. "So has my father succumbed to the feminine charms already? That wasn't a very long interview."

"Perhaps you and I should conduct one for our own benefit." Stella flashed her half-smile. "Although she does seem to be a competent young woman. She's very neatly presented, well-spoken, and pleasant."

"We'll see." Grant straightened the already perfect knot in his tie and turned toward his father's office. "Looks aren't everything, even if it makes work more 'pleasant.'"

"Grant, I'd like you to meet Meredith Winstone." Frank stood as his son entered the room. "Miss Winstone . . . my son and partner, Grant Bascombe."

Meredith turned in her chair, suddenly unsure whether to stand up and shake hands or to remain seated, but as she looked up she was unprepared for the darkly imposing looks of the man standing beside his father—striking looks that were beset by a slight frown as he stared straight at her. For a few seconds she squirmed slightly under the directness of his look, then she broke his gaze by glancing at his father.

Grant coughed as he stared at the girl from the graduation ceremony . . . the one girl that he'd found so difficult to ignore among the hundreds of graduates, the only girl that he'd taken a second look at in years; she had to be the one that Charles had recommended.

"Um . . . I'm pleased to meet you, Miss Winstone. I hear you come with excellent references."

Even to *his* ears his voice sounded hesitant and stilted, and it certainly took Meredith by surprise. "I . . . apparently." She made herself smile as he spoke again.

"And I believe you know Charles . . . quite well." His tone was slightly more abrupt for some reason, and Meredith looked straight at him. Her family would have recognized the way she braced her shoulders and lifted her chin.

"Not well, Mr. Bascombe. I am acquainted with your cousin through our legal studies, but as I explained to your father, Charles's recommendation of this job to me, and of me to you, came as a complete surprise."

"But you obviously thought enough of him . . . or his suggestion, to follow it up." For some reason he found himself not only resenting Charles's association with this woman, however she might be downplaying it, but also perversely enjoying her discomfited response to his questions.

Meredith bit her lip and briefly studied the knot on his tie, unsure how to respond to his statement.

"His suggestion was different enough to be intriguing, Mr. Bascombe, but then I did my homework and found out more details about your firm." She hesitated, then clasped her hands together and rested them in her lap. "*At that point* I was impressed enough to apply for the job."

Frank pursed his lips to suppress a grin as she'd placed emphasis on "at that point." He watched Grant's shoulders straighten and knew his son had caught her meaning as well.

"I see. So do we measure up to your requirements, Miss Winstone?" Grant's tone was suddenly guarded as he found himself noting the way she sat, her shoulders and back naturally straight and confident, her long legs crossed neatly at the ankles.

Ouch! Keep going, son, and you'll lose me the best applicant I've seen since you joined the business. Frank frowned and found himself waiting for Meredith's reply. It was as if he were watching a fencing match, and the parries and thrusts were intensifying.

She took her time answering before she inclined her head toward Frank. "I believe Bascombe and Bascombe offers me a broad spectrum of work that I would enjoy being a part of . . . and a warmth and stability that your father obviously works very hard to maintain."

Touché! Frank grinned and put his hands in his pockets.

"I see . . ." Grant nodded slowly, then turned to his father, and, for the first time, Meredith noticed a similarity in their stance that didn't show in their looks. They were both obviously strong-willed individuals, and she found herself wondering if they ever had disagreements . . . and if they did, who usually won. She noted that Grant's eyes had slight frown lines between them, which intensified as he put his hands into his pockets and nodded slowly as he inclined his head toward her.

"Well, I guess I'll leave you two to continue extolling each other's virtues. I have some cases to prepare." He turned toward the door, then hesitated and looked back. In that split second Meredith had visibly relaxed and run her hand through her lightly blonded hair, tucking it behind her ear. He checked himself as he noted the fine gold earring that shone in her ear lobe. "It was interesting to meet you, Miss Winstone. I hope Charles is right . . . this time."

This time? Something trembled in Meredith's chest as she watched the firmness of his stride as he turned and walked out the door. Her heart pounded unreasonably fast and she shook her head very slightly. *No, there's absolutely no way I could work here. He obviously has mixed feelings about me, and, besides, I've practically insulted him as well.*

As she resignedly bent to pick up her briefcase, Frank closed the door and went to stand behind his desk. There was a short silence as she waited for him to speak, but when he said nothing, she slowly stood up herself and held out her hand.

"Thank you very much for the interview, Mr. Bascombe. I appreciate your time."

"When could you start, Miss Winstone?" Frank said abruptly.

"Start?" She felt her eyebrows pull together in confusion as she stared at him blankly.

"Working here." He pointed downward as if explaining to a small child. "With us."

"I . . . ?" She hesitated as reason clamored for a hearing, but she listened to her heart. "Straightaway, if you want me to, Mr. Bascombe. I don't have any other commitments right now."

CHAPTER 6

"Yes, I'm definitely staying in Auckland, Mum. Mr. Bascombe offered me the job on the spot." Meredith waited patiently on the phone as her mother offered a final plea, and then she drew a deep breath. "I know I was going to try for work closer to home, Mum, but this job is a really great opportunity. I'd be silly to turn it down, and besides . . ." She stared at the wall in front of her. "Besides, it may not work out, and then I will come home."

It was a weak substitute for the real thoughts that had been plaguing her since she'd sat in her car directly after her interview at Bascombe and Bascombe. *I'll prove to Grant Bascombe that I'm worth employing. He may think I'm just another of Charles's irresponsible friends that's out for a good time, but I'll prove I'm a good choice.*

"Yes, Mum." She made herself concentrate. "I'll try to get home for Ryan's farewell. If I can't, maybe I can meet him before he goes to the mission training center in Hamilton. He could even come and stay with me for the night if you can't travel up. I'd love to spend some time with him before he goes." She paused, listening. "I know he's only going to Australia, Mum, and you really wanted him to go to England, but isn't it the work he'll be doing that counts, not where he's going to?"

My goodness, that sounded like a me I haven't heard in a while. She pulled a face as her mother made a similar comment at the end of the line.

"What do you mean that sounded like the old Meredith?" she answered her mother. "I may not attend church, Mum, but it doesn't mean my testimony has changed . . . look, I really need to go now . . .

give everyone a big hug for me and I'll call next week. Okay . . . love you too."

Meredith sighed as she lowered the phone onto the receiver. It was hard to decide whether it was her mother's persistence or her own sense of inadequacy that made her keep the phone calls brief, skirting the inevitable subject of the Church. She loved hearing what her family was doing, but it seemed as if every subject ended up relating to her inactivity.

She clasped her hands in front and extended her arms, stretching them slowly, then rolled her shoulders back as if shrugging off any burdens.

"Maybe that's because their whole life *is* church . . . just like mine used to be."

She glanced down at her skirt, fashionably clinging halfway up her thigh, and tugged at it self-consciously. As a teenager she had sometimes challenged her parents about the length of her skirts or wearing short shorts, but she'd never really considered wearing a skirt as short as this, or the sleeveless lycra top that now hung on her slim figure. She pulled her neckline higher. She realized that after she'd stopped attending church, her progressively less-modest clothing had been a measure of her movement away from the standards she'd always observed—the standards that had begun to change when she had started dating Mitch more seriously. "Maybe it is time for an overhaul. New job, new image, new life . . . or maybe old life again," she said pensively.

* * *

It was barely seven thirty in the morning when Meredith backed in through the front door of the office with her arms full of buff-colored folders, quickly sidestepping to allow the door to swing shut behind her. After two weeks of the same routine of taking cases home to study, she had perfected the movement.

"Nice footwork," Stella commented dryly as she straightened up behind the desk and glanced at the clock. "And you're early again, too."

"Oh! Stella, you startled me," Meredith turned quickly. "I wasn't expecting anyone here yet."

"Well, I decided to satisfy my curiosity about whether you were actually sleeping here or not." Stella frowned slightly. "You've been leaving after me each day and you're always here before me. I'm not used to that."

"I'm sorry." Meredith clasped the folders more tightly as her handbag began to slip off her shoulder. "I'm just trying to get the feel of everything."

"All at once?" Stella raised a well-shaped eyebrow and folded her arms.

"Well, no . . . at least . . ." Meredith shook her head. "I didn't realize there would be quite so much to learn, and I want to justify Mr. Bascombe's trust in me."

"Oh, I'm sure you're doing that, but I just think you need to be careful about doing too much too soon." Stella's voice was almost kindly, though still brisk. "Sometimes it pays to work smarter, not harder. You might need to ask more questions."

Meredith nodded at the suggestion and then she shrugged. "But I haven't seen Mr. Bascombe very much since I started."

"Mmm, he has been rather busy with that big case, but still . . . he's not the only one in the office. Young Grant is a great source of information and he's an excellent lawyer."

There was a brief silence while Meredith pretended to concentrate on juggling the folders again. How could she tell Stella that she found it almost impossible to be around "Young Grant," let alone ask for his advice? In the two weeks she'd been working at Bascombe and Bascombe, he'd only talked to her a few times, and most of those had merely been an instruction issued from her office door. The rest of her office orientation had come from Stella.

"I guess I'll have to work on that." Meredith moved forward, then bent her knees slightly to hold the wobbling load as her handbag again slid down her arm. "Whoops, I'm going to drop the lot in a second."

She failed to notice Grant come quietly in through the door until she heard the deep voice behind her shoulder.

"Maybe you should ask for more help before things get messed up."

Meredith's mouth dropped open and she momentarily relaxed her grip on the folders. One fell on the floor and a few papers scattered.

"You see what I mean?" He bent to pick them up. "You're trying to take on too much."

Somehow, when Stella had made the same sort of comment it had been in a kindly fashion, whereas Grant's words sounded more like chastisement.

"I . . ." Meredith glanced at Stella. "I'm just trying to get to know what's happening. I'm sorry . . ."

"You don't need to be sorry, Miss Winstone," he interrupted her to take a few of the folders out of her hands. "You just need to be sensible."

"But I am!" The objection burst out and she felt her cheeks burn as the memory of the last few days flashed through her mind. She'd been desperate to please, even impress, her new employers by working extra hard . . . but she realized she hadn't really been sensible.

She studied the top button of his suit jacket. "I just wanted to make sure that . . . you felt you'd made the right decision in employing me, Mr. Bascombe . . ." she faltered, partly from tiredness and partly from embarrassment, and she swallowed hard to regain her composure.

"It wasn't really my decision, Miss Winstone," Grant answered quickly. Then, as the color seemed to drain from her face, he tapped a file against his hand and took a deep breath. "I'm sure you'll learn just as much if you slow down a bit."

There was a brief silence, and then he turned abruptly toward his office. Meredith looked up as the door closed behind him.

"Now, don't take him too seriously," Stella almost whispered, coming around her desk and taking the rest of the folders. "He's not really all that bad. He's just getting used to having another woman around."

"Great . . . lucky me." Meredith smiled weakly, then consciously straightened her shoulders. "But anyway, point taken. Do less work after hours and ask more questions while I'm here. Work smarter rather than harder." She grinned at Stella. "The problem is, now that I'm so used to studying, I'll have to figure out something else to do after work. That could be the difficult part."

"There you are then—something that you and Grant have in common. Neither of you seem to have a life or know how to relax." Stella gave a short, abrupt laugh. "Maybe the two of you should get together."

"Aah!" Meredith rolled her eyes in a look of genuine horror. "I think that would definitely be hard work and not at all smart. No thanks, Stella. The files are infinitely more appealing." She turned toward her office, then hesitated. "But what do you mean . . . that Grant doesn't have a life? I mean, I don't want to pry, but . . ."

"No, no, it's fine." Stella followed Meredith into her office and set her armload of files on Meredith's desk. "It's probably only fair you should understand what causes Grant to be such a driven person . . . and why he can be a bit difficult to work with at times." Stella raised an eyebrow. "Although he has been a bit more out of sorts lately than usual."

Stella moved to the door and closed it, leaning back against it. She paused for a moment, gazing beyond Meredith and out the window.

"I came to work for Frank Bascombe when he first started in practice. His wife and I were good friends and she recommended me. When young Grant graduated and came into the practice, they were both thrilled. He really is a wonderful son and he's worked very, very hard. I think he wanted to establish his own worth . . . prove that he hadn't gotten the partnership just by being the boss's son. Anyway, it was fortunate he was here for Frank, because not long after he began working here, his mother was diagnosed with cancer." Stella swallowed hard. "Barbara was an amazing woman—so positive. She fought it well for a long time, and toward the end she even insisted on helping plan Grant's wedding . . . she was so happy. She loved Hannah just like her own daughter, and when Emily was born . . . it seemed to give her a new burst of life."

There was a long silence, Meredith's heart going out to the Bascombes. "Hannah and Emily?" she finally asked.

Stella coughed and shook her head. "Hannah was Grant's wife and Emily their baby girl. They were both delightful and everyone doted on them. They almost filled the void for Frank and Grant when Barbara finally died. Then . . ." Her voice faltered again and Meredith was surprised to see the older woman's eyes glisten behind her glasses. "Then a short time later, Grant took Hannah and Emily away for a few days to the Coromandel Peninsula. On the way back home the car spun on some newly laid gravel and they went off the road. Hannah and Emily were both killed." She took a deep breath. "Hannah died instantly. Emily died in Grant's arms just before the ambulance arrived. She was eleven months old."

There was a very long silence as Meredith felt a coldness encompass her whole body. It felt like her blood had turned to ice. *Off the road . . . both of them killed . . . she died in his arms.* She felt the room close in around her as she stared at Stella.

"I had no idea," her voice was barely a whisper.

"There's no reason why you should, but I somehow had the feeling that it's important for you to know. I can't fully explain why Grant is behaving the way he is right now, but it appears you are bearing the brunt of it." She straightened her suit jacket as if to resume the official secretary persona. "But if it's any consolation, Mr. Bascombe thinks you're doing a great job."

Meredith smiled weakly and toyed with the papers on the edge of her desk. "Thank you, Stella. I think I did need to know that . . . all of it. It really makes a difference."

Stella smiled and nodded, then paused with her hand on the door-knob. "Just a word of advice, though. Don't be too nice to Grant, just because you know. He doesn't want or need pity . . . from anyone."

"Point taken. Increase tolerance, decrease pity."

"Good case summary, counselor." Stella opened the door and nearly collided with Grant, who was reaching up to knock.

"So you're moving into counseling, Stella?" He slid his hands into his pockets and tilted his head back slightly. Meredith found herself watching the small muscle that worked at the side of his jaw. It was difficult to read his mood, so it came as a complete surprise when he gestured toward the window. "How would you like to counsel us all over lunch later?"

"Excuse me?" Even Stella looked surprised.

"Lunch." Grant pointed to his stomach with a slight smile and Meredith felt an inexplicable surge of happiness. "A regular eating activity at midday. I though we could shut up shop for a while and go to one of the cafés up the road."

"I . . . well, yes . . . certainly."

"I'll check with Dad later, but he should be able to join us." Grant glanced at his watch then at Meredith. "Twelve fifteen, then?"

"I . . . yes, I'd love to." She swallowed hard, trying to reconcile this new Grant with the tragic image she'd held of him just a few seconds before, or even with the man he'd been since her arrival.

"Good. Don't be late. Oh . . ." He hesitated as he turned at the door and said, "I should go over that Stratford case with you after lunch. It's going to trial soon, and I'll need your help. It'll be as good an introduction as any to the criminal side of our practice."

"I'll be in court?" Meredith's eyes widened in astonishment, and again the smallest smile lifted the corner of Grant's mouth.

"Well, maybe not right away, although I'm sure you're capable of it. No, for now you'll just follow through all the proceedings and interviews with me."

The two women stared at each other as he left the office, and neither spoke until Stella rolled her eyes in such an uncharacteristic gesture that Meredith barely suppressed a laugh.

"Increase tolerance, decrease pity. Work smarter, not harder. Shall I throw in mind reading as well?"

As she completed work on a smaller file that Grant had given her, Meredith glanced at her watch. *Eleven thirty . . . just a while to go before lunch.* She rested both elbows on her desk and stared blankly at the black vinyl corner of the desk pad. *You just have to relax and behave normally. He's obviously trying to improve company relations. There's only four people in the office . . . they're bound to do things together occasionally, so you just have to get used to him.* She pressed the slight curl on the vinyl until it sat flat. *Just treat him normally.*

The small café was reasonably full when the four of them arrived, and Grant glanced quickly around for an empty table.

"Nothing inside, so it'll have to be outside. Anybody mind a bit of sunshine?"

"I'd prefer it with a boat and a rolling ocean, but this'll do fine," Frank answered jovially as he moved to an empty table. As he held out a chair for Stella, Meredith silently noted the ease of their relationship. She failed to see Grant holding out another chair for her until she bent forward to reach for her own chair and Frank's chuckle made her hesitate.

"We must have employed a feminist, Grant. She doesn't want your help."

"What?" Meredith glanced around and, realizing what she'd done, impulsively put her hand on Grant's arm. "Oh, I'm so sorry. I didn't mean to be rude. I didn't see . . ."

As he glanced down at her hand on his arm she pulled back quickly, then stood helplessly, unsure which chair to sit down on.

"I didn't mean to compromise your independence, Miss Winstone. I was just trying to be polite in the company of my elders." Grant's tone was mildly cynical as he inclined his head toward Frank and Stella. "They sometimes worry that I might have forgotten how to treat women properly."

"Well then, I'd better make sure you get plenty of practice." Meredith moved in front of the chair he held out and sat down.

"I must say it's good to have a lady around." Frank picked up the menu. "It's been a while."

"I'm not sure I like that remark." Stella arched an eyebrow at her boss. "What are you implying?"

Frank chuckled. "You know what I mean, Stella. A young lady."

"Which makes me?" she persisted with a half-smile.

"Um . . . reassuringly mature."

"Which makes me?" Meredith quickly asked, imitating Stella's eyebrow, and unable to suppress her own impish smile.

"Oh heck, they're ganging up on us already, Grant." Frank raised his hands in mock surrender. "This is meant to be a 'Welcome aboard, Miss Winstone,' not an introduction to a battle of the sexes."

"Well then, thank you," Meredith put in. "It's very good to be aboard."

"And I'm sorry I haven't been much help lately." Frank looked straight at her. "Has my son been working with you or are we relying totally on Stella to train you?"

"Well, both actually." Meredith glanced at Grant. "I'm working on the Stratford case with . . ." She hesitated, suddenly finding herself unable to say "Grant." " . . . with your son, now."

"Good, good. That's an excellent one to start on. Should be fairly cut and dried." He nodded approvingly. "Now, what say we order and then you can tell us all about yourself?"

While they studied their menus, Meredith's mind was racing, unable to concentrate on the food items. *Tell them all about myself? What am I going to say? Do I focus on family? No, maybe not. That could be too delicate.*

"Miss Winstone?" Grant's voice interrupted her thoughts. "What are you ordering?"

"Um . . ." Meredith looked quickly at the menu, realizing that everyone else had already ordered. "Gosh, there's so many to choose from. I'll have the caesar salad, please."

"That's an excellent choice." Frank nodded. "They have great homemade dressings here. Now, tell me, Meredith . . . if I may call you that?" He waited while she nodded. "So what does Meredith Winstone do when she's not studying and working?"

"Oh, not much." She swallowed quickly and coughed.

"Well, that's not good enough," Frank grunted. "Come on, Grant. Use your courtroom tactics . . . help me interrogate the woman."

There was the briefest silence as Grant finished pouring a glass of ice water from the fish-shaped carafe, then sat back in his chair and stared at her intently. "Well, let's narrow the questions a bit. Tell us, Miss Winstone, how have you been spending your time since you completed your studies?"

Meredith felt her back prickling as he stared at her, and she gave an involuntary shiver before toying deliberately with a small dessert menu. "Actually, I took a holiday over on the Gold Coast in Australia."

"Ah . . . a rich student!" He leaned back and eased his hands into his trouser pockets.

"Oh no, not at all!" Meredith responded quickly, disconcerted by his approach and illogically becoming aware of the width of his chest. "The . . . the flight was a graduation present from my parents, and my aunt manages a small motel at Broadbeach on the Gold Coast, so I stayed there for a couple of weeks."

"Oh, I see . . . nothing to do but get a tan," Grant commented dryly, and she found it hard to decide if he was serious or just mocking her. Either way, she responded defensively.

"Actually, just after I got there, I ended up helping clean the motel each day when one of the girls got sick."

"But you still managed to get the tan." Stella held out her own slender, pale wrist beside Meredith's olive brown arm. "You practically radiated sunshine when you first came into the office."

Meredith laughed, trying to relax. "It's easy for me to get a tan. I'm a bit of a throwback to some Maori and French ancestors."

"Okay, enough of the beauty stuff . . . let's get back to the Gold Coast." Frank tapped his fingers on the table. "I haven't been there for years. Is it still packed with tourists?"

"Absolutely." Meredith nodded her head. "Although when I was there, it was more packed with lifeguards."

"Lifeguards?"

"Mm-hmm. It was the national lifesaving carnival, and it was a huge event. I was told it was one of the largest competitions in the world, after the Olympic games."

"It must have been impressive." Grant nodded and took a drink of water. "Lots of bronzed bodies everywhere."

Meredith frowned at the faintly mocking tone in his voice, refusing to be ruffled by his words. "They're definitely bronzed, but they do some great work and I'm quite sure it's not all just to impress people."

"Oh, I'm sure they do. It must be hard sitting out in the sun all day."

"But there's so much more to it than that!" She heard her own voice, briskly decisive and defensive, and felt a sudden desire for the earth to open up and swallow her whole. Why was this man able to make her react so readily . . . and so abruptly? This was meant to be a friendly introduction to the firm and she was retaliating to his comments.

"And you'd know?" Grant showed a mild reaction to the vehemence of her response.

"Actually . . . yes. Yes, I would," Meredith answered more quietly. "I've been a lifeguard for years and we work and train very hard."

There was a long silence following her words as Stella and Frank nodded and Grant raised his eyebrows in genuine surprise.

Meredith realized she was still sitting very upright in her chair and she forced herself to relax. "I find it very rewarding," she finished quietly, unsure how to continue the conversation.

"Well, I'm sure you do, but I really just wanted to know about the weather on the Gold Coast," Frank interrupted, frowning at his son. "I've been thinking I need a holiday."

"Oh, the weather on the coast was wonderful, although the sharks were a bit of a problem." Meredith deliberately turned away from Grant. "I couldn't believe it! The warm weather brought thousands of tiny baitfish in close to shore, and all of these sharks followed them in."

"Sharks?" Stella grimaced. "Delightful."

"It was a bit scary to think of it, but the surf patrol scared them away by running jet skis and boats at them."

"Another example of their dedication?" Grant spoke quietly beside her and watched as her shoulders straightened and her head went up.

"Absolutely." She didn't turn toward him. "I found it very reassuring."

There was a slight pause in the conversation as the waitress delivered their food, and Meredith concentrated on her salad. It really was a delicious meal and she ate heartily.

"Well, it's good to see you've got a wholesome appetite." Frank pointed his fork at her plate. "I get frustrated when I see women picking at their food and leaving half of it."

Meredith paused and self-consciously wiped her mouth with her napkin. "I guess that's a legacy of having much larger, younger brothers. Eating was always a bit of a competition at home."

"It obviously hasn't hurt you," Stella commented wryly. "I don't suppose you're a gym fanatic as well, are you?"

"No, not really," Meredith shook her head. "I enjoy mainly outdoor exercise like running and swimming." She looked at Frank. "Don't you do a lot of sailing?"

"Not nearly enough." He gazed longingly out toward the blue waters of the Auckland Harbor that lapped onto a small beach barely a hundred yards away. "If only Grant would work harder, I could get away on the boat more often."

"Ha!" His son gave a short laugh and Meredith turned, surprised as a wide smile transformed Grant's face. The difference was remarkable and she felt the tension leave her own body. "We hardly see you now, Dad . . . and don't tell us it's all the Murphy case—or that *your* tan is a result of your ancestry."

Frank shook his head, grinning broadly as well, and Meredith glanced from father to son, noting the resemblance when they both smiled. "Those mobile phones are a wonderful invention. The guy on the other end has no idea where you're calling from."

"Until they hear the seagulls calling in the background," Stella commented dryly. "Bryan Murphy remarked on that the other day."

"Good old Bryan," Frank chuckled. "He was probably calling from his golf cart. It's one of the advantages of old age. We understand each other." He looked at Meredith, suddenly serious. "Bryan Murphy has been a client and a friend for years. We trust each other. It's a personal and company policy to establish that trust. You can't put a price on integrity."

She nodded. "My father always says, 'It's better to be trusted than to be loved.'"

"Then I think I'd like your father."

* * *

"Meredith?" Frank's head appeared around the doorway of Meredith's office just as she was closing her briefcase at the end of the day. "Are you busy?"

"Just finishing up." She smiled. "I'm just off to find an apartment somewhere close to Devonport."

"Right, then I won't keep you long." He walked in and closed the door behind him. "I just wanted to explain something to you . . . about Grant."

You too? Meredith set the briefcase down. "There's really no need, Mr. Bascombe. I think I'm getting used to him."

"Well, you shouldn't have to 'get used to him.'" Frank stood at the window. "Stella told me that she'd explained about Hannah and Emily . . . and Barbara."

Meredith nodded and swallowed. "Yes, she did. I'm very sorry."

"It was a dreadful time and it still is very hard to comprehend." He paused and took a deep breath. "After the accident there was a lot of investigation. Grant was very nearly charged with 'reckless endanger-ment.' There was so much pressure on him, on top of the trauma of losing his family." Frank suddenly didn't speak for a long time and Meredith found she couldn't breathe properly. "In the end he was completely exonerated, as they discovered the road hadn't been cleared properly after road repairs, but . . . Grant still blames himself for Emily and Hannah dying. He just buries himself in his work to try to forget. I think having a young woman around the office might be making it more difficult for him to maintain that forgetfulness. I think you somehow remind him of his wife . . . or something. But I don't want you to worry about it. We all think you're doing a great job and, as far as Grant is concerned, I'm sure he just needs a little time to adjust.

CHAPTER 7

"So . . . are things good with Bascombe and Bascombe?" Telesia juggled her bag with a bottle of orange juice and a sandwich as she sat down on the low concrete wall bordering Cheltenham Beach. The girls had finally arranged to meet for lunch at the small beach near Meredith's office in Devonport village.

"I think so." Meredith kicked her shoes off onto the sand below them and sat down beside Telesia on the wall. "I mean, the company has a really good reputation, there's plenty of work, and Mr. Bascombe is great," she nodded thoughtfully. "He's very friendly and helpful."

"Then why did you only say, 'I think so'?" Telesia took the wrapping off her sandwich and studied the filling before carefully extracting a piece of pickle. "Is there another Bascombe or is he one of those long-dead partners?"

There was a very long pause as Meredith contemplated some cone-shaped shells lying on the sand in front of her. "Actually, there is another Bascombe . . . Mr. Bascombe, Jr. . . . Grant," she finished quietly.

"So, why do you hesitate? Is Mr. Bascombe, Jr. a problem?" Telesia chewed thoughtfully as she watched her friend's face.

"Not . . . exactly. He's an excellent lawyer . . . from what I hear." She squinted at the sun. "I haven't worked much with him yet . . . which is probably a good thing."

"Why? Wouldn't he be good to work with if he's such a great lawyer?"

"Oh, yes . . ." Meredith hesitated. "And we have just started working on a case. It's just that . . ."

"It's just what?" Telesia shook her head. "Come on, Mele, tell me about Mr. Bascombe, Jr. Full details, please." She waited as Meredith slowly undid the plastic wrapper on her own sandwich.

"Okay . . . Mr. Bascombe, Jr. is tall, dark-haired, and handsome in a rugged way . . . about thirty . . . maybe thirty-two years old. He's very . . . confident and hard-working . . . and, like I said, I get the impression he's a very good lawyer. It's just that . . . it's hard to know how to act when he's around. One minute he appears to almost resent me being around . . . then he'll be really helpful, even . . . charming." She took a bite and chewed quietly. "Even at the initial interview, he was quite . . . abrupt, and I'm afraid I was too. I almost up and walked out before the interview finished because I thought they'd never employ me."

"But now you're working there." Telesia looked puzzled. "Am I missing something?"

"No." Meredith took another deep breath. "He left the office and, next thing, Mr. Bascombe, Sr. offered me the job, on the spot . . . and I said yes." She shook her head. "I still can't quite believe it. I love working there, but at the moment I don't feel I can really relax when he's around."

"Because he intimidates you?"

"No, not really . . . I mean, he does, but he's had a very difficult time . . . which is probably why he's so unpredictable." Meredith closed her eyes. Intimidated? That was just one of the myriad of emotions she experienced whenever Grant was around. "You see, his mother died and then his wife and baby were killed in a car accident. Evidently, he was driving, and to make matters worse, he was nearly charged with reckless endangerment."

"So you feel sorry for him?" Telesia spoke quietly.

"No . . . I mean, I didn't know any of this when I took the job. His father and Stella, our secretary, both told me later. I don't even know exactly why I took the job. I just . . ." she shrugged.

"You just felt . . . compelled to?" Telesia nodded at her significantly.

"It was almost like that, yes." Meredith nodded. "I don't know why I even said yes. He hasn't gone out of his way to make me feel welcome, but then he's not actually antagonistic either." She frowned. "I really can't explain it . . . but then, when I found out his story . . ."

"Ahh . . . then you felt sorry for him."

"Sia, stop it! You're not in court. No, I don't feel sorry for him," she exclaimed, her jaw tightening defensively. "Besides . . . whether I feel sorry for him or not has nothing to do with my becoming a lawyer. I said yes to the job because I think I can get really good training there."

There was a long silence as they both contemplated the sea quietly lapping onto the elongated mounds of bright orange-and-red shells that stretched over the sand.

Telesia finally spoke. "So, do you still want to keep working there?"

"Of course I want to." Meredith shook her head. "It already feels like . . . like I belong there. Mr. Bascombe, Sr. is a great lawyer and I think he recognizes what I can do. And as for Grant . . . he keeps to himself and that's fine with me. Knowing about his past doesn't have to have any effect on our professional relationship."

"As long as it stays that way." Telesia raised one eyebrow knowingly.

"Of course!" Meredith quickly bit into her sandwich. Then, still chewing, she wagged a finger at her friend. "Besides . . . that's enough about me." She swallowed. "What about you?"

Telesia shrugged and smiled. "Who . . . me? Not much happening, except I now have a great job at the district court and an income, which is really nice. But I also have no home . . . and no fiancé."

"What?" Meredith choked on her sandwich. "What about Tavita? What happened?"

"We decided to take time out for a while." Telesia's eyes suddenly glistened. "My family started putting the pressure on about having a huge wedding with lots of bridesmaids and a huge feast and big bridal cars. It would cost so much that they would have to go into debt to pay for it, but still, when Tavita told them that we were planning to be married in the temple and that we didn't want a huge wedding . . . my stepfather got very angry and threatened Tavita . . . physically." She hung her head and Meredith could see tears glistening on the ends of her thick, black eyelashes. "Later, after the argument . . . Tavita said that it was up to me . . ."

"Oh, Sia, I'm so sorry." Meredith temporarily forgot her own problems and moved closer, touching her friend's shoulder as it shook slightly. It was usually Telesia who offered her comfort or counsel when she got discouraged or upset; now it felt strange to see her friend's composure crumble and to hear her crying quietly. She awkwardly patted her on the back until Telesia rubbed her face with her hands and smiled weakly.

"I just got so confused, Mele. I was annoyed with my family for trying to force us to do something that we didn't want, but . . . I also know how important it is for my stepfather to be seen giving me a huge wedding . . . and it really would be so much easier to just go along with all of the plans. But I didn't want a big wedding either, and I wanted to do things the way Heavenly Father has told us is right. I wanted to focus on the temple and not on all the expense and fuss." She shook her head miserably. "I know Tavita just wanted to do the right thing as well, but then I got frustrated with him for making me choose between them. So I told him I didn't want to get married . . . and then my stepfather told me to leave the house anyway."

"So where are you staying?"

Telesia shrugged. "At a backpackers' hostel in town . . . until I find somewhere else. It's quite funny, really. I get up in the morning and leave in my suit as everyone else leaves in their hiking clothes."

Meredith remained silent, trying to find words to console her friend, then suddenly her face brightened and her eyes sparkled.

"Sia, why don't we get an apartment together? I've been looking for a small place around Devonport, but it's quite expensive here. Together we could manage it! What about it? I think it could really work."

Telesia recognized the tone of her voice and the look on her face; it heralded another of Meredith's "brilliant" ideas that would fast become a reality given her natural persistence.

Telesia nodded slowly, not quite convinced. "It could be good. You don't think I would cramp your style?"

Meredith laughed and leaned over to give her an exuberant hug. "Style? We create our own style, and besides . . . I've really missed not having you around every day like at university. "

"Do you mean legally, professionally . . . or spiritually?" Telesia glanced sideways at her friend with the beginnings of a smile.

"Oh . . . okay." Meredith pursed her lips, then grinned. "Let's start with professionally. Maybe—and I mean maybe—we'll work on the rest later."

* * *

Grant flipped the light switch on the brass table lamp and watched as the warm light shone downward to illuminate the top of the desk in the darkened study. He walked around and sat down in the large leather chair, opening the file he had brought home. The Stratford case. It appeared to be a fairly straightforward case of sexual molestation—his client, of course, fiercely denied being guilty.

He began to read the case notes again, trying to decide how he would introduce the case to Meredith Winstone. He had put off going over it with her for too long, he realized, probably because of the sensitive subject matter. How much would she be able to handle? He frowned as he studied the notes. He knew he was most likely being silly. *She's probably already been over the notes . . . several times.*

He felt his frown unwillingly change to a slight smile as he thought about the enthusiasm with which she seemed to tackle everything. *Is it all for show, or can she keep up that intensity?* Even as he considered that possibility he shook his head. *No, she's not one to pretend. She appears to be genuine about everyone and everything.*

"*Not a deceitful bone in her body.*" He could almost hear the mellow tones of his mother's voice whenever she described someone that she trusted. He suddenly felt sure that his mother would have liked Meredith Winstone.

Just as Dad and Stella obviously like her . . . and Charles.

He began to toy with his pen, rolling it between his fingers while he stared unseeing at the pages in the folder.

So why don't I know how to behave when she's around? As soon as she looks at me with those brown eyes I say something unreasonable that makes her uncomfortable. That's obvious from the warning looks I get from Dad and Stella.

Grant closed his eyes and leaned his head back against the leather armchair. *Meredith Winstone, with all her fresh-faced enthusiasm and vitality, seems to personify* . . . his eyes flicked open. His thoughts had been leading to her capabilities as a lawyer, but suddenly Meredith's face became an older version of Emily's face in his mind.

His hands gripped the arms of the chair until the knuckles showed white.

Meredith Winstone, with all her fresh-faced enthusiasm and vitality, seems to personify everything . . . that Hannah can never be. Everything that Emily can never become . . . because I killed them!

Was that why he had been so abrupt with Meredith? Not just because of her attractiveness or her genuinely likeable personality . . . but because she somehow represented everything his wife and child could never be. Grant inhaled deeply as the pain of remembering again made his whole body begin to shake.

For years he had successfully blocked out the memory of his family from his daily life, refusing to think about them or what might have been. Now Meredith Winstone, just by being here with her youthful exuberance, was bringing back all the pain.

He closed the folder and pushed it aside, then reached for the photos on the desk. For several minutes he contemplated the framed images of his family . . . his wife, his daughter, his mother—and their perpetual postures and smiles frozen forever onto pieces of glossed paper.

"Forever." He leaned his head back against the cool leather and stared at the ceiling. "Gone forever . . . dead forever," his voice was a harsh whisper in the empty room. "While I spend forever trying to forget them . . . and what I did to them."

He slowly bent forward.

"I took away your life, little Emily. I'm so, so sorry." He gently touched the baby's face, and for the first time since he'd held his daughter's tiny lifeless body in his arms, tears began to roll down Grant's cheeks. "If only I could see you or touch you . . . know where you are."

The frame slipped from his hands as he leaned forward on the desk and cradled his head on his arms.

* * *

"Is there another big case on?" Meredith leaned against the reception desk and quietly broached the subject with Stella. "I was meant to meet with Grant several days ago about the Stratford case, but . . . it hasn't happened, and he seems to be working awfully hard."

"Work is often the panacea for other things." Stella adjusted her glasses and peered over the top of them at Meredith. "There's not much on at present. I get the feeling he's just busy being busy."

"Oh." Meredith nodded lamely, unsure what to say. "I guess he'll let me know when he wants to go over the Stratford case then."

"Possibly. I could ask for you, but maybe he needs a bit of a shake along from you." Stella smiled. "He's too used to ignoring me."

"I think I'd rather be ignored as well," Meredith put in quickly. "Anyway, I've got plenty to work on. Mr. Bascombe gave me a bunch of new files to look at."

As if he'd been listening, Grant's door suddenly opened and he stood observing them both for a long moment. Then he took a deep breath and looked directly at Meredith. "Are you free tomorrow morning, Miss Winstone? I believe we have a case to review."

"Ah, yes." Meredith swallowed and avoided Stella's glance. "What time?"

"As soon as you get into the office. About eight o'clock. The sooner we get started the better, because we've a lot to catch up on . . . oh, and we'll probably need to work late. The initial hearing is in a few days."

"Of course." Meredith hesitated only briefly before relegating the continued search for an apartment to another night.

* * *

"So, considering all of the evidence we've looked at, what do you think? Is he guilty?" Grant sat back in his chair and pressed his fingertips together, waiting for Meredith's reaction.

She took a final look at the last page of the file before closing the buff folder and placing it carefully on his desk. They had been carefully going over the case for the last two days since the hearing, analyzing all the evidence and reviewing statements. It seemed to be a clear-cut case of a family acquaintance accused of molesting a thirteen-year-old girl. The man had pled not guilty, but the girl was adamant in her accusation.

"I think she's lying. I think he's innocent." Meredith spoke quietly but decisively, addressing her words to the folder.

There was a long pause but she didn't look up, concentrating instead on the white sticker that bore the name of their client. Finally Grant leaned forward and spoke deliberately.

"The evidence is very conclusive. She is very clear about what happened. And he really doesn't have any alibi at all. What is your justification?"

"I just think she's . . . fabricating." Meredith picked up a pen and twisted it in her fingers. It was so difficult to explain to Grant all the thoughts and feelings that she'd been experiencing the last forty-eight hours, especially lying awake in the early hours of the morning.

"And what do you base your opinion on? Women's intuition?" Grant's voice sounded faintly mocking and Meredith glanced up quickly.

"It's a little more than that, I assure you." She swallowed hard. "I just feel that her story is a bit too clear, too definite." Again she sensed Grant's doubt and suddenly wished she hadn't interrupted the easy flow of communication that had developed as they'd worked together the last few days.

"Too definite?" He stood up slowly and tapped his fingers on the desk. "Some judges would call it fairly conclusive evidence. An open-and-shut case."

Meredith took a deep breath. "That's just what it appears to be. I guess I just see it from . . . a slightly different angle."

"Which is . . . ? You haven't mentioned anything else until now."

She could sense Grant trying to keep the tone of his voice polite and wished again that she'd never said anything. Then she thought of their client and her voice became stronger.

"Well, I don't know if you remember a story in the Bible." She hesitated, hardly daring to look at him. "It was about Joseph, when he was a prisoner in Egypt, and about how the pharaoh's wife . . . wanted him."

She waited until Grant nodded slowly. "I am acquainted with the story . . . go on."

"When Joseph refused her advances and ran from her, she got very angry and tried to grab him. He got away but she had a piece of his clothing she'd ripped off him, so she tore her own clothes and called the guards . . ."

"And she pretended that he'd raped her," Grant finished.

Meredith nodded her head. "I don't know if that's what the girl's motives are, but I just feel that she's lying."

"But we can hardly base our whole defense on a Bible story." Grant thrust his hands into his pockets. "Or your gut feelings. There's got to be a whole lot more to it than that."

Again Meredith took a deep breath. "I do actually have another reason for doubting her."

"Which is . . . another story?" Grant raised his eyebrow, noting the way the pulse in her throat was beating faster.

"Not . . . just another story." Meredith put the pen down, and, as she folded her hands in her lap, he noticed that she was shaking slightly. "I was . . ." She pressed her lips together, then with an explosive sigh, finished, "raped . . . when I was eleven."

The words seemed to hang in the air. Meredith looked straight at Grant. "I know exactly what she would have gone through. The things she would have felt, the images, the smells, the same things playing over and over in your mind . . . the things you don't remember because . . ." She paused and her voice shook slightly. "I don't see any of that here. I don't see fear or zero self-esteem or wondering what she might have possibly done to cause it . . ."

Meredith hesitated. "Part of the reason I became a lawyer was to help young girls and women who have suffered . . . like me, at the hands of men like that." She swallowed again. "When I was going over the materials, the written statements all made it seem so clear-cut, and I was angry at him for hurting a young girl like that . . . I was actually angry at having to defend him. But the other day, after the first court hearing . . ." She shook her head. "In this case, I just don't feel this man is guilty."

"I've gotten that same impression myself," Grant said thoughtfully. "Though I couldn't be as certain about it as you seem to be. But how can we prove it? We have no direct evidence. I think our only hope would be to get the girl to admit she's lying. In this sort of case, all the sympathy is with the alleged victim—as it should be." He smiled wryly. "It's not considered in good taste to question the credibility of such a witness, so I had been going to concentrate on the fact that the prosecution's physical evidence is too weak to prove Stratford's guilt conclusively enough. It will be a very delicate thing to question her in such a way as to elicit what we want without appearing like ogres ourselves. But . . . it could work." Grant rose from his chair, staring into space as if deep in thought.

Meredith sat pensively as he slowly paced to the window and back again, then reached over to pick up the file in front of her. He opened it and flicked through the pages before closing it and putting it on the desk again. Then he leaned heavily on it.

"I hope you aren't going to disrupt every case like this."

Meredith quickly glanced up at him, then relaxed as she saw the slightest smile twist at his lips and a look of sympathy, or perhaps respect, that reached his eyes as he studied her closely.

"I assure you . . . I didn't mean to be disruptive at all, but I couldn't agree just because it's . . . your case." She felt herself warming under the directness of his gaze and deliberately looked away.

"Fair enough . . . and I don't expect you to just agree. I'm paying you to be a thinking lawyer." He hesitated and his voice softened. "And compassionate, too."

Neither spoke for several seconds as Grant sat down and leaned forward, resting his elbows on his desk, his hands clenched together and pressed against his lips.

Meredith hesitated before blurting out suddenly, "So where does this leave us? They're expecting us to defend next week."

"I guess we do some fast reviewing." Grant shrugged as he emphasized the "we." "Don't think you're going to get out of this now after making me rethink my whole defense."

"I'm sorry." Meredith ran her hands over her thighs, unsure what to say next.

"And never say you're sorry, Meredith . . . especially if you don't mean it."

Again she looked quickly at him, surprised at the softness of his tone and the slight smile that accompanied it. She tried to relax and smile in response, but his next words sent icy fingers down her spine.

"It seems we've both been marked by tragedy." Grant sat back in his chair. "How did you cope with your situation?"

Meredith licked her lips, which had suddenly become very dry, and exhaled slowly. The preparation for the case had brought a lot of buried memories to the surface.

"I'm not sure that I did cope. I think my parents coped for me." She nodded, remembering the priesthood blessings her father had given her, reassuring her of her personal worth, and of the many weeks spent sleeping in her parents' bedroom because she was too afraid to sleep alone.

"They supported me physically and spiritually, but the emotional side was a bit more difficult to handle. I fluctuated a lot—my self-esteem, trusting other people . . ."

Grant nodded as he swiveled in his chair to face the west wall of his office. "Do you think it'll always be with you? Will you ever get over it?"

Suddenly Meredith sensed that he wasn't just talking about her, and she carefully considered her answer.

"As a tragic experience, yes, I think it will always be there. Sometimes a dim memory, other times like it was just yesterday . . . but I've worked hard to replace the pain and the torment."

"Replace?" He was still contemplating the wall, but she became keenly aware of his heightened attention to her answer.

"Well, I was quite skinny when it happened, so at first I sort of associated the pain with my size. I thought if I was fatter, no one would be interested in me, so I basically started eating all the time. My parents tried to stop me, but then one day they enrolled me in self-defense classes—martial arts. They kept telling me that it was a much better way to protect myself than overeating, and they sent my younger brothers along with me to keep me company. After a while I started to believe them, and I became the best student in the class." She smiled wryly. "I guess I had a lot more motivation than the others. I still do."

"You still do martial arts?" Grant swung his chair around so that he was facing her, his face furrowed in a slight frown of disbelief.

Meredith nodded almost apologetically. "I gained my black belt in Taranaki, then I began teaching younger children. My parents also got me into swimming, and that led to the lifesaving training." She gave a small laugh. "I was so busy doing physical things that I wasn't constantly hungry, so I overcame the food issue. But I've been committed to exercise and teaching the young children ever since. I guess at the back of my mind there's the thought that if I keep training or helping others, that it . . . it won't happen again . . . to me or them."

There was a long silence. Grant could have been contemplating her, but his eyes seemed to be looking right through her. Finally, he leaned his head back against the chair.

"I suspect Stella or my father will have talked to you by now . . . about my . . . situation." His voice was low and slightly husky as he made the statement, and Meredith hesitated before she nodded.

"They did mention . . . the accident," she stammered. "I'm very sorry."

"That's why I asked you how you coped with your tragedy." He hesitated. "Because I don't know that I have. Physically, I work hard at my job and that sometimes fills a void." He stopped and stared directly at her. "Frankly, I thought I was coping . . . until you came here."

"Me?" Meredith felt a sickening weight drop to the base of her stomach and her throat seemed to constrict. She didn't know how to respond, but Grant didn't wait for an answer.

"I've kept feeling annoyed with you for some reason. I really didn't know why . . ." A deep frown creased his forehead, and she watched as his long fingers rubbed at the furrows before he looked directly at her. "Until the other day. It hit me that in some obscure way . . . you . . . your youth and vitality . . . somehow you represent what Hannah and Emily, my wife and daughter, can never be . . . what I took away from them."

Meredith felt the color drain from her face as she realized again the extent of his pain, and she felt powerless to help him. Then he leaned forward.

"Miss Winstone . . . I've spent the last few days and nights doing a lot of soul searching. Thankfully, you have been otherwise occupied because my mind has been elsewhere a lot of the time . . . but, in all honesty, I've realized that I've got to stop blaming you for things you're not responsible for." He stopped and ran his hand through his hair in an unexpectedly childlike way. "The trouble is . . . I've never been very good at apologizing."

There was a long pause as Meredith fought to control the lump growing in her throat, then Grant walked slowly around the desk to stand directly in front of her and it felt as if the room had shrunk to the few inches that surrounded the two of them.

"Miss Winstone, I've started badly and I've made your beginnings here a bit . . . unpleasant. I want you to know that I appreciate you sharing your personal pain with me." He extended his right hand toward her. "Please forgive me for my rudeness, and be assured that I really do want to help you become the excellent lawyer that I think you're capable of being."

Meredith stared at his hand, noting the lean fingers and well-manicured nails and an unexpected callus on the palm. She stood up and looked straight at him. Her first inclination was to say there was no need to apologize, until she heard her mother's voice in her mind. She had been speaking after Meredith had quarreled once with Ryan. *"Let him say 'sorry,' Meredith. A boy becomes a man when he learns to say 'sorry.'"*

"Apology accepted, Mr. Bascombe, and . . . thank you . . . for trusting me." She swallowed hard and placed her hand in his. There was a second's hesitation before she felt his hand tighten around hers and give it the merest shake. Then he relaxed his grip but didn't let go. She couldn't look up, but as she began to pull her hand away, he briefly squeezed it again.

"Thank you . . . Meredith."

* * *

"Meredith! Hey!" Telesia's voice carried to her as she strode out briskly along the paved walk of King Edward Parade, the early evening breeze just cool enough to be exhilarating. "Meredith! Slow down!"

"Sia!" Even as she said her friend's name and turned toward the small, blue car pulling onto the curb beside her, Meredith clapped her hand to her forehead. "Oh, my goodness, I completely forgot!"

"You did, didn't you?" Telesia switched off the engine and leaned over to the open window.

"I did. I'm so sorry!" Meredith glanced at her wristwatch. "Have we still got time?"

"The agent said she'd wait for another fifteen minutes. Jump in." She waited while Meredith settled herself into the car, then pulled out along the parade. "Did your car break down? I saw it still parked outside the office when I came to look for you."

Meredith shook her head and ran her fingers through her hair to settle the windblown strands. "No, the car's fine. I just needed to get some fresh air and I guess I just kept walking. I'm sorry. I completely forgot about seeing the apartment."

"Well, whatever was on your mind must have been pretty big." Telesia raised a dark, shapely eyebrow. "You were the one who was so excited about this place."

"I know, I know." Meredith stared straight ahead. "Actually, I had a meeting with Grant . . . Mr. Bascombe, Jr."

"And?" Telesia prompted. "Oh, wait. Here we are, and the agent's still here. Tell me later."

Both girls jumped out of the car and ran up to meet the red-haired woman waiting outside the front gate of a neatly renovated villa. She glanced primly at her watch, then assumed a businesslike smile.

"You're just in time. We only have a few minutes."

"I'm very sorry, it was my fault . . ." Meredith's apology was lost as the agent turned and quickly led the way along the wooden veranda that wrapped itself around the entire villa.

"The apartment is at the back. It used to be the servants' quarters, so it's all self-contained and, of course, fully restored."

Meredith followed Telesia as the agent held open a door for them, and then in an instant she forgot her recent worries. The small lounge with its polished wooden floors and French windows with cream-painted joinery held her spellbound.

"Oh, Sia, don't you love it! Look at the view . . . and the garden!"

"It is lovely. How big are the other rooms?" Telesia was always practical.

After being shown the rest of the apartment, Meredith was even more entranced than ever.

"Look, Sia, we could sit out here on the veranda and watch the sun rise over Rangitoto Island and go swimming every day."

"I'll stay with watching the sun rise." Telesia grinned and turned to the agent. "What are the terms and bond required?" she asked smoothly.

Even to Meredith, Telesia appeared especially efficient and businesslike, and the agent looked slightly taken aback.

"So . . . you really are interested?" She sounded slightly flustered and looked directly at Meredith, as if for reassurance.

"You didn't get that impression?" Telesia laughed.

"I . . . well, I wasn't sure. This is quite an exclusive area."

"I assure you we can manage the rent." Telesia smiled but the agent still didn't look at her.

Meredith nodded. "My friend is correct. She is legal counselor at the district court and I'm at a private legal practice in Devonport. The rent really is not a problem."

"I'm sure." Still the agent hesitated. "Do you both have family?"

"Yes . . . but I'm not sure what that has to do with renting this apartment." Meredith frowned.

"Shall I say, the landlord is very—particular—about who rents the apartment?"

Suddenly the agent's words sank in, and Telesia glanced at Meredith. "I get the feeling that your brothers would be acceptable as visitors, but maybe not mine."

"Is that right?" Meredith looked squarely at the agent.

"Well, it's just that we've had problems in the past."

"And so you anticipate problems? Would that stop you renting the apartment to us?"

"I might just have to include a few extra conditions in the agreement. Perfectly legal," she laughed nervously. "As you'd both know, I'm sure."

"Of course." Telesia moved so that she was looking directly at the woman. "I'd be happy to meet the landlord personally."

"No, no, that won't be necessary. Just as long as you give me your word . . . that there won't be . . . excessive family gatherings on the premises."

Meredith tipped her nose in the air in imitation of the agent a few minutes after finalizing the lease. "No excessive gatherings on the premises," she said in a snooty voice as they drove away. "You know," she added, "we could take her to court for some of the things she said."

Telesia laughed gently, then frowned. "Let's not worry about it. I know what she's talking about, and I don't know if I should be offended. I see so many cases about this sort of thing in court, where people just destroy houses because they don't own them and don't care."

"I can understand that, and we'll just be extra careful. But I could just as easily be irresponsible. She didn't have to single you out like that. Are you sure you're going to be happy here?" Meredith looked at her friend. "Don't just agree because I get all carried away."

"No, not at all. I do love it here." Telesia sighed. "And I'm so looking forward to being out on my own. I really think it's important for me to take a break from my family as well as Tavita so that I can sort myself out."

Meredith nodded. "Yes, I can see that. I'll do my best to help you, though I'm not sure exactly how."

Telesia smiled and wiped a hand across her cheek. "Just pray for me, my friend . . . and promise me that you'll keep that wild family of yours under control when they visit."

As they pulled up behind Meredith's car, Telesia gasped. "Hey, you never finished telling me about your Mr. Bascombe, Jr.!"

"Well, he's not 'my' Mr. Bascombe, for a start." Meredith felt the color rise in her cheeks. "And actually, nothing much has happened really."

"Just enough to make you forget our appointment and be out striding along in your suit after work. I haven't seen you walk that fast since you got your first C grade at university." Telesia shook her head. "What happened?"

Meredith hesitated. "It's quite strange really. Grant . . . Mr. Bascombe . . . has not been particularly friendly since I arrived. Then we were meant to be working on a case together and we had one brief meeting, but then he just didn't come out of his office for several days." She shrugged. "Today, he suddenly confessed that he realized he hadn't been very pleasant, and apologized, but . . . he told me that in some obscure way, I represent everything his wife and baby could never be and it has made the pain come back all over again."

"Oh dear, and he's been taking it out on you?" Telesia nodded in understanding.

"I guess so. I appear to represent whatever disturbs him most."

Telesia sat quietly for some time, and then she ran her hands lightly over the steering wheel and glanced at her friend. "I really wonder if you're meant to be here right now. For him. For them."

Meredith glanced quickly at her friend, then up at the windows, "Bascombe and Bascombe" etched on their length. "What makes you say that?"

"I really don't know." Telesia shrugged. "It just occurred to me that you might be the right person for them right now."

"But what can I possibly do, apart from being a good lawyer?"

"Just be a good lawyer, perhaps." Telesia pursed her lips. "Or maybe it's more like . . . you're somebody who knows what they need to know."

"Meaning?"

"Oh, Mele, don't you see? This family is still in a lot of pain because they've lost a mother, a wife, and a baby. Do they have any idea where their loved ones are now?"

Meredith hesitated then she shrugged. "I don't know."

"Well, put it this way then. Do you know where Grant's wife and baby and mother are now?"

"Ye . . . es," Meredith took a deep breath. "Yes. I do."

"Then perhaps this is why you are the right person for now." Telesia's soft tones seemed to sink into Meredith's thoughts.

"But . . . I don't even go to church," Meredith almost groaned. "Why would they believe me . . . even if I happened to say anything?"

"Maybe you need to become believable," Telesia smiled. "Maybe you need Grant and his father as much as they need you."

Meredith drove home without registering any details of the trip, and it was almost a surprise when she pulled up outside the dark gray building with its numerous narrow windows. She climbed the stairs to her room, walked straight to her bedroom, and sank onto the bed.

"*Maybe you need Grant and his father as much as they need you.*" Telesia's words had played over and over in her mind on the way home and now she heard them again.

"But why me?" Meredith moaned as she rested her head on her hands. "I just want to be a good lawyer, that's all. I didn't ask to upset my boss!"

Even as she uttered her thoughts out loud, Meredith closed her eyes, then shook her head and slid off the side of the bed. In a matter-of-fact way, prayer had always been a part of her life until she'd moved to Auckland. Even in the first year she had routinely offered morning and evening prayers, asking for help with studies, with adjusting to her new ward and being away from her family. It had been that way until the evening she'd spent with Mitch and they'd flirted a bit too much and kissed too long—it had been too embarrassing to kneel down when she got home . . . or the next day . . . or the day after. And then the desire or the need to pray had left her completely. She had driven herself forward with a growing conviction of her own skills and ability, with no need for spiritual confirmation . . . until now.

For a long time, Meredith sat back on her legs and gazed at the ceiling, then with a groan of resignation she drew herself up onto her knees and leaned against her bed, resting on her elbows with her head in her hands.

"Heavenly Father . . . I know it's been a while . . . a very, very long while . . ."

CHAPTER 8

"I must say, that went surprisingly well." Grant held the court-room door open to allow Meredith to walk through. "Your intuition certainly paid off."

"I'm just so relieved that Mr. Stratford wasn't convicted." She frowned as she stepped past him. "It's so different when you study these cases at university . . . they're just words on a page and you learn only the clinical details, but when it's real people involved . . ." She shook her head. "It just makes me cringe to think that Mr. Stratford may have been punished for something he is innocent of."

She had unconsciously screwed up her nose in an almost childlike expression of concern, and Grant found himself suddenly watching her rather than thinking about the case as they made their way out into the corridor. Did she realize that her lips pursed when she was concentrating or that she put her head at a distinct angle and always to the left when she was about to make a statement? Even when he had been presenting in court he'd noticed the same mannerisms, as though she could have stood up and taken his place at any time because she was so involved in the proceedings. He jerked his attention back to her words as she spoke again.

"But I also feel sorry for the girl. She must be a very mixed-up child."

Grant blinked and coughed as if to clear his mind and his throat. "Ah, yes . . . looks like a pretty troubled relationship with her family, and this will only make things worse, I would imagine."

Meredith stopped as she thought about the verbal abuse that had ensued after the charges had been dismissed. During her testimony, the teenage girl had broken down and confessed to lying about her attack, and her parents had not been pleased to discover her deception.

Meredith looked at Grant. "I think it takes times like this to help me realize how amazing my own parents are—were—when I went through my situation. I never realized how fortunate I was."

"How fortunate . . . or how sheltered?" Grant countered as he stood aside and held another door open for her. As she walked close by, he caught the subtle mellowness of her perfume—it was a fragrance he had come to appreciate at the office. He caught his breath and hesitated slightly before following her through the door. *Keep your mind on your work, Bascombe. She's a good lawyer . . . and that's all.* He continued speaking abruptly. "Sometimes it can affect your attitude toward clients if you're too . . . protected. You're going to come up against some pretty nasty cases . . . especially in family law, and you're not going to be able to solve them all with a Bible story."

Meredith wondered if she should be defending her upbringing but for some reason it didn't seem to matter, and instead she smiled as she stopped and turned to face him. He had his head down as he was following behind and almost ran into her. He neatly sidestepped but his chest brushed against her shoulder, and the second of close contact made her skin prickle. It was the same sensation she'd felt when Grant had shaken her hand in the courtroom at the conclusion of the case. Distracted, she resumed walking, this time by his side.

Concentrate, Meredith. You've just won the case. You're excited . . . it's nothing more. She bit her lip when he briefly put his hand against the small of her back in an instinctively protective gesture as some people brushed by. *But I'd like it to be more.*

She drew a quick breath and glanced around the corridor as awareness of her own thought translated into confusion and she struggled to remember what she had just been going to say. "Um . . . I noticed how well you presented that 'Bible story' in court. I don't believe I've ever heard it related with such . . . flair. It was almost as if you knew it really well."

She noted how quickly the color spread from his face down his neck, until it reached the top of his pristine-white shirt collar, and then he actually laughed.

"I confess, I actually dug out the family Bible and read." He shook his head, chuckling, and she began to relax again as he smiled openly. "I was really getting into the whole story, but it just about gave my father a heart attack when he came into the study and saw me reading the Bible again."

Meredith put her hand to her mouth. "What did he say?"

"Absolutely nothing. I just walked past him with it and made some comment that a good lawyer uses all the resources at his disposal. I didn't wait for an answer."

She smiled, enjoying this more amiable Grant. In the weeks that they'd worked on the Stratford case, Grant had been pleasant and informative, and even expressed appreciation for the extra hours of work she'd put in by leaving her a gift voucher for a CD from the local music store. She had found herself looking forward to their sessions each day, and now winning the case only brought an increased sense of satisfaction.

They continued walking up the long, wood-paneled hallway, ill lit by high overhead windows. Small groups of people stood quietly discussing their own problems, awaiting their turn in the numerous courtrooms off the main corridor. Meredith found herself absently noting the appearance of people and wondering what crime they might have committed. How would they be defended? *How would we . . . Grant . . . defend them?*

Her train of thought was suddenly interrupted as Grant stopped and turned to her. "I was thinking . . . to recognize our—your—winning this first case . . . that is . . . perhaps you'd like to get a bite to eat after we finish work this evening?"

The cumulative noise of the crowds seemed to become a whisper as Meredith's pulse beat faster and louder in her ears. Was Grant Bascombe actually asking her out, or would it just be at company expense?

"I . . . I'm sorry. What . . . ?" she stammered, then clamped her jaw tightly to stop from saying anything else.

"I just thought . . . after the long hours you've put in over the last few weeks . . . and after winning the case . . . you might like dinner," Grant finished lamely, and waited for her reaction.

"That would be . . ." Meredith stared back and then swallowed hard. "I can't."

Her answer sounded abrupt, even to her own ears. She closed her eyes and turned her head away as Grant nodded and fixed his gaze on the wall behind her.

"I see." He switched his briefcase to his other hand and straightened the front of his jacket. "Well, that's fine, then."

He turned abruptly toward the large double wooden doors beside them, but Meredith quickly touched the sleeve of his jacket to restrain him.

"No . . . I mean, I really can't—not that I don't want to." She swallowed. "It's just that I have to leave straight after work. It's Friday, and I'm driving down to Taranaki for the weekend. It takes about six hours in my old car . . . and Mum gets worried . . ." Her voice trailed off as she realized she was still holding onto his arm.

"I understand." Grant nodded as she moved her hand away and clasped her briefcase tightly with both hands. "Family priorities."

"It's just that my brother is leaving. He's going on a mission." She bit her lip as she imagined Grant's internal reaction to that excuse. *More Bible stories.* "I won't be seeing him for quite a while . . ." Meredith trailed off again, staring at his jacket collar and the way his dark hair was beginning to touch on it and curl slightly.

"Then you'd better make sure you get there in good time." He glanced at his watch and turned abruptly. "There isn't anything too pressing at work. Why don't you just leave straightaway when we get back to the office?"

* * *

Meredith closed the drawer of her desk and tidied the buff-colored folders into a neat pile. It really was thoughtful of him. Now she could travel during the daylight and spend some extra time with her family tonight before bed. She hummed quietly as she picked up her briefcase, paused in front of her office doorway, and quickly scanned the room to check if she'd forgotten anything.

"When were you planning to travel back?" The voice seemed disconcertingly close to her ear.

"What? Oh! You startled me." She swung round to face Grant as he stood in the doorway.

"I was just wondering when you were planning to travel back."

"Oh . . . um . . . late Sunday night. We're having a big family dinner in the early evening, so I'll leave after that." She nodded as she mentally calculated her travel time. "Don't worry, I'll be here for work on Monday morning."

"That's exactly what I want to be sure of." His tone was surprisingly grim, and Meredith reacted sharply.

"I assure you I won't be late, and my work is all ready to go."

"Your punctuality was not the reason for my concern," he said, still abruptly, and a pulse beat rapidly in the side of his jaw. "I was just going to suggest that you come in later on Monday . . . or even on Tuesday."

"But . . ." Meredith swallowed the lump in her throat that had formed instantly at his suggestion. "I can't take two days off! I've only just started working here. I mean, I'm very grateful, but . . ."

"Miss Winstone." Grant held up his hand to silence her. "If this was a family funeral you would be entitled to the days off. I'm just ensuring that it's not your funeral—which it could be if you have to drive back on those winding roads in the middle of the night." He turned on his heel, but she heard his last comment clearly: "I expect you here promptly at eight o'clock Tuesday morning. We have another case to review."

Meredith stood quietly as the door to his office closed behind him. *How can he be so kind and so abrupt at the same time? Just a couple of hours ago I was laughing with him and feeling . . .* She put her hand to her throat, unable to even think about the feelings she had been experiencing. *Then I feel like he's telling me off, and then a few minutes later I'm feeling totally grateful and thinking what a kind person he is. How can I feel . . . attracted to somebody so unpredictable?* She shook her head. *Because I am.*

"Isn't it time you left?" Stella stood up behind her desk and pointed at the wall clock.

"Ah, yes." Meredith sheepishly realized she had been standing in her own doorway staring off into space. She looked questioningly at the secretary. "Stella, why do I feel grateful and confused all at once? Grant just gave me one and a half days off to visit with my family . . . which is wonderful. But it was almost like an order."

Stella nodded knowingly. "It was an order and you'd better obey it." Her voice softened as she moved around the desk closer to Meredith. "Don't forget that Grant had his accident driving on winding roads late at night. He just doesn't want the same thing happening to you."

* * *

"Well, I think it's great. I imagine it'll be months before I get any time off. Just enjoy it, girl." Telesia's voice was reassuring.

"You'll be okay for the weekend, then?" Meredith walked around her bedroom with the mobile phone, packing clothes into a large sports bag as she talked.

"Positive." Telesia's voice dropped a tone. "I have a feeling I may be busy, anyway."

"Busy? I thought you said you were going to find a good book to read."

"Oh, I was, but . . . Tavita called a little while ago."

"Tavita?" Meredith stopped packing and switched the phone to the other ear. "And?"

"Well, we're going to spend some more time together . . . and talk," Telesia spoke quietly. "I'm not getting my hopes up, but Mele . . . it was so good to hear his voice again."

Meredith nodded with a broad smile on her face. "Then I hope you have a wonderful weekend, and I want a full report when I get back. Just remember that I won't be here to chaperone you."

"Okay, mother," Telesia giggled over the phone. "I'll remember. Take long walks along the beach, say good-bye at the front door, and give a full accounting of my activities on Monday night."

As she pressed the button to end the phone call, Meredith stared at Telesia's neatly made bed across the other side of their large bedroom. A neatly hand-sewn quilt made up of bright Polynesian floral prints was folded tidily at the end of the bed, and a honey-colored bear in black graduation robe and hat sat perched on top of it. The bear had been Tavita's gift at graduation, and in the weeks since they'd broken their engagement, Telesia had often sat just holding it and staring out the window.

Maybe they just needed time out. Maybe they needed a crisis to make a break from the traditions that were holding them back. Maybe . . . She stared at the bear. *Maybe a crisis really can be a blessing in disguise.*

* * *

Meredith glanced in the rearview mirror for the last glimpse of Auckland city. The distinctive green hills of extinct volcanic cones were striking among the sprawl of urban buildings. She straightened her arms against the steering wheel and flexed her shoulders for the drive ahead. Within minutes the surroundings had changed from city concrete to rolling green hills, their pleasant, contoured shapes soothing to drive through as they demanded no attention. She didn't even turn the car stereo on, preferring her own thoughts.

The road signs flashed by . . . Mere Mere . . . Huntly . . . Ngaruawahia . . . Te Awamutu. Meredith found her attention wandering. She blinked rapidly and rubbed the back of her neck. She'd only been driving a couple of hours and already she felt fatigue threatening her concentration.

Te Kuiti soon. I'll stop at the Bus Stop Café. That'll wake me up, and then it's all straight home from there.

The cold air seemed to wrap itself around her body as soon as she got out of the car at the small rural township of Te Kuiti. She shivered slightly and reached back inside the car for her jacket.

"I must be getting close to home. It's getting colder," she muttered as she shrugged on her thick, tan leather jacket and made her way quickly into the roadside café. It was surprisingly full of people, and while Meredith waited to be served, she smiled at the inevitable entertainer crooning a song in the corner. There was always somebody singing here whenever she passed through, but never the same person.

"It's a darned shame. They wouldn't have had a show . . . not on that bend."

Meredith turned as the voice seemed to stand out from the hum of the crowd.

"Just look at that mess. Doesn't even look like a car," another male voice joined the first.

"That Mount Messenger road is always bad when it's windy . . . and if it's icy as well . . ." The man cursed and shook his head. There was another silence as the two continued reading the cover page of a newspaper spread on the table in front of them.

"What will you have, miss?" Meredith turned suddenly as the girl behind the counter spoke to her.

"Um, just a meat pie and an orange juice, thanks." She hesitated. "Oh, and could I have a newspaper, please?"

Although she had intended to keep driving while she ate, instead Meredith found a seat at a small window table and quickly opened the newspaper. The right-hand columns were headed with a picture of a car that was nothing more than a twisted mass of metal with most of the left side crushed. She scanned the article beside the picture. *Mount Messenger . . . family returning to New Plymouth from Mokau . . . driver asleep . . . steep bank . . . three killed . . . driver in critical condition.*

The moist pie seemed to dry in Meredith's mouth as she stopped chewing, and she had difficulty swallowing. *This is what the newspaper probably looked like after Grant's accident.*

She forced herself to look at the picture again, and suddenly the similar newspaper articles that she'd read over the years took on a new meaning. They had never mattered much to her because she wasn't personally involved, but in that instant they mattered a great deal to Meredith.

He had to look at photos . . . at the car . . . at their bodies. He must have relived it over and over. She drew a deep, shaky breath. *No wonder he still has trouble dealing with it. You'd want it to just go away, but then . . . that would be forgetting the ones you loved so much.*

Meredith folded the paper and slid it slowly to the side of the table, then rested her forehead on her hands for a long moment. Her eyelids closed, but there was no feeling of tiredness.

Heavenly Father . . . how can I help Grant? How can I help him find peace?

* * *

Meredith swung the Volkswagen around yet another bend in the road before emerging from the dauntingly rugged confines of the Awakino Gorge. As always, she felt a faint tremble of relief as a yellow road sign announced the township of Mokau just a few miles ahead. Since early in her childhood, Mokau had meant "home" because from there she and her family could see "their mountain." A smile played on her lips as she recalled the inevitable competition between her siblings to see the mountain first, and then forgetting who actually won as they all spotted the majestic andesitic cone of Mount Egmont rising in wonderful symmetry out of the dark, green forest at its base.

Even as she thought about it, Meredith spotted the mountain in the distance. *Home soon. I wonder if the family that crashed were thinking that.*

Her foot automatically lifted off the accelerator, slowing the car as she gripped the steering wheel more firmly. A few more miles and she would wind round the perilous bends of Mount Messenger, probably passing the scene of the accident.

I wonder if Grant has ever gone back to where he crashed. That would just be so hard. I think I'd probably stay away . . . to stop the pain from surfacing again. She shook her head. *I just can't imagine losing anybody I loved.*

Her mind suddenly filled with images of her family. Of sitting together in church, of activities at family home evening, of trips to the temple in Hamilton as each of them reached the age of twelve and were able to perform baptisms for the ancestors her mother had carefully researched. Meredith breathed deeply then, and as if her mind were flicking through the pages of a photo album, a clear image of each family member came in rapid succession:

Her mother, hair slightly damp and cheeks flushed as she wiped her hands on a tea towel and surveyed rows of freshly bottled fruit; her father, tall and distinguished in his suit, white shirt, and tie, and peering over the top of his glasses while he laughed the deep, happy chuckle that Meredith loved to hear; her older sister Wendy holding baby Matthew in faraway Austraila; Ryan in his rugby uniform, trying to look taller and broader than his father; young Cam with tousled hair, cheeky grin, and the inevitable sticking plaster or bandage.

Meredith felt the tears begin to brim in her eyes and she blinked hard. No, it was impossible to imagine losing any of them.

But you are losing them . . .

Her breath caught as the thought cut into her heart and mind with a swift thrust.

You're losing your eternal family . . . because you're the one who's dying spiritually.

* * *

Grant picked up the Adams file for the third time, flicked through the typed notes, and tried to make sense of his scribbled pencil notes in the margins. He'd already been through them after he'd arranged to work with Meredith on the case next week. It really was time to leave for the weekend, but he felt an odd reluctance to go home on his own.

He moved restlessly to the window and observed the parking space that Meredith's Volkswagen usually occupied. A large, four-wheel-drive truck now dominated the space, and it looked out of place to Grant. He sighed and turned his back to the window, glancing at his desk clock. It was nearly six thirty. *She should be nearly in Taranaki by now . . . although why I'm even thinking about it is beyond me.* He put his hands in his pockets and rocked slowly onto his heels. *You're thinking about it because you can't think of anything else . . . and you don't know how to handle it. You've never even looked at another woman since Hannah died.*

"So why am I thinking about Meredith Winstone?" He rocked again and stared at the ceiling as he interrogated himself. "What is different about Meredith Winstone that makes you want to make sure she travels safely . . . and gets back home safely. And that makes you anticipate working with her every day?"

He closed his eyes, but couldn't dispel the image of Meredith smiling broadly earlier in the day as they had won the case in court—a generous, uninhibited smile that went right to her eyes. Then he'd seen the genuine concern on her face as she watched the parents of the girl angrily berating their daughter.

She's just different . . . like she's interested in everybody and really cares about them. He opened his eyes and moved slowly to the desk. *But could she care for me?*

"Are you intending to stay here all weekend?" Frank grinned as he spoke to his son from the doorway. "There's a much better view from the yacht than from that window."

Grant turned and slowly smiled. "You're not going sailing for a change, are you?"

His father straightened as he detected the almost lighthearted tone in his son's voice. "Actually, we are. I've even convinced Stella to come tomorrow." He raised his thick, silvery eyebrows. "Can you be tempted?"

There was a long pause. Then Grant sank both hands deep into his pockets and shrugged. "I don't see why not, although it's been a while. I may be more of a hindrance than a help."

Frank walked into the room and laid his hand on his son's shoulder. "You'll never be that, son. You always were a better sailor than your old man." He coughed self-consciously. "It'll be good to have you back on board."

CHAPTER 9

Meredith hesitated just before the turnoff to her parents' home, then suddenly accelerated past. It was still light and she felt a sudden urge to drive around the area where she had grown up. Just a few streets up the road, the primary school that she and her brothers had all attended had been given a new coat of paint and there was a new hall, but it still evoked vivid images from her childhood. She remembered running across the playground, patrolling the pedestrian crossing outside the gate, and sitting on the slatted wooden benches eating lunch. It had been her responsibility to get Ryan and Cam safely to school each morning, and she had looked after them diligently.

She smiled as she drove farther up the road, past the park where they'd taken their dogs for runs, and the local swimming pool where her father had patiently taught them all to swim. Farther on, the larger buildings of the high school loomed more impressively, and Meredith drove past the main buildings and pulled into a driveway beside the fields. She turned off the car engine and sat quietly as more memories flooded back.

Academic achievements had come easily to her as a teenager, as had the physical challenge of sports once she had been channeled into them by her parents. It wasn't until she was fifteen that she even realized that not all her fellow students handled school with the same ease, some even resenting her natural ability.

Meredith smiled ruefully as she remembered once trying to fail a test to become more acceptable. At the last minute she had quickly corrected her answers, unable to settle for anything less than giving her best.

"Latter-day Saints cannot afford to be mediocre. We know too much to settle for less than the best we can give." Her father's gentle words filtered through the memories and Meredith sighed. Her parents had always expected them to give of *their* best even if they weren't the best. *"You don't need to be top of the class to know that you tried your hardest. And if you are the best, then it's your job to help those who struggle with what's easy for you."*

The outlines of the buildings blurred as tears began to build up, and she made no attempt to stop them. Her parents had been wonderful to her, guiding her through years filled with tragedy and triumph. They had always been there when she needed them, always counseling her to ask Heavenly Father for direction after they'd given their advice.

Meredith quickly wiped the tears away and started the car engine. Shortly, she had pulled up alongside the church building where she'd spent so much of her youth. A few cars were in the parking lot and people were unloading boxes.

"There must be an activity on tonight," Meredith murmured as she wound down the window and tried to make out the faces of figures in the gathering dusk. "And there's Sister Morgan to supervise everybody." She smiled as the familiar, generous figure of her former Young Women's leader eased out of a too-small yellow car.

Adele Morgan had been her teacher in early morning seminary, and then later as her Laurel adviser, she had cheerily organized Meredith into achieving the goals she had set for herself. "Because if a thing is worth doing, it's worth doing brilliantly!" Chanting the expression, Meredith closed her eyes and leaned her head back against the seat. Her life really had been full of positive influences, all helping her make good decisions and paving her way to success.

They've all helped me get where I am today. Now I'm a qualified lawyer working in a good job, surrounded by good people, good family, and good friends . . . and . . . they're right . . . when you have the best, you should give to those who don't have as much. She unconsciously paraphrased her mother's advice. *Grant has worldly things but he doesn't have the spiritual knowledge that I have. I could tell him so much . . . but how do I share it with him when I don't even go to church anymore? He'll never believe me if I don't practice what I preach.*

Meredith twisted her hands tightly around the steering wheel as her stomach clenched. *But how do I go back?*

"Hey, Sis . . . what are you doing here?"

She jumped as the car rocked and Cam's freckled face loomed through the open window. "Mum and Dad are expecting you at home."

"Oh, my heck! Don't frighten me like that!" Meredith laughed as he pulled a face at her, then swung the door open and climbed inside. "I just came to check the place out. I haven't been home yet."

"I was just helping the Young Women unload some stuff for their activity, and you're just in time to pick me up, but we better hurry or Mum will be leaving soon to get me." Cam closed the door and turned to rest his long arm along the back of the seat.

Meredith started the car and pulled out as he finished speaking. "How come you didn't drive yourself down?"

There was a brief pause while her brother ran his hand through his already tousled hair. "Actually, Dad suspended me from driving for a bit. He reckons it's better that he does before the police do."

"Police?" Meredith looked startled. "Cam, what have you been up to?"

"Nothing! Honest." Cam tightened his hand into a fist and thumped it gently against the window. "I just got home late a few times and landed the car in a ditch once, so dad decided to 'take precautions.'" He pulled another face. "Trouble is, I lost my job because I couldn't drive to work."

"Oh, Cam." Meredith spoke softly, unsure what to say. She'd always enjoyed Cam's outgoing personality and his ability to have fun in any situation, but suddenly his irrepressible ways seemed to conjure up possibilities of him getting into an accident. "At least you aren't hurt. I couldn't bear to lose you."

Her quiet statement seemed to hang in the air, and Cam turned to look straight at her, studying her face as the tips of his ears turned pink.

"Would you really miss me, Sis?" he finally said, and she nodded silently. He looked back at the dashboard and slumped in his seat. "I never thought of it like that."

"Well, you'd better." She reached out and briefly patted his arm. "When you do something wrong or silly . . . you hurt a lot more people than just yourself."

They drove without speaking until Cam suddenly pointed past her. "Quick, there's Mum! Beep her!"

Meredith reacted by quickly flicking the headlights at the approaching car, and Cam leaned over and pressed the car horn hard. Their mother's car swerved slightly and they glimpsed her startled face as she pulled onto the side of the road, then her quick wave as she recognized them.

"Good old Mum." Meredith watched in the rearview mirror as her mother calmly negotiated a three-point turn and followed them down the road. "Just goes with the flow."

"Not so much lately." Cam shook his head. "She's been getting kind of upset about Ryan leaving, and then she got a bad result from the doctor."

"Bad result?" Meredith frowned at him. "What's wrong with her?"

"I'll let Mum tell you." Cam looked uncomfortable. "I think she was waiting until you came down."

The window lights cast a welcoming golden glow across the front lawn as Meredith swung her car into the small space beside the garage. She switched off the engine and sat still for a moment, savoring the comfort of being at home. *But Ryan's leaving, Mum's sick, and Cam's in trouble. What is happening to home? They're all meant to stay the same and be happy.* She smiled wistfully at her own naive hope that things would remain unchanged. *Just like Mum hopes that I'm going to church every Sunday.* A thickness swelled in her throat, and Meredith glanced out the window as her mother's car drew up behind her. *Maybe it's not too late to make Mum's hopes come true. It can only change things for the better . . . for her and for me.*

"Hello, darling!" Nan gave Meredith a warm hug as she stepped out of the car. "That was lovely of you to pick Cam up. I was running late and I couldn't call the chapel . . . and it seems like everybody who has a cell phone is using it. What did we ever do before we had those little telephones? Cam wants his own, and I've resisted, but now I'm thinking it might be a good idea. At least we might be able to keep track of him. He's going through such a difficult patch." She paused for breath and put her hand to her heart. "Just listen to me prattling on. Let's go inside. Dad will be pleased to see you down early. We weren't expecting you till much later."

Meredith laughed as she took her mother's arm and walked into the house.

"I was lucky to get away early. Grant . . . my boss . . . told me to leave straight after court so I wasn't traveling late. He even gave me Monday off so I could stay and enjoy Sunday dinner with you."

Nan stopped and patted her daughter's hand. "Well, you tell him a big thank-you from us. I always worry about you traveling over those roads in that little car. He must be a very nice man."

"Yes . . . yes, he is." Meredith fought the color suddenly moving up her cheeks as she thought of Grant. "He's a very nice man. A bit intimidating sometimes . . . but he can be very . . . charming."

Nan glanced at her daughter. "Charming? How old did you say he was? I had the impression he was quite elderly."

Meredith shook her head. "Actually, Mr. Bascombe, Sr. . . . the one who interviewed me . . . is quite old. You know . . . tall, distinguished, silvery hair. Then there's Mr. Bascombe, Jr. . . . Grant." Again she fought the heat in her cheeks. "He's . . . well, they're both . . . charming." She laughed awkwardly and moved past her mother. "I'm very lucky to have a job there."

"Did I hear my girl's voice?" Stewart Winstone crossed the small hallway and enveloped Meredith in his arms. "So how long have we got you for?"

"Until Monday morning." Nan rested her hand on her husband's shoulder. "Meredith's boss has given her time off so she doesn't have to rush back."

"That's considerate of him." Stewart nodded and squeezed his daughter. "We appreciate any time we can have with you children. It seems the older you get, the more precious it is."

There was a sudden silence as Nan glanced at her husband. Then she smiled happily at Meredith. "Then let's not waste it. Put your things away in your room, love, and dinner will be ready in ten minutes."

Stewart slipped his hands into his pockets as his wife turned away toward the kitchen, and as soon as the door swung behind her, he turned to Meredith. "Cam said he told you that Mum had been to the doctor."

Meredith nodded, noting the subdued tone of his voice. "He said Mum would tell me what's going on." She hesitated. "Dad . . . is it bad?"

Her father pulled her back against his chest and she felt his heart beating hard against her shoulder as he took some time to answer. "There's every possibility she'll be just fine. There's nothing conclusive yet, and you know your mother . . . she's not even thinking about it until Ryan is away safely."

"Mum always says if you don't think about it . . . it'll go away," Meredith whispered as she looked up at her father. The evening stubble was showing on his jaw and she saw, with surprise, that many of the little hairs were silvery gray. Her father really was getting older. She nestled in against him, appreciating the familiar, warm smell of his aftershave and the way his arms tightened around her.

"Dad?"

"Yes, love."

"Can we talk this weekend?" Meredith swallowed hard. "Seriously."

* * *

"I can't believe you're actually going to be a full-on missionary." Meredith finished stacking the dinner plates into the dishwasher. "I mean, I knew it would happen. You've always been so set on it since you were little . . . but now it's actually here." She shook her head as she straightened up and glanced around the kitchen for more dishes. She and Ryan had volunteered to tidy up after dinner, and the rest of the family had happily left them to it.

"Not quite here." Ryan opened the drawer and slid a pile of placemats in neatly. "Six more sleeps and then you may call me Elder Winstone."

"Elder Ryan Winstone." Meredith smiled weakly as she reached up to touch the top of his head. "I was always the one leading you off into adventures . . . now you're big and going off on your own . . . and leaving me behind."

There was a brief silence, then, "What happened, Meredith?" Ryan spoke quietly, but when she didn't respond, he folded his arms and leaned against the kitchen bench. "You know, I always thought we knew each other pretty well, but I've never been able to understand how you just . . . stopped going to church. You were always the one that made sure we all went."

Meredith tried to smile as she mirrored his posture and folded her arms, but the smile didn't last. Somehow it was easier to listen to and ignore her mother's constant interrogation about her Church activity than to face her younger brother's single question. There had always been an especially close bond between Meredith and Ryan, and she felt it now as strongly as ever.

"I don't know, Ryan." She took a deep breath. "It never even occurred to me when I left Taranaki that I would stop going to church."

"So why did you stop? Did somebody do something?"

Meredith shook her head. "No, not really. I think . . . it was just so different when I got there. I missed the first couple of weeks in my ward because I went to the wrong chapel. Then it was video conference, and then . . ." She hesitated, then finished quickly, "When I did get to the right ward, it felt . . . different. I didn't know anybody and most of the members there were from different cultures, so . . ."

Ryan nodded slowly. "So you didn't get involved right away . . . because you felt like a stranger?"

"I know it was stupid of me, but all of a sudden my family wasn't there . . . I didn't have anything to do—no calling or anything—and sometimes I was the only native English-speaker there." She shrugged.

"But Telesia is Polynesian, and she's one of your best friends." Ryan frowned slightly.

"Telesia and Tavita are wonderful." Meredith folded her arms more tightly in frustration at her inability to understand or explain how she'd felt over the last four years. "And maybe if I had been attending their ward . . . but I wasn't, and it just seemed more difficult to get involved at church and easier to get lost in the crowd. I was studying law and no one else was. Then I joined up at the surf club and started work at the bakery and suddenly . . . I felt needed. I could set my own program and work hard, and when I was on duty . . . I really felt like I was doing something important . . . that I was contributing. Then one day I filled in for one of the guys on a Sunday duty, and I felt like I was doing much more good than just sitting in a Sunday School classroom talking about being of service."

"So you rationalized your way through it . . . or out of it," Ryan stated simply, then waited as Meredith stared at the ceiling.

"I guess I did . . . and after I started working at the bakery the owner got sick, so I would work in the evening for her. I'd justify doing my class assignments on the weekend because I had to help her, and pretty soon I didn't even notice that I was missing church. I still did my own scripture study occasionally, but I didn't . . . feel anything . . . and sometimes Telesia would drag me down to the institute building for lunch, but . . ."

"But you'd already lost the Spirit."

Meredith glanced at him quickly and nodded. "If you want to put it like that . . . I guess I did." She licked her lips, hesitating before she finally spoke again. "The clincher came when I was out on a date with a guy from the surf club . . . Mitch. He was a good man, but we didn't have the same standards . . . at least, not at first."

"At first?"

"We dated a while and he was really understanding about . . . chastity and everything," she hesitated. "Then one Sunday night . . . I guess I felt like we'd gotten closer than we should have, so I didn't take the sacrament the next day . . . and all of a sudden, I felt like I was under a microscope . . . like everybody thought I'd been really bad . . . and that made me angry because it wasn't like they knew me that well, anyway."

"And you didn't go back after that?"

Ryan watched her thoughtfully as a mixture of emotions passed over her face. Then he slowly straightened and stretched his arms up behind his head. As he lowered them he brought one arm down to rest around her shoulders and squeezed her hard. It was strangely comforting, and Meredith relaxed against him. When had their roles reversed?

"I'll be praying for you, little sister," Ryan said, with another quick squeeze.

The remark was totally unexpected and Meredith gave a short laugh. "Now you're really getting to me, 'big' brother. I'm meant to be sending you on your way with my profound words of wisdom to help you . . . not the other way round."

"Well, you are kind of helping me." Ryan smiled. "Once I get out in the mission field, I'll be watching out for people and making sure they feel included." He hesitated. "I don't want them to become another statistic like my sister."

"So I'm a statistic, now?" Meredith grunted and punched him gently. "That makes me feel good."

"But you don't have to be. Seriously, Meredith . . . it's hard enough going away, but it's even worse thinking of going away with you being where you're at and Mum being so worried about both of us."

The mention of her mother made Meredith swallow hard, and she leaned away from her brother.

"Has Mum told you what's wrong?" she asked quietly.

"Nothing specific." Ryan shook his head. "I think she's trying to protect me from anything bad so I can concentrate on my mission, but I'd be an idiot not to notice how she and Dad have been behaving." He scuffed at the tiles on the kitchen floor. "Meredith . . . it would make a difference if I could go away knowing . . ." He paused and swallowed hard, so she finished for him.

"Knowing that I was back at church." It was a statement, not a question, and she spoke hoarsely, suddenly recognizing the pain she had been causing everyone in her family. Could she even be the cause of her mother's sickness? She'd read that stress or grief often brought on an illness, and hadn't her mother been grieving for her these last four years? As if he could read her thoughts, Ryan nodded toward the lounge.

"I don't think you had anything to do with Mum being sick, but I'm sure it would also help her get better a lot quicker if she knew you were . . . safe."

"Safe?" she repeated almost dumbly. Grant had wanted to make sure she was safe as well. So many people cared for her. She fought back the tears. *Safe . . . with her family . . . forever. Not grieving about what might have been.* Meredith laughed weakly.

"Wow . . . you sure know how to make a farewell speech, Elder Winstone. Just come right out with it." She reached out and hugged him again. "I was going to talk to Dad about . . . everything, this weekend, but you've managed to cut straight to the point."

"And?"

Meredith detected the hopeful tone in his voice. "And . . . I think you have your first . . . convert. Or something like that."

Ryan held his breath. "You mean, you think . . . ?"

"I'm not sure what I think right now, except I feel like I've avoided the issue long enough. Oh, Ryan . . . I've wanted to come back . . . but

I just didn't know how." The tears began to flow down her cheeks as she realized how much it meant to talk to him, to feel like her little brother understood. To realize for herself how she really felt.

"Hey, you two! Are you making dessert? Because I'd like chocolate sauce . . . oops . . . intimate family moment . . . sorree!" Cam's tall figure burst through the kitchen door, then retreated just as fast.

"That boy has a gift." Meredith couldn't help giggling through her tears as she reached for a paper towel to wipe her face. "You just can't stay serious for long with him around."

"Oh, I don't know about that. Mum and Dad have been pretty serious about him lately." Ryan wiped at his own eyes with the back of his hand. "I think it'll be better when I leave. They've been paying me a lot of attention lately."

"You don't think Cam is jealous?" Meredith looked surprised. "I can't imagine that. He's always idolized you."

"Hey, he's sixteen. Things change." He shrugged.

"And I probably helped that process." Meredith took his arm. "I definitely haven't been the finest example, but maybe I can change that."

Ryan groaned and opened the door for her. "Oh no, Meredith's got a project. I wonder if Cam realizes what's in store?"

They were both laughing as they entered the lounge, and Meredith could see the relief on her mother's face as she watched them come in. The gray shadows under her eyes seemed to lighten as she smiled and patted the cushion on the couch beside her.

"So come and tell me what's so funny about doing dishes. I must have been missing something all these years.

* * *

"Now you see it, now you don't," Meredith whispered the words, pursing her lips to blow a long breath. The icy cold turned it into a white vapor that swirled around her face as she stared up the street.

"Typical Taranaki weather." Her father nodded in agreement as they walked in step. "You can see the mountain for five minutes, and then the cloud settles around and it's like it was never there."

"I always hold my breath after driving through the gorge, just hoping I can see the summit," Meredith laughed. "Not that it's ever going to change or anything, but it's just always been a thrill," she finished quietly. "It means I'm home."

"I heard there was a bad accident up that way just before you came through. Your mother was worried." Stewart rubbed his fist against the palm of his hand.

"So was my boss . . . Grant. I mean, he didn't know about the accident . . . he was just worried about me—driving late, that is. That's why he gave me time off. He wanted me to be safe."

They continued walking in silence along the tree-lined street, their feet leaving prints among the fallen terra-cotta-colored leaves that covered the pavement and grass verge. At six o'clock on Saturday morning there was very little traffic or movement other than the occasional person jogging or walking their dog. Meredith moved closer to her father and slipped her hand into the crook of his arm.

"It's so good to be home, Dad. I work away up in Auckland with this image in my mind of everything staying the same down here." She took a deep breath. "What sort of picture do you have in your mind of me . . . up in Auckland?"

Stewart glanced at his daughter, her nose and cheeks tinged pink by the cold air, her hair pulled close against her face by the tight-fitting woolen hat she'd grabbed off Cam's head as they'd left the house. She wore no makeup, and suddenly she felt like his little girl again. He patted her fingers with his other hand, and it took him a while to respond.

"Mmm, well . . ." He coughed and blew another frosty breath. "My Meredith in the big city . . . how do I imagine you?" Stewart grunted. "You know, love, I'm not sure I really have an image right now. For the last few years I've sort of seen you amongst big university buildings, but now . . . I don't know where you work or who you work with . . . or where you live. I only really know Telesia. And by the way, I'm very pleased you're flatting with her. She's a fine girl."

Meredith nodded and squeezed his arm. "I was so happy when she agreed. She keeps me tidy and . . ."

Her hesitation caused her father to stop, and he looked at her sideways. "What else does she do, Meredith?"

"She's strong, Dad . . . when I'm not." Meredith kicked at the wet leaves with the toe of her boot. "She's always just kept talking about the gospel and sharing things with me . . . even when I was quite rude. Even when I started dating Mitch . . ."

"Mitch? That's a new name." Stewart raised an eyebrow, then nodded slowly. "Mitch wasn't a member of the Church, I take it?"

"No . . . no, but he could've been. It was quite a long time ago, just at the beginning of my second year. He's one of the nicest men I've ever met." Meredith smiled. "He was one of my lifeguard buddies."

"Oh . . . Mitch, the lifeguard." Stewart grinned. "Sounds a bit like *Baywatch* to me."

Meredith giggled and shook her head. "He got teased about that so much, and he loved it. He reckoned it was his only claim to fame, so why not use it."

"So where is Mitch now . . . in the Meredith stakes?"

"Mitchell Johnson Savage II was last heard of building log cabins in the icy wastes of Canada. We dated for a few months and then he went overseas." There was another long pause while Meredith stared toward the mountain. "I think I could have . . . enjoyed being with Mitch. He respected me . . . my standards. We had some good talks . . . long talks, often about the Church."

"So what happened?" her father asked quietly, watching his daughter's face.

"Absolutely nothing . . . for quite a while," Meredith shrugged. "Then one time . . . just once . . . we got a bit too intimate and . . . well, soon after, he had the opportunity to work overseas. I cried at the airport . . . and that was that."

"Except that you were farther away from the Church," Stewart murmured quietly, and his daughter looked up quickly and nodded.

"I guess it did happen a bit like that. We'd do patrol duty and then just spend the rest of the day together . . . usually Sunday." Meredith tilted her chin. "I did actually take him to a couple of Church activities with Telesia."

"How did he react to that?"

She nodded thoughtfully, remembering. "Actually, he really enjoyed himself. One night was a luau and he just loved the whole atmosphere . . . and everybody loved him. I almost felt left out." She hesitated again.

"So when Mitch left, you didn't go back to church?"

Meredith slowly pulled her hand away from her father's, finding it much more difficult to express to him the same things she had shared with Ryan. "It was just so much easier to be involved in my studies, and I soon found that I could be the best in class if I worked that hard . . . and I liked being the best. It was much better than just feeling different like I did at church."

"But what happened to your testimony, Meredith? You were always so . . . outspoken—the most of all our children." Stewart pushed his hands deep into his pockets. "I have such vivid memories of you in your little plaid skirt and white blouse, bearing your testimony when you could hardly reach the top of the pulpit."

"And I'd thank Heavenly Father for all the 'pwecious' things, and you'd have to ask me to stop because other people wanted to bear their testimonies." Meredith gave a short laugh but quickly grew serious again. "I can't remember when I last bore my testimony."

Her father didn't answer, but just took her arm and began to walk again.

"So what sort of testimony would you bear now, Meredith? What sort of 'pwecious' things would you thank Him for?"

She studied the wet leaves that curled on the pavement and clung to her shoes.

"My family . . . my job . . ." She trailed off and then shook her head. "You know, Dad . . . I always thought I had a testimony . . . of everything. I could stand and repeat all the things that you and Mum would say in prayers. But now I don't know that I ever really . . . thought about it."

"You mean nothing challenged your testimony?"

Oh, I think I had challenges," she corrected quickly. "But even when I was . . ." She swallowed. ". . . raped . . . I relied on you and Mum. You were my strength and you gave me my answers—found my solutions."

"Do you think we protected you too much?" he asked seriously.

"No." She squeezed his arm reassuringly. "Well, maybe . . . or maybe I was just a slow learner, or I just liked the attention I got when I said the right thing." She sighed. "I really don't know, except that once I got to Auckland and university, there were so many things that challenged what I thought was true—people being cruel or indifferent or saying one thing and then doing something else. I found more peace in doing my surf club duties and my job because I felt like I was contributing in my own way, like I didn't need the Church structure to be a good person."

"And you are a good person," her father affirmed quietly. As they reached the outskirts of the park Meredith had passed the day before, he pointed toward the swings and slides in the playground area. "Do you want to see how high you can go?"

"Can I let my hands go at the top?" Meredith grinned, repeating the familiar conversation from her childhood as she pointed toward her favorite green swing.

"Nope . . . you have to hold tightly onto the iron rod." Her father winked as he closed both of her hands firmly around the straight metal rods of the swing as she sat down on it.

"But . . . it's more exciting if I let go." Meredith's voice lost the challenge of her childhood protests and she looked up at her father with tears in her eyes, knowing exactly what his response would be.

"It only feels better for a second. But if you hold on tightly, Meredith . . . you'll be able to see forever."

The cold air made the tears icy on her cheeks as she swung higher and higher on the swing. Each downward rush, she felt the reassuring pressure of her father's hands against her back, then the pull on her stomach as the swing carried her higher again. Finally, it carried her to the point where she could see above the rooftops of the nearby houses, and it seemed as if there was nothing between her and the mountain. She felt the childlike thrill of pleasure as her feet rose in line with the mountaintop.

"I see forever, Dad!" She felt the words slip off her lips and waited for the familiar response, smiling when it came.

"That's my girl; you just keep holding tight."

They walked for nearly an hour, with Meredith sharing a lot of the experiences that she'd had in Auckland, even managing to confide more about her situation with Mitch and her feelings of inadequacy at church. It seemed as if physical and spiritual barriers had been lifted, and she finally clamped her hands over her mouth and stared wide-eyed at her father as they reached the end of their driveway.

"I can't believe I've talked so much. You hardly said a thing."

"I didn't need to." Stewart nodded and smiled. "I only wanted to listen . . . and you told me a lot."

"You're being deep, aren't you?" Meredith wrinkled her nose. Then she swallowed hard. "Dad, what do I have to do . . . now? Can I just clear things up with you?"

Her father's chuckle was reassuring as he gave her a quick hug and rested his hand on her shoulder. "Not quite, my dear. I think we've covered a lot of ground this morning . . . but I'm not your bishop. You need to go and talk with him. He'll be there, close by, to help you through the next part of the journey."

"'The next part of the journey'—you make him sound like a tour guide." Meredith tried to smile but ended up frowning thoughtfully. "I don't even know who my bishop is, Dad. How can I just go and talk to a complete stranger? 'Uh, hello, Bishop . . . you don't know me from a bar of soap, but I'm Meredith. I've been avoiding everything to do with the Church for quite a while but, hey . . . here I am again!'"

"And he'll say, 'Was that Meredith with an *M*? I've been waiting for you to arrive.'" Stewart laughed and squeezed her hard again, gently pushing her inside the front door. "I'll be happy to give him a call. Bishop Brown is a great man. He went to school with your mother."

Meredith stopped. "You already know who my bishop is?" her voice rose slightly.

"Of course." He winked again. "What did you expect? We've been worried about you, you know."

Meredith wondered why that was so reassuring.

CHAPTER 10

"You're handling those ropes well. Just like riding a bike, eh?" Frank ducked beneath the boom and straightened up beside Grant as he tightened some thick rope around the polished metal stay. "Great day, isn't it?"

"Let me answer that when I get the feeling back into my face and fingers." Grant grinned as he completed the final coil of rope and rubbed his hands together briskly. "I'd forgotten about the chill factor out here."

"Best thing to get the blood pumping." Frank was irrepressible as he inhaled deeply of the wind that whipped his jacket about him. "Besides, at this time of the year we don't have to worry about lots of traffic in the gulf. It's just us and the waves."

Even as he spoke, the boat slewed slightly and a large wave crested over the bow, thoroughly wetting them. Both men gripped hold of the stainless-steel railing and braced themselves against the swell.

"Are we still going out past Kawau Island?" Grant had to speak louder as the boat crashed into another wave.

Frank raised his head to study the sky and then the horizon, the water beginning to run continuously off the brim of his cap. "Maybe we'll just head for Kawau and moor in the Mansion House Bay for a while. This looks like it could turn into a bit more of a storm than they'd predicted." He motioned with his head toward the interior of the boat. "You'd better go down and tell Stella we'll wait and have lunch at the island."

Grant nodded, wiping the water off his face as another blast of spray showered them. "Hey, Dad." He leaned closer to his father. "I'm glad I came today." He hesitated, then clapped the older man roughly on the shoulder. "I'm glad Stella came, too."

Another large wave pounded the boat as Frank turned and grinned. "Me too, son. It's been the best day I've had in a very long time."

* * *

The chorister was already leading an enthusiastic rendition of "Called to Serve" when Meredith sat down with her mother and Ryan a few rows from the front. Her father was giving her mother a quizzical look from behind the pulpit, so Nan gave a surreptitious charade of the car failing to start and Stewart responded with an understanding nod and comforting wink and smile.

I wonder if I'll ever have that sort of communication with my husband. Meredith moved closer to her mother. *I wonder if I'll ever have a husband. Mum was married with two children by my age.* She watched as her mother focused her attention on her husband as he began the meeting. *I wonder if I'll ever have a husband like Dad . . . a Church leader—a strong, spiritual man. Ryan's going to be just like Dad.* She glanced along the row as her youngest brother caught the attention of a small toddler and made the boy laugh. *Cam will too . . . in his own way. And then there's me . . .*

Instead of hearing the words of the sacrament hymn the congregation had begun singing, she was suddenly recalling all the activities she'd confided to her father the day before. The images seemed to run through her mind in quick succession, keeping weird time with the rhythm of the music, and then the young deacon was standing beside the pew presenting her with the sacrament tray. A knot of panic formed in Meredith's throat as she lifted her hand and then quickly dropped it onto her lap. In an instant, she felt her trembling fingers covered with her mother's warm hand and was given a reassuring squeeze.

The soothing movement was like a balm to her soul as Meredith kept her eyes tightly shut and let the words of the next sacrament prayer wash over her.

". . . that they do always remember Him."

I haven't remembered Him at all. She suddenly recalled putting the small picture of the Savior facedown in her bottom drawer with her scriptures.

". . . that they may have his Spirit to be with them."

She was five years old again and telling her mother, "*I want to have the Holy Ghost with me all the time, so I can be good all the time.*"

I do want to have the Spirit with me . . . and I want Grant to be able to feel it . . . to know what I know. The tears began to flow silently down her cheeks. *Heavenly Father, where do I start? Can You forgive me for being so stupid?*

Meredith felt her mother's hand move, pressing a tissue between her fingers, and then the heavier weight of Ryan's arm come to rest behind her back as the tears continued. There were no thoughts left as she absorbed their combined strength—only a strange emptiness.

"Hey, Sis." Cam's voice was a deep whisper from the other side of Ryan, and she opened her eyes. As he passed her a Book of Mormon with startlingly colorful markings, he pointed to a spot on the open page. "I like this one," he whispered again and gave a quick thumbs-up sign. "I stayed awake in seminary one morning."

"But as oft as they repented and sought forgiveness, with real intent, they were forgiven." Even as she silently mouthed the words, Meredith felt her whole being begin to tremble . . . *as oft as they repented and sought forgiveness*—she felt her mother's hand on hers again, strong and soft—*they were forgiven.*

Her father's voice from the pulpit broke in on her thoughts. "We'd like to invite Brother Ryan Winstone forward to bear his testimony. Ryan will be leaving on Wednesday to serve in the Australia Adelaide Mission, and we wish him well as he moves forward on his new errand for the Lord."

Stewart Winstone watched his family as he invited his son to come forward. He saw the tight hug Ryan gave his sister before he stood up and the way she smiled through tears at him. He saw the new serenity on his wife's face, a peace that he hadn't seen for a long time. And he watched his youngest son slide along the seat closer to his sister, taking his brother's place and putting his arm along the seat behind her and his mother.

* * *

"Whew . . . that was quite a meeting." Meredith sank down in the corner of the long couch, turning her face to the sun that filtered through the lace curtains. She raised a hand and pressed the reddened puffiness under her eyes. "You'd think someone would have marketed Mormon mascara by now . . . extra-strength waterproof kind for people like me." She laughed weakly as her mother sat down beside her. "I think vanity is another way of humbling me."

Nan didn't respond immediately. A shadow of discomfort flittered across her face, and she pressed a hand against her chest in an unconscious movement that Meredith had noticed happened quite often. It only lasted a second, and then her mother smiled as she took a slow, shallow breath.

"It was so lovely to have you there . . . so lovely." Her voice faltered. "So complete."

Meredith avoided her mother's gaze as she felt an all-too-familiar knot welling in her chest; instead she gestured toward a tiny wooden rocking chair sitting on top of the piano.

"No empty chairs, eh, Mum?"

They both smiled at the memory. When Meredith was fourteen, Nan had returned from an evening Relief Society session with a paper bag full of wooden clothespins. Over the next few days, she had worked on the project when the children weren't around, fending off their questions as to what she was making with a quiet, "You'll have to wait till family night."

When Monday night finally arrived, they had waited expectantly in the lounge until the lesson, when their mother had finally produced the miniature rocking chair. Carefully placing the neatly constructed chair, complete with tiny hand-quilted cushions, on the floor in front of them, she had set it rocking gently. No one had spoken at first, then Cam had tipped it with his finger. "It's cool, Mum. It really rocks."

"Expecting leprechauns, Mum?" Ryan had chuckled, then gone quiet as his voice cracked in its newly acquired squeak.

"Is it for a pot plant, love?" Stewart had leaned forward, studying it respectfully.

Meredith remembered saying nothing, but refusing to look at her sister Wendy for fear of laughing. Then her mother had turned the tiny piece of furniture gently and brought her scriptures out before stating quietly, "Our lesson tonight is No Empty Chairs."

Nan laughed, remembering. "I've often wondered why that family night turned out to be so memorable."

"Because we didn't know how to react?" Meredith screwed up her nose apologetically. "It was just such a tiny little chair, and I remember thinking you were joking until you gave us the lesson about families being eternal and that your goal was to see that there would be no empty chairs around the Winstone table in the eternities. And the chair has always been there to remind us," she added.

She watched as her mother tilted her head and lightly smoothed her eyebrow with one finger, as she often did when she was thinking seriously. It had usually prefaced a quiet reprimand when they were growing up.

"I've held that little chair in my hands often over the last few years . . . and prayed so hard to Heavenly Father that He'd watch over you . . . even if you didn't want Him to."

It was a simple statement, without any tone of reproach, but Meredith suddenly felt her mother's pain and she couldn't speak.

"I used to read the passage in Mosiah where Alma prays for his son . . . and I would tell Heavenly Father that that boy Alma was naughty, but my girl wasn't like that . . . that you were a good, good girl." Nan smiled. "I just wanted to protect you . . . from everything."

There was another long silence as both women wrestled with their own thoughts. Then Meredith slowly rose and walked over to the piano. The shine of the dark wooden lid was dulled to a matte finish by the finest film of dust, as were the neat stack of hymn books and an antique clock that had never worked. She picked up the small rocking chair. There wasn't any dust on it, although one armrest wobbled as she carried it back and placed it in her mother's lap.

"It was a great lesson, Mum . . . I'm just sorry I was such a slow learner." She leaned forward and laid her head on her mother's shoulder. "No more empty chairs, Mum . . . you've made sure of that."

* * *

"I wonder if you can send roasted potatoes through the mail." Ryan forked more crispy golden potatoes onto his plate and poured a generous amount of gravy around them. "I am going to miss these Sunday roast dinners so much."

"It's always good to have something to look forward to," Nan quoted happily as Cam followed his brother's example. "And you can be sure I'll have a big pile of crispy potatoes waiting for you when you come home."

There was an immediate silence around the entire dinner table until she dug her own fork emphatically into a slice of meat. "You can be sure of it!"

As if on cue, the telephone shrilled behind them, and everybody began to talk at once as Stewart went to answer it.

"Yes, she's right here. I'll get her for you," came through the din.

Meredith didn't even look around until her father tapped her shoulder. "It's for you. It's a lady calling from your office. Stella?"

"Stella?" She slid her chair back, frowning as she took the phone, then quickly placed her hand over the mouthpiece and whispered, "Did she say what for?"

As her father shrugged and shook his head, Meredith stood up and moved away from the table. "Hello, Stella. How did you find me? Is anything wrong?"

There was a long silence at the dinner table as she listened, then gasped.

"Oh, my goodness, is he going to be all right?" Her parents glanced at each other as the color drained from Meredith's face, and her father instinctively moved closer to his daughter. "Yes. Yes, of course I can do that. I'll leave first thing in the morning . . . or I could leave now if that's any help." There was another silence, then she nodded and the color began to infuse her cheeks again. "All right, I'll come tomorrow . . . carefully. Thanks for calling, Stella."

The whole family waited expectantly as she cradled the phone thoughtfully before replacing it.

"Well?" Cam broke the silence.

"Oh, sorry . . . that was Stella, our office secretary. There's been an accident. My boss—bosses—were out sailing and a storm came up suddenly and the boom broke." She faltered and shuddered as she recalled Stella's description. "Mr. Bascombe was struck on the head by the boom . . . he's only just regained consciousness."

"Oh, dear, that's awful." Nan stood up. "Which Mr. Bascombe was it?"

"Mr. Bascombe, Sr.," Meredith drew a deep breath. "But Grant is with him at the hospital, so he needs me to cover some work for him tomorrow. I offered to go back tonight but Stella said Grant's already given instructions that I wasn't to rush back."

An hour later, as she packed her belongings into her bag, Meredith heard her parents voices in the hallway on the way to their room. First her father's deep voice, then her mother's light laugh as she responded. Suddenly Meredith realized how much those voices meant to her. They were the voices that had guided and counseled her for so long.

"Mum, Dad . . . have you got a minute?" She folded the last shirt in and zipped the bag shut as they came to the doorway. "I have some questions . . . at least . . . I need some answers."

"Sounds like the same thing to me." Stewart raised an eyebrow as he stood in the doorway behind his wife, his hands on her shoulders.

"No, it's not quite." Meredith frowned and sat down on the bed. "It's just that . . . this accident with Mr. Bascombe . . . it's like the third time. Not for him," she quickly amended. "But a few years ago, his wife died after a long battle with cancer, and then not long after that, Grant's wife and baby were killed in a car accident."

"Oh no . . . the poor men!" Nan's sympathy was genuine, and her hand went to her throat. "Oh, I can't imagine . . ."

"Neither can I, Mum." Meredith shook her head. "But do you remember, when I took the job, that I said I felt like I needed to be there? I really did feel that way, but I thought it was as a lawyer." She paused, staring at her hands as she pressed her fingertips together. "Then on the way down here I was thinking about the family that crashed at Mokau, and then about how it must have felt for Grant and Mr. Bascombe to lose their family like that. Now, since the phone call, I can't get it out of my mind that Grant must be feeling devastated by this accident . . . he must be reliving everything." She swallowed hard and looked up with tears in her eyes. "After this weekend, after being here with all of you and really understanding and appreciating again what it means to be with you for eternity, I realize how precious that knowledge is, and I know that I need to have some answers for Grant . . . for them. The right answers."

"Are you sure he's going to want them?" Stewart asked quietly.

"No, I'm not sure . . . I just keep feeling it." She smiled weakly. "And it must be a pretty strong feeling because I haven't listened to those sorts of . . . promptings . . . for a while. I think I've deliberately blocked out the Spirit for a long time . . . so I may be a very limited spiritual resource, but I think I may be the only one for him at the moment."

"And you want to be prepared?" Nan walked across and sat down on the bed.

Meredith nodded. "I don't even know if Grant is that . . . religious. They do have a Bible . . . and he used a Bible story in a court case—but I just know that I want to be able to say the right thing to him if it comes up."

"Well, you know it's been said that the Lord sends prepared people to His prepared servants." Stewart pulled up a desk chair from beside the bed. "Although this sounds like a harsh preparation for them."

"But maybe crisis can bring good with it," Meredith finished quietly, recalling her thoughts from days before. She drew a deep breath and looked at her mother. "I know it has for me, Mum. I've been sitting on the other side of the fence for a while, but seeing you and realizing that you . . ." Her voice broke and then she felt her mother's arm around her shoulders and she breathed in the familiar perfume. "I know you don't want to talk about it too much . . . just yet . . ."

"There's nothing much to talk about." Nan gently stroked her daughter's head. "I've been more tired for a while, and they thought I was anemic, but then they found a small lump and I'm just waiting for the biopsy results." She smiled as Meredith sat up straight. "It's just old age getting at us. If it isn't your father's back and shoulder then it's my insides. We have to have something to talk about."

Stewart gave his wife's shoulder a firm squeeze. "We're literally fulfilling prophecy about becoming as one . . . between us we have one body that works."

Meredith shook her head as she laughed quietly and held out her arms to hug them both. "Just promise me you won't keep any secrets from me. I'm a big girl now, and seeing how Wendy is so far away in Australia . . . I expect to be relied on."

"We'll do that, love." Stewart nodded. "Although I think after this weekend your mother will just go from strength to strength."

Nan nodded as she squeezed Meredith's hand. "You've come back . . . the least I can do is stay around to enjoy watching you happy."

They were all silent for a moment, then Stewart cleared his throat. "So . . . what about those questions . . . now that you have our undivided attention."

"Okay, questions . . ." Meredith wiped her eyes and glanced at her watch. "You have approximately nine hours to teach me everything I need to know."

"What you need to remember," her father corrected as he settled back on the chair beside the bed. "I just have one question before we start. How important is this young man?"

"Excuse me?" Meredith frowned.

"How important is this young man . . . to you?" Stewart emphasized the last two syllables, watching his daughter carefully and ignoring his wife's quick glance.

"Important to me?" Meredith shrugged, but she became aware of her heart beginning to beat more quickly as she stammered. "He's . . . very important. He's my boss. He's a very good lawyer—and he's very thoughtful." Her cheeks colored as she thought about Grant's concern for her safety, and just as swiftly came memories of their working together—a quick smile, a contemplating look as she asked endless questions, a disbelieving glance followed by a sudden laugh as she challenged his defense. She swallowed and looked directly at her father. "Grant is a very special person . . . to me."

CHAPTER 11

The office seemed unusually empty as Meredith let herself in just after midday on Monday. Even compared to the early mornings she had put in when she first started work before everyone else, it seemed more empty . . . more solemn. She glanced over Stella's desk, but everything was neat and tidy, as it was always left on a Friday afternoon.

"Even Stella hasn't been in," she murmured to herself as she pushed her own office door open. "I'd better listen to the messages first."

It was hot in the office from the morning sun and being closed up for several days, so Meredith slipped off her suit jacket and hung it up before going back out to the reception area to play back the phone messages. There were a few repeat calls from a distressed-sounding woman, a couple of dial tones, promises to call back, and then Meredith started as she heard Grant's voice on the end of the line.

"Hello, Meredith." His voice sounded weary and there was a long pause. "I guess you'll have safely arrived at the office . . . if you followed instructions. Ah . . . just to let you know, Dad is doing fine now. His eyes and his mouth opened at the same time and all he can talk about is getting the boat fixed as soon as possible." There was another pause. "Thank goodness. Um . . . I'll be in tomorrow. If you could just go over the files for the Stephens case and call Mrs. Henry to arrange another appointment . . . and . . . thanks for being there."

She pressed the replay button without thinking and listened to the message again. She could hear none of the crisp, clipped tones she was used to. *He sounds so tired. He probably hasn't slept at all. I can't imagine what he's been through, but at least his father's all right.* She leaned her elbows on the desk and covered her face with her hands, closed her eyes, and breathed deeply as she contemplated the whole weekend.

"Falling asleep on the job already?"

Meredith's eyes flew open as Grant's voice sounded above her head. He was leaning against the reception desk in the usual stance he adopted when talking with Stella, but there the similarity ended. There was no crisp shirt and silk tie, and no well-cut suit. Instead Meredith looked at a man whose face bore the darkened stubble of a couple days' growth and whose plain navy sweatshirt and crumpled chinos looked like they'd been slept in.

"Oh my," she whispered, then realized how she must have sounded when he glanced down at his attire and rubbed his roughened cheek. "I mean . . . how are you—how's your father?"

"Dad's fine." Grant smiled and ran his hand through his hair, making small strands stand on end. "But from the look on your face I must look a bit worse for wear."

Meredith stood up. "No, no, you look fine . . . I mean . . ." She paused and shook her head. "You look tired. Have you been home at all?"

"Not since we went sailing. After the accident I went straight to the hospital with Dad and stayed until he came to. Stella's still at the hospital with him."

Meredith frowned and glanced at her watch. "But that was quite a while ago . . . where have you been?" She shook her head and held up her hand. "I'm sorry . . . it's none of my business."

He said nothing, so she glanced around and then quickly bent down and picked up a pile of mail. "I'll go and get these sorted and you go home and get some rest. Things will be fine here." He still didn't respond as she walked around the desk toward her office. She turned when he still hadn't moved. "Grant . . . please, go home. I've been here a couple of months now. I think I can cope for a few hours."

She waited while he absently ran his finger up and down the handle of the brass bell that Stella kept on the desk, then raised his head and stared at the ceiling. Somehow, it didn't seem right to leave, so she stood quietly until he looked straight at her.

"You asked me where I'd been." He shook his head. "Physically . . . after I left the hospital, I just walked along Takapuna Beach. Mentally . . . emotionally . . ." He took a deep breath and his voice rasped. "I think in the last twenty-four hours I've been to hell and back."

Meredith felt her stomach clench at the torment in his face. Her mind raced as she tried to find something appropriate to say, but suddenly she knew to say nothing. Grant had slowly turned and leaned back against the desk, folding his arms and dropping his head forward.

"We were heading for Kawau Island and a storm came up suddenly," he began slowly. "The wind got really strong so Dad went to tell Stella to stay down below, and then he took the helm. He told me to go up and reef the sail—lower it so that the sail area is reduced," he explained absently. "It takes the pressure off the mainsail, but the problem is, if you ease it wrongly, the boom can flap about. I haven't done it for a while, and the wind caught it. The next thing, the boom swung down on Dad." He shook his head.

Meredith watched as his fists clenched on the edge of the desk.

"I panicked," he stated simply. "The boat was dipping like crazy, Dad was lying unconscious with blood pouring out of his head, and I was trying to yell to Stella but she couldn't hear me. I felt so useless!"

Meredith finally spoke quietly. "How did you get out of it?"

Grant looked sideways at her before closing his eyes. "I prayed. Actually, I just begged for help. Not that that helped me the last time . . ."

Meredith winced at the pain in his voice as he struggled to control his emotions.

"Anyway . . . Stella came up then . . . and I managed to lash the helm. She looked after Dad until I got the engine going." He shrugged. "After that it all ran together pretty quickly. We got to Kawau Island, the helicopter came for Dad . . ."

"But how are you feeling now?" Meredith asked the question quietly.

Grant folded his arms and then rubbed his forehead as if trying to draw out an answer.

"When Dad was lying there all I could think was that he was dead . . . and that I'd killed him . . . just like Hannah and Emily." His voice broke and she watched him fight for control as a surge of emotion wracked his body. Finally, he stared at the door without seeing it and his voice was barely audible. "I just don't understand why . . . why does it happen? When I'm just beginning to forget—to get on with life—this happens and brings it all back again. I mean, if there is a God, why does He let people keep suffering?"

The question seemed to hang in the air. Meredith slowly moved forward until she was standing beside him. *Please, Heavenly Father . . . please help me know what to say to him.* Her heart seemed to fill her whole chest with its beating and she struggled to keep her voice steady.

"Maybe you're not meant to forget. Maybe they don't want you to forget them, Grant."

Time seemed to stand still as neither of them moved.

Please! "Hannah and Emily—your mother—they're part of you, Grant. You can't just lock them out and pretend that they didn't exist. Maybe you're supposed to—"

His expression contorted in confusion, then pain as his voice became harsh and he interrupted her. "You know . . . after I left the beach I was planning to go straight home, but instead, I found myself driving here to the office. I knew that you'd be here and I kept thinking of you." He gave a rueful half-smile that disappeared quickly into a grimace. "And when I thought about you, I felt peaceful and I wanted to feel more of that peace. I wasn't really looking for answers . . . just comfort." He shrugged. "Actually, I don't know what I was looking for or thinking . . . but it certainly wasn't that." He continued, his voice was growing slightly louder. "My wife and child and mother are dead! My father nearly died! Suggestions like that don't really bring me any peace." He sighed heavily. "Thanks for nothing, Meredith. Somehow, I thought you'd be more understanding."

He began to walk toward the door, then turning abruptly, and still looking past her, he said formally in the clipped tones she was so used to, "I take it your weekend went well. Thank you for coming back so promptly."

Meredith stared at him—the defensive way he'd braced his shoulders, the small pulse beating beneath his gritted jaw. Her heart felt as if it were being put into a vice. "It's nothing . . . but thank you for giving me the extra time . . . especially with my . . ." Her voice broke as the emotion of the whole weekend seemed to suddenly drain the energy from her body.

In the silence, she sought refuge in thoughts of her family. On her departure from Taranaki, the pressure of leaving quickly had helped to keep the farewells with her mother and Ryan deliberately happy and positive. Even the long trip back had been more of a mental journey for her, going over and over in her mind the hours of discussion with her parents the night before, and rehearsing ways she could explain eternal concepts to Grant.

A few seconds before, as she had responded to Grant's plea, she had felt a surge of hope that her prayers had been answered. *"Thanks for nothing."* Her answer had meant nothing to him . . . it had only hurt him more.

"Especially with my mother," she finished in a whisper and turned abruptly. The door to the reception area closed as she reached her desk.

"Thanks for nothing?" She shook her head, trying to fight an overwhelming sense of failure as their conversation repeated itself rapidly in her mind. *Why did I even say anything? Why did I even think I could? Dad says the Lord sends prepared people . . . not people like me.* She gritted her teeth and stared at the brass lamp on her desk until its outline blurred as she fought the tears that were determined to come. "So much for helping . . ." She directed bitter words toward the lamp. "So much for listening to the Spirit. Now he hates me even more."

"I don't hate you at all," Grant spoke quietly behind her. "Meredith . . . I'm sorry—I shouldn't have spoken to you like that."

She felt, rather than heard, the flatness in his voice, and she couldn't make herself turn around. He continued.

"You're probably right . . . about locking them out . . ." He paused for a long moment. "But how else does the pain go away?"

How does the pain go away? Oh, Father . . . please help me . . . not for my sake, but for Grant and his family . . .

Meredith spoke quietly as she finally turned around and looked straight at him.

"I don't think the pain does go away . . . you just have to learn to temper it with hope."

"But what if there isn't anything to hope for?" He asked the question quietly, without expression.

Meredith tried to fight a swell of panic as she felt the answer—she now dreaded saying anything. She stared at the tiny insignia on his sweatshirt, trying to formulate the right words. Then she lifted her chin almost defiantly, clenching her jaw and willing her lips not to tremble.

"I . . ." She felt her determination begin to fade immediately and closed her eyes. *Please . . . give me the right words.* She opened her eyes and tried to look directly at Grant. "I was always taught that faith is the hope for things which are not seen, but are true." She cleared her throat and rubbed her forehead. "I don't know . . . what you believe in, but I get the feeling . . . that you think you've lost your family forever. That you'll never see Emily and Hannah—or your mother—again."

She watched the muscles working on Grant's face and saw him fighting to control his response. He finally rubbed his lips together and thrust his hands into his back pockets.

"So, if I think that—and I don't have any reason to believe anything else—what makes you think, or believe, any differently?" Grant's tone was resigned rather than defiant now, and Meredith began to feel more strength. She straightened up from the desk.

"I've always believed that this life is just part of a process." She licked the side of her mouth and took a deep breath. "I believe that we existed before now as intelligent beings, and that when we die, our spirit lives on. I don't believe for a moment that you've lost your family permanently. There is a way you can be together forever."

Grant studied her face carefully, but then shook his head. "I can tell you really believe that, Meredith. But what if I don't—what if I can't?"

"That's because you don't know what to believe, Grant." Her voice was barely a whisper. "If you knew what I knew . . . then you would have hope. We can't see Emily right now, but I have faith her spirit still exists—and that gives me hope that you'll see her again."

At the mention of his daughter's name the pain resurfaced on Grant's face, and he closed his eyes. "Meredith . . . you can't know . . ."

"But I have faith, Grant—and an understanding." She shook her head and swallowed the lump in her throat. "I found out this weekend that . . . my mother has cancer. I don't know what the future holds, whether I'll lose her yet . . . but I have faith that we weren't just put here to love people and then to lose them and live in pain for the rest of our lives. We're meant to have hope . . . and happiness. We just have to know where to find it."

Her voice trembled and her shoulders began to shake as all that had happened over the last few days suddenly found expression. With a final effort, she looked straight at Grant, biting her lip. "I know, because I nearly lost it."

She covered her eyes, pressing her hand hard against her forehead in an effort to gain control, but the emotion was too strong. Without thinking, Grant responded by moving to her side. Then he hesitated, lifting his arms, then dropping them again.

"Meredith . . . I . . ."

She was unaware of his arms closing around her until he drew her gently against his chest. The unexpected comfort only gave vent to another wave of tears, and she cried against his shoulder, her whole body shaking. For several minutes, as Grant held her close, her stifled sobs were the only noise in the room.

As the last tears fell, she drew a deep, shuddering breath and instinctively put up a hand to push away, but Grant's arms only tightened around her, encouraging her to relax against him. She felt his head against hers and then the slightest pressure of his lips against her forehead.

"I feel really silly," she finally said against his wet shoulder, unable to look up at him.

"Don't . . ." She felt his chest rumble with a weak chuckle. "It's been a weekend of storms. I don't mind getting wet for a good cause."

She stood still, unsure what to say or whether to move until Grant slowly eased away, holding her at arm's length and looking at her steadily.

"I'm really sorry about your mother. If I'd known . . ." He stopped and shook his head. "I guess it's one thing I can relate to you on."

Meredith clasped her hands together, aware of his hands still resting on her shoulders. Then of a feeling of emptiness came as he let her go and folded his arms.

"I'm sorry, maybe that wasn't completely appropriate. I better keep my hands to myself or you'll be charging me with harassment."

"I don't think so. In fact, I'm sorry if I said too much. I get a bit carried away . . . especially when I feel strongly about something." She rolled her eyes. "Sometimes really, really carried away."

"But I know you really, really meant what you said . . . and I do appreciate that," Grant's voice was surprisingly gentle. "Even if I can't quite grasp it yet."

* * *

The next three days Meredith was kept busy as she covered for Stella as well as doing the work that she would find on her desk early in the morning. Frank was out of the hospital and recuperating at home under Stella's watchful care. Grant was even busier than usual, handling his father's cases as well as his own, so he was out each day for court appearances and business appointments, often returning just before five o'clock.

He was openly friendly whenever he entered the office and greeted Meredith, but he made no further mention of the incident on Monday. Sometimes she found herself touching her forehead and wondering if she'd imagined the whole thing. Then she'd spend the evening lying on her bed, going over and over their conversation . . . and wondering what else she could have said . . . or what she could have said better. She found she was trying to analyze it like a court case. Sometimes she would pick up the scriptures and try to find the answers in print, but the words would cloud as feelings of inadequacy and frustration would wash over her again, and she'd put the scriptures down. But occasionally, she would remember a scripture or a doctrinal expression from when she was younger and a sensation of peace would settle over her, and at those times she would almost cry with relief.

At four thirty on Thursday, Meredith was finalizing appointments for the next day when the phone rang. Stella was on the other end of the line.

"Meredith. I've called with a royal summons for you. Mr. Bascombe asked if you could come over after work and stay for dinner." The secretary's normally brisk voice suddenly dropped a tone. "I think he's sick of his own company, not to mention mine, and Grant is going to be out, so it's just the three of us."

The unexpected request and the way Stella worded it took Meredith by surprise. She hesitated only briefly, then nodded.

"Yes . . . for sure. I'll be there about five thirty. Should I bring anything?"

"Goodness me, no . . . just yourself," Stella chuckled. "I'm having fun actually having time to cook meals—and for someone other than myself."

As she replaced the telephone, Meredith was thoughtful. Stella had sounded so different . . . almost lighthearted.

An hour later she had parked the car in the driveway next to a large one-level villa. The white plaster walls and terra-cotta-tile trim, although Mediterranean in appearance, were as much part of the English style of the older home as the tidy but rambling gardens that Meredith walked through to the front door. Even as she raised her hand to lift the solid brass door knocker, the door opened and Stella waved her in.

"I saw you coming up the drive. Right on time . . . good girl." She ushered her through a tiled foyer and into a large room overlooking the city and harbor. "Dinner will be ready in about fifteen minutes."

Unsure of what to do next, Meredith stood still and looked around as Stella whisked out again. The room appeared empty, so she made her way uncertainly to the open French doors.

Outside, bright green lawns spanned out from a generous arc of red-tiled steps in front of the windows, and the perfume of carefully nurtured roses mingled with the clean smell of the freshly mown grass. Meredith drew an appreciative deep breath as she took a step farther out onto the narrow patio.

"Glad you could come, Meredith." Frank spoke from close beside her and she jumped. He laughed. "Sorry. Didn't mean to give you a fright. I just got tired of sitting in there." He gestured with his head back toward the lounge, then grimaced. "Ouch . . . forget this head of mine doesn't like sudden movements."

As he turned she saw the large dressing taped to the side of his head, and she pulled a face. "Ooh . . . that looks serious." She studied his face. "But you look pretty cheerful. You must be a quick healer. I was expecting to see you in a wheelchair or something."

"Been there, done that." Frank grinned as he motioned her to an elegantly wrought-iron patio chair. "I'd be back at work tomorrow except I'm quite enjoying Stella's cooking, so I think I'll ham it up a bit longer." He pulled his cell phone out of his cardigan pocket and waved it. "Still work if I want to."

Settling himself into a matching chair opposite her, Frank stretched his legs and crossed his ankles. He looked so happy and relaxed that Meredith found it hard to reconcile the image with that of an unconscious man lying in a pool of blood, as Grant had described.

"So, how is work going?" He patted his head carefully. "I've tried not to think about it too much, it makes my head hurt on a normal day."

He spoke lightly, but Meredith immediately detected an undertone of genuine concern. Since their initial interview, she had developed a profound respect for Frank Bascombe that had grown steadily as she watched his interaction with clients and other lawyers . . . and her. He managed to convey his trust in her in a way that made her want to give her best; at the same time, they had come to enjoy an easy camaraderie. She knew how much he loved his work and the business he had created, and how being forced to recuperate at a distance would be a challenge for him.

She nodded thoughtfully. "It's been very busy, but I've explained the situation where necessary and everything is fine. Grant has been covering a lot of your cases, as I'm sure you've discussed, and . . . well, I have a new and healthy respect for Stella's skills, because she has everything structured so well that even I can follow the system and still do my work. In saying that . . ." She grimaced. "I really miss her . . . and you."

Frank nodded. "That's good . . . very good. Grant has been keeping me informed . . . in fact, he's been very diligent about everything. And as for Stella . . . I certainly don't know what I'd do without her at the office. She's been a pillar of strength to me since this accident. When I woke up in the hospital, she was right there, and she's been buzzing 'round ever since. I told her I could get a nurse, but she told me not to be silly." He lifted his hands in a happily helpless gesture. "Who am I to argue? Like I said, her cooking is a dream compared to my and Grant's efforts."

Meredith smiled. "She said she was enjoying cooking for you . . . that she gets tired of cooking just for herself."

"Mmm . . . I think I've learned more about her in the last few days than . . ." He grunted a small laugh. "You know, Meredith, you can know someone for so many years . . . and not really know them. I mean, Stella was Barbara's friend . . . not mine."

"So how long have you known each other?" Meredith waited as he calculated.

Finally he frowned. "It must be the best part of thirty-five years. The girls were friends from university, and Barbara and I were high-school sweethearts before that." He nodded again. "Yes . . . at least thirty-five years."

"And you've never tasted her cooking?"

"Well, I must have . . . I just never really thought about it."

"Then why have you noticed now?" Meredith leaned forward, her elbows on her knees and her chin cupped in her hands. "What's different?"

Frank took a moment to consider, and then furrowed an eyebrow. "Why do I suddenly feel like I'm being interrogated? I asked you over to check how the office is running."

"The office is running fine and I commented on what a good job Stella does." She grinned, feeling suddenly confident in his company. "You were the one who started extolling her virtues. Being a good lawyer, I just asked a few more questions—and I just have one more."

"I don't know that I dare ask what it is." Frank watched the young woman in front of him carefully. For some reason he could talk to her easily, and he knew she felt comfortable in his presence. At this moment, he felt more like her father than her employer. "All right, Miss Winstone . . . what is it?'

"Well . . . having listened to all the evidence in the case . . ." Meredith paused, pursing her lips. "It seems to me that the person in question, Stella, being of extremely sound reputation in all areas of expertise, as extolled by you . . ." She raised her eyebrows. ". . . is, however, blissfully unaware of the high regard in which you hold her. The question I have—sir—is, why are you telling me and not Stella?"

Not a muscle moved on Frank's face as he listened to Meredith. He sat still for so long after she had finished that she began to feel her newly acquired bravado slipping away.

Then he spoke very quietly. "I don't know. I'm just so used to her . . . being around."

"Well, most people like to hear that they're appreciated," Meredith responded gently. "Especially after thirty-five years."

Frank was silent again. Then he suddenly started laughing out loud until his head hurt too much and he held it gingerly. The look on his face made Meredith laugh as well, although she wasn't sure why he was laughing.

"I'm sorry," Frank chuckled. "I was just thinking that I really didn't know what I was getting in for when I took you on. I just can't imagine ever having this sort of conversation with any of those other applicants."

Meredith smiled hesitantly. "Well, I certainly never imagined talking to the senior partner like this either. My father always told me my mouth would get me into trouble. I'm really sorry if I've said anything out of place, Mr. Bascombe."

"Not at all." Frank raised his hand to stop her apology. "I appreciate your openness. It's given me a lot to think about. But now tell me . . . how was your weekend?"

* * *

Grant pulled into the driveway and sat for a moment, his fingers drumming the steering wheel. He was supposed to be meeting a client for dinner, but had spilled some ink on his shirt and rushed home to change. Now, the unexpected sight of Meredith's car brought an increasingly familiar sense of anticipation to the surface again. He'd been experiencing it more and more as he returned to the office each day, expecting to see her sitting at Stella's desk and welcoming him with a hesitant but warm smile.

He began to loosen his tie as he got out of the car and walked deliberately past Meredith's little Volkswagen, but his hand dropped to his side as he noticed some dents on the rear bumper and a patch of rust by the driver's window. The little car was neat and clean but definitely needed some repairs at the panel beaters, he thought.

He glanced back at his own BMW, its shining bronze chassis a stark contrast to the unpolished cream paintwork of the Volkswagen.

"She may not have all the fancy trimmings, but she won't let you down." He shook his head and gently thumped Meredith's car with his fist. "She won't let you down."

He turned and looked toward the house, then exhaled slowly as he pulled his cell phone from his coat pocket and dialed.

"Hello, Steve." He looked up at the sky as a voice responded. "Look, sorry about this, but I won't be able to make it for dinner tonight. Um . . . something's just come up at home."

CHAPTER 12

"Meredith . . . it's going to be okay." Telesia finished twisting her thick, black hair up into a coil at the back of her head, and fixed it into place with a large tortoiseshell comb heavily set with a floral pattern of mother-of-pearl. It matched the tortoiseshell pendant she wore with a simple cream dress. "That suit will do fine."

"You don't think it's too . . . lawyerish?" Meredith turned again in front of the mirror, then glanced at Telesia. "Maybe I should wear a regular dress like you."

"Meredith . . ." Telesia patiently picked up her scripture case and pointed to her watch. "If we don't hurry, it won't matter what you wear—everybody'll only notice that we're late."

"I'm sorry . . . you're right." Meredith took a deep breath and bent to pick up her own scriptures off the bedside cabinet. She'd been up late reading them every night since getting back to Auckland, enjoying the sense of recognition she'd felt as she reread the many marked verses from her seminary days. She zipped the case shut firmly. "You know, Sia, it really has felt so good finally making the decision to get back into the Church, reading the scriptures and prayers and everything, but . . . the thought of actually going to our new ward is scaring me silly."

"You'll be fine." Telesia pushed her gently but firmly through the doorway. "Nobody's going to eat you—and besides, Tavita will be coming, so we can sit on either side of you and protect you."

Meredith's wish to slip quietly into sacrament meeting wasn't fulfilled. The girls were greeted as soon as they entered the chapel.

"Sisters, it's good to meet you," said an elderly woman leaning on a walking stick. She smiled graciously at them, then peered more closely through her bifocals and frowned. "But where are your name tags? I can't tell who you are."

There was a moment's confusion, then Telesia smiled. "Oh no, we're not the missionary sisters. I'm Telesia Leota and this is my friend Meredith Winstone, and we've just moved into the ward. I've come the last two weeks, and I've seen you, but it's lovely to meet you properly."

"Och, how silly of me. I just assumed that you were missionaries because there were two of you." The lady smiled sheepishly and took Meredith's hand between both of hers. "I'm a bit new to this. I'm Lydia Crowsen. I was just baptized a wee while ago. I think Bishop Brown gave me this job of welcoming everybody so that I'd get to know them quicker."

"And has it worked?" Meredith felt immediately drawn to this small, wiry woman with white hair and the faintest Scottish accent.

"Oh, indeed." Sister Crowsen nodded her head, then leaned toward Meredith confidentially. "I might even give you two a wee turn at it if you want to . . . just to help you get settled."

She chuckled as she looked beyond them to the family that was entering next, and the girls moved on into the chapel.

"Now, that wasn't too bad a start, was it?" Telesia sat down near the window and turned to Meredith. "First day here and you're already mistaken for a missionary. What on earth were you worrying about?"

"It must be the suit," Meredith commented wryly as she tugged at the hemline, turning to watch as people rapidly filled the seats. A couple of minutes before the meeting started, she leaned over to whisper to Telesia.

"Have you ever counted how many nationalities are in this ward?"

Telesia glanced up from reading the newsletter they'd received and looked around.

"No . . . at least, not specifically."

"I think I've counted eight already." Meredith opened her eyes wide. "And that's only the ones I can see the differences immediately or tell by their accents."

"There's probably more." Telesia began counting on her fingers. "Our Relief Society presidency has a South African, a Kiwi-Canadian, and a Filipino sister, with a Korean secretary. And I just found out that our visiting teachers are Australian and Japanese."

She was suddenly quiet as the bishop stood to open the meeting, but leaned over quickly as Tavita slipped into the seat beside them. "There's no way you could feel out of place here . . . so there's no excuse now."

By the end of the three meetings, Meredith was left wondering why she had ever felt apprehensive about coming. Bishop Brown, obviously under direction from her father, had found her, and after regaling her with a few interesting stories about her mother's school days, had invited all three of them to dinner and family night the next evening. Meredith made sure to request a few minutes to talk with him privately later, and felt as if a weight had been lifted off her shoulders as she made the appointment. Telesia had introduced her to their visiting teachers, and the activities chair had rushed up to remind them about the cultural evening item that they'd promised to perform.

"Telesia . . . I don't even know how to do Samoan dancing . . . let alone in front of a group of strangers," Meredith moaned good-naturedly at her friend as they headed down the driveway, waving to a group of children who waited for their parents. "How could you volunteer me? You didn't even know I would be at church."

"Just call it faith." Telesia smiled. "I needed someone to dance with me, and you're the only person I know that I can teach how to do the siva in three weeks—and by then they won't be strangers."

"Oh, that's all right then." Meredith rolled her eyes, laughing ruefully. "Why do I suddenly feel like I'm right back in Young Women's?"

They spent the rest of the day reading, talking, and preparing a light meal for dinner, which they ate out on the veranda. The trees at the bottom of the garden were beginning to create a black silhouette against a deepening blue ocean when they finally finished dessert and sat back in the wooden deck chairs they'd bought that week.

"So has it been so bad today?" Telesia glanced sideways at Meredith. "Any regrets?"

"No, not really," Meredith shook her head slowly. "I was nervous, but it's made a big difference feeling like I'm involved straightaway in the cultural evening project . . . which I'm sure you're aware of—and planned." She frowned good-naturedly and rested her head back on the canvas chair. "You know, everybody was so nice there today, but spending last weekend with my family was the turning point for me. It's given me a completely new perspective on how I've been . . . denying everything all these years. In fact, Ryan came right out and asked why I'd been inactive and then said that I'd rationalized my way through it all."

"Good one Ryan." Telesia nodded. "He's already got the missionary spirit with him—he's not afraid to speak up."

Meredith sat silently watching the darkening sky. "It's the first time in a long time that I actually felt . . . the Spirit. When I was talking with Ryan, and then with my family in church . . . it was almost overwhelming." She gave a rough laugh. "Actually, it *was* overwhelming. I blubbered like a baby all through church—and just because I realized how much I loved them and wanted to be with them always."

"But that's how it's meant to be," Telesia added quietly. "We can know about being families forever, but it's only through the Spirit that we can actually feel it . . . feel the joy."

"Feel the joy," Meredith repeated thoughtfully. "That is what it's about, isn't it?"

"If you'll let yourself. Sometimes I think we fool ourselves that we're happy in our work because we're busy and accomplishing things, even if there's no Spirit there." Telesia raised an eyebrow. "Speaking of work—has it been any different?"

"Ye . . . es," Meredith answered warily. "In fact, this whole week has been so full, what with Ryan going on his mission, and Mr. Bascombe's accident, and trying to catch up with work, and spiritually, and . . ." She trailed off.

"And . . . ?"

"And talking with Grant," she finished quietly and clenched her hand around the hard teak-wood armrest.

"Aah . . . Mr. Bascombe, Jr. . . . and what did you talk about? I get the feeling it wasn't anything to do with law."

"No . . . no, it wasn't," Meredith sighed. "He had such a terrible experience when his father got hurt on the boat. It brought back all the pain of losing his family, and it's been on my mind all week, especially since Monday."

Telesia nodded knowingly. "I did wonder what happened on Monday. You walked in here looking like you'd seen a ghost, and then you've been so quiet all week and going to bed early. I've been worried . . . but I thought it best not to ask. I figured you'd tell me when you were ready."

"I'm sorry . . . I didn't realize. But it has been strange. After my experiences last weekend . . ." She trailed off, then began again, "I really felt like I needed to talk to Grant, so before I left home on Sunday night, I asked Mum and Dad for lots more information about eternal families and . . . things like that—things that I thought Grant might ask questions about, or that I could tell him." Meredith rested her chin in the palm of her hand. "He came to the office straight from the hospital and . . . he looked dreadful. Then he began to tell me all about the accident on the boat, and that it was his fault. And that brought back the memories of his car accident and his family dying—and how he just wanted to forget."

"Oh, dear. That must be dreadful for him." Telesia's brown eyes moistened. "What did you say to him?"

"Well . . . I had one of those instant prayers—that I could say the right thing—and then I suggested that maybe his family didn't want to be forgotten and that there was a way he could be with them again."

She looked alarmed when Telesia's eyes widened in surprise.

"Do you think I said too much—or the wrong thing?"

"No . . ." Telesia shook her head. "I'm just surprised you said it at all."

"So was I . . . but I just wanted to reassure him so much."

"And how did he react?"

Meredith swallowed hard. "Actually, he was pretty negative at first. And then, I thought about my mother and how I've been rejecting it all and I realized how much I wanted an eternal family and . . . I sort of lost control and started crying."

"What happened then?" Telesia leaned forward.

Meredith blew a long breath. "And . . . next thing he was . . . comforting me."

"Ooh . . . I see," Telesia nodded slowly. "So how have things been at work since then? Has it been difficult?"

Meredith pulled a face. "Actually, no it hasn't. I was sort of dreading going to work the next day, but it's been fine. We've both been so busy doing all the work for Stella and Mr. Bascombe that I didn't really get to talk to him again . . . until Thursday evening."

"Thursday evening . . . ? You said you were having dinner with the boss—singular." Telesia frowned. "Did that change?"

"Mm-hmm . . . I thought it was just to report on the week at the office. Then Grant came home unexpectedly." She pulled at her ear. "It turned out that after dinner we sat around talking—"

"Until midnight." Telesia grinned. "I heard you come in late."

"I thought I was being quiet."

"Oh, you were . . . it was your humming that woke me. I take it the evening went well?"

Meredith sat contemplating the darkening landscape, then looked at her friend.

"Sia . . . everything is happening so fast. It seems like I make the decision to come back to church and it's been an emotional roller-coaster ever since. From not praying at all, suddenly I feel like I'm talking to Heavenly Father constantly—asking Him to help Mum and Ryan. And then Mr. Bascombe. And then Grant."

"You think you've used up your quota already?" Telesia chuckled. "Maybe it's just that you've been a bit selfish the last few years . . . and now you're thinking more about others."

Meredith frowned. "Thanks, Telesia," she said sarcastically. "Cut right to the point. What did I do to deserve such an honest friend?"

"Some people are just lucky." Her friend grinned. "Just like Grant—the Bascombes—are lucky to have you around. Now tell me how the evening went."

"It was good. Mr. Bascombe is so funny and Stella was so . . . relaxed." She smiled. "It was really good."

"And Grant?"

"Fine." Meredith nodded. "He was very pleasant. We all talked business at first . . . then he and his father started telling stories about each other, and Stella added a few. I'm not sure what I was expecting, but I really enjoyed it. He was like a different person."

The girls were silent with their own thoughts for a long time, until the chill night air sent them inside to bed. Later, Meredith lay in her bed, with her hands clasped behind her head, silently watching the gray shadows lengthening across the ceiling. She heard her flat-mate's voice through the darkness.

"Mele?"

"Mm-hmm?"

"Forgive me if I'm being too personal." Telesia coughed delicately. "But . . . how do you feel about Grant?"

Meredith watched the shadows move gently. "I respect him a lot. He's a great man—who's had a lot of pain. I really want to help him. Although I'm not sure how or why I want to."

"I understand that. But how do you feel?" Telesia was quietly persistent. "Really?"

As if on cue, the feeling of Grant's arms around her and the slight pressure of his lips on her forehead were as real as if they had just happened.

"How do I really feel?" She shook her head. "I really enjoy him being around. I really look forward to seeing him each day and working with him. I really feel confused because he's my boss, and . . . I really, really wish I'd gone to work in Wellington."

CHAPTER 13

"You know, I think I got spoilt by being at home so long." Frank glanced at the clock in the lobby. "It's three thirty and I'm expecting an afternoon snack to turn up."

He patted his stomach meaningfully and looked at Stella, who kept her eyes directed at the computer screen while her fingers moved rapidly over the keyboard. She stopped briefly to backspace, and rolled her eyes at Meredith.

"I think we created a monster."

"We?" Meredith looked up from the pile of folders she was perusing at the reception desk and pointed at Stella. "It's your fault. You pampered him too much."

They were all laughing when Grant's door opened and he peered out. "Does anybody else do any work around here?"

"It's your father . . . he keeps interrupting everybody." Stella kept typing while Meredith grinned at Grant and backed away toward her office.

Frank put his hands into his pockets and produced his wallet. "It sure is hard to get good help these days. I'll just go get something for myself. But while you're all here . . ." Meredith stopped, Grant's head reappeared, and Stella stopped typing. "How about we have a company picnic this Saturday? We'll sail over to Rangitoto, and we could spend the day at the old cottage . . . or maybe we could even go for a hike up to the summit."

There was a moment's silence while all three looked at each other, then back at Frank.

"Well, don't get excited all at once." He frowned. "Don't tell me you had other plans?"

Meredith thought about the cultural evening she had been practicing for with Telesia. "What time would we be back?"

"Oh . . . about sixish." Frank shrugged. "But if you've got something else happening we'll make it another time."

"No, no . . . It's fine. I've got a concert thing later in the evening but—I'm in." Meredith nodded and smiled. "I'd love it. I've never been to Rangitoto Island, even though I've lived here for four years."

"I confess, I haven't either," Stella said quietly.

"You're joking!" Frank looked startled. "How long have you lived in Auckland?"

"Oh, about forty years." Stella shrugged her shoulders. "I don't know why . . . it's so familiar sitting out there in the harbor. I've just never gotten around to actually going there."

Grant shook his head. "Looks like these girls need a bit of educating about the finer points of life in our fair city. What time are we going to leave?"

* * *

Meredith waited on the wooden jetty as Stella handed down a small carry bag to Frank and stepped carefully after it. Meredith followed suit, hesitating slightly as the boat moved gently, and instinctively putting her hands out to steady herself.

"Don't worry, you'll get your sea legs soon enough." Grant spoke from behind her, reaching out to hold her elbow lightly as she stepped onto the deck. "Have you done any sailing before?"

Meredith glanced around and upwards at the tall mast above her, then shook her head. "Nothing like this. The closest I've got is paddling a surf ski at the surf club . . . not even a jet ski."

"Well, this doesn't require nearly as much effort," he responded easily, and guided her to the cockpit. "It'll only take about twenty-five minutes to get over there, although Dad will probably go for a sail around the harbor before we stop at the island."

Once Frank had the motor running and had nosed the boat out of the Bayswater Marina, he checked the wind and nodded happily.

"There's a good easterly wind, so we can take you for a bit of a jaunt along the bays and then scoot round Motutapu Island before we put down the anchor."

Within minutes of reaching the channel, he and Grant had the sails up and soon had the yacht cutting through the water toward the southern tip of the harbor, both men looking relaxed as the sea breeze pulled at their clothing.

Meredith leaned over to Stella as they settled themselves on the comfortably padded cream vinyl seats. "It certainly doesn't seem like Mr. Bascombe's had any setbacks from the accident."

Stella nodded. "This is the best remedy for him. He's been muttering about 'getting back on the horse' ever since he regained consciousness. I'm surprised he waited this long."

Meredith inhaled deeply, letting the wind whip her hair back from her face and enjoying the crisp, taut feeling of the salt spray drying on her face. "I'm just so pleased I got to come." She smiled happily. "This feels wonderful! No wonder Mr. Bascombe enjoys it."

They sailed past the shining panorama of glass, steel, and concrete of the inner-city buildings and large, impressive passenger liners that sat patiently while small businesslike ferries jostled for a place at the docks. Occasionally, a sleek, beautifully appointed yacht would veer past, riding low in the water as if driven by a different wind.

"I never realized there was so much activity out here." Meredith glanced back over her shoulder to watch a small sailboat skip jauntily over the waves. "Oh, is that the museum?"

Stella followed Meredith's pointing finger to the large, gray, Grecian-styled building set against a hillside of green parkland overlooking the city and harbor. "Certainly looks different from this angle. Quite majestic."

"Everything does." Meredith nodded. "You can get a completely different perspective on things."

"Mmm . . . places and people."

And people. She stood up to watch as Grant responded to an instruction from his father and went forward to do something to the sails. He worked quickly, the muscles obvious under his white T-shirt. *Amazing what a suit covers up.* Her hands tightened on the rail she was holding onto. *And amazing how you'll let your thoughts wander—*

this is a company outing, and don't you forget it, Meredith Winstone! Just be grateful you have such a good boss—bosses!

For nearly an hour they made their way past ivory-colored beaches and small green-tufted islands spread throughout the harbor. At all times, the towering cone of Rangitoto rose in the middle of the harbor, in perfectly symmetry from wherever they were as they circled it.

"I never realized that Rangitoto looked the same from everywhere." Meredith held her face to the wind as Grant joined her near the front of the boat.

"Neither did I until I was about eleven." He leaned closer so she could hear him better. "I really got a shock when I went to a school sports day and someone from a school over in the city had the same profile of Rangitoto on their uniform as I did. I felt like they were stealing my island."

The reference to his childhood combined with his physical closeness brought a swift color to Meredith's cheeks, which he noticed immediately. "You can't imagine me as a little boy?"

"Not really." She shook her head. "I think you were an instant adult."

"Sometimes it felt like it . . . especially when Charles was around."

She looked up quickly, surprised at the reference to his cousin. "How come?"

"Charles and I spent a lot of time together when we were young—until he was about fifteen. He was always charging into things which I thought were . . . stupid, mostly."

"Not quite correct or logical?" Meredith suppressed a smile.

"Mmm . . . like I said . . . stupid." Grant smiled even as he shook his head. "Even more stupid, I felt an older cousin's responsibility to protect him, which he neither wanted nor needed, because he could always charm his way out of whatever trouble he got into."

"He'll probably make an excellent lawyer one day because he'll be able to relate to most of his clients," Meredith laughed, suddenly grateful for Charles Unsworth's impulsive nature and for his decision to go overseas and recommend her for this job.

Grant studied her face carefully before staring past her shoulder toward the island's coastline. "I am glad he did one thing . . . although I never thought I'd admit it."

Meredith's heart seemed to stand still and she felt her breath stop. "Oh? What was that?" She tried to control the tremor in her voice. "Another stupid decision?"

Grant continued to look past her for a long time, and she found herself concentrating on the row of double stitching on his sleeve, hoping he couldn't hear the pounding of her heart. He finally looked straight at her and shook his head then, dropping his voice to the softest she'd ever heard it.

"No . . . not a stupid decision . . . and you know darned well what I mean, Miss Winstone."

Meredith stood still. Her legs wouldn't have moved if she'd tried to force them. In fact, the only movement in her entire body seemed to be the color that was spreading rapidly up her neck and cheeks.

Frank's deep voice sounded over the silence. "Grant . . . we'll drop the girls at the wharf first. Can you get ready up front? Meredith . . . you'd better grab your gear."

"Uh—right . . . gear." She jerked awkwardly, running her hand through her hair, and called toward the cockpit. "I'm there!"

She turned to Grant. "Um . . . do I need to help you?"

"Not yet." Grant bent to pick up the end of a thick coil of rope. "Maybe later."

The next few minutes were busy with activity as Frank steered the boat close to the wharf. She watched as Grant leaned out to wrap the rope around the heavy wooden strut.

"We can't stay here because the ferries come in here to dock," Frank explained as he maneuvered the boat against the wharf. "Grant and I'll go and anchor offshore and row back in."

After they'd off-loaded and the men had taken the boat back out, Meredith and Stella strolled down the wooden jetty and along the foreshore pathway, taking their time reading the information posters presented in tidy wood-and-glass frames.

"My goodness, I never realized there was so much to do over here." Stella nodded at another poster. "I feel bad now . . . that I've been here nearly forty years and it's only been two miles away and I've never made the effort. Isn't it amazing how we take things for granted?"

Meredith watched the older woman as Stella studied the posters. Stella's meticulously cut bob was blown about by the wind, and the severe lines of the suits she wore at the office had been replaced with red, three-quarter-length trousers, white T-shirt and sneakers, and a navy zip-up sweater. She looked years younger as she read the information, glancing frequently out to sea to watch Frank and Grant row to shore in a small aluminum dinghy.

Grant was rowing, and the oars cut through the water in a steady rhythm that brought them rapidly to the shore. They pulled the dinghy well up on the beach and secured it, then quickly made their way over to where Stella and Meredith were waiting. Grant pulled some chocolate bars out of his bag and passed one to each of them.

"Bit of an energy boost for our walk. We can eat lunch at the summit."

"Actually," Frank hesitated and looked around, "I'm thinking I'll pass on the summit walk and show Stella the old bach we used to stay in at Islington Bay. It's a flatter walk along the coastline—better for my delicate state." He winked at Meredith.

"You used to stay in a cottage here?" She pointed at the ground. "I didn't think people actually lived on this island."

Frank grinned and pointed to a solid concrete pool area to one side of the path. "I used to come over every Christmas for years when I was a boy. During the summer, I used to swim in that pool and watch the ferries bringing all the visitors over."

"So do people still stay here?"

"Not anymore. Most of the baches were built in the '20s and '30s, so they're historical now—looked after by an historic trust. The whole island is a protected reserve," he chuckled. "That makes me feel really old. My parents started coming over with friends just before World War II. Then, when the war got going, the island was made into a strategic defense area."

"I didn't think we were really part of the war." Meredith looked puzzled.

"We weren't. Our soldiers went away to fight and New Zealanders were ready to defend themselves, but nothing ever happened down here. I was born just before the war, but I remember my folks telling me about all the secret roads and military installations that were put here on Rangitoto and on Motutapu Island." He laughed. "The old ranger here used to tell us stories about the war years. I like the one about the first enemy submarine. Everyone got really excited and then it turned out to be a whale."

They all laughed as they walked along the stony pathway to where the path divided.

"So you two hit the summit, and we'll go to the bay." Frank looked at his watch. "We'll need to be out of here by five at the latest if Meredith is to get to her show."

"Right. We'll see you in . . . six hours." Grant nodded and began to walk toward the left-hand track, not noticing that Meredith was standing still.

Six hours—alone—with Grant. Suddenly her courage failed her. *How can I spend all that time with him? What do I talk about?* She looked at Frank and Stella, unaware of the look of desperation on her face.

"It'll be fine." Frank was suddenly serious. "Let him do the talking, Meredith."

In that instant she realized that this trip was no spontaneous outing—Frank never had any intention of walking with them. She swallowed and put her hand to her heart, trying to still its rapid beating as she looked from Grant's tall figure back to his father.

"Walk and listen." She blinked hard and smiled weakly. "And if all else fails . . . admire the view?"

"Exactly." Frank smiled. "He could use a friend, Meredith."

CHAPTER 14

The first few hundred yards of the track were reasonably wide and level, and Meredith walked silently alongside Grant, concentrating on the track and the scrunching impact of their boots on the gravel path. Within minutes the shallow band of trees had given way to knotted vegetation that clung grimly to the dark red scoria rock base.

Grant finally broke the silence by pointing to a particularly twisted mass of gray-green shrubs, a curious mix of tangled roots and branches. "There's hardly any topsoil on most of the island, so the plants have to fight for food." He pointed back at a stand of Pohutukawa trees. "You watch how much smaller the same trees are the farther up the summit we go. Charles could never accept that they were the same trees."

"You used to come here with Charles?" Meredith looked around. "It doesn't look like his type of country."

"It's not." Grant motioned with his head toward the track. "We used to come here as kids, but he only really wanted to swim or find some girls to walk with."

She glanced sideways at his boots, which were solid leather and very well worn, as were his long beige shorts. He looked lean and comfortable, and she was glad she'd opted to wear her own light tramping boots and similar shorts.

"Do you do a lot of hiking?" She lengthened her stride as they walked up a slight slope.

"I used to, mainly at university." Grant looked at her boots. "You too?"

Meredith nodded. "I used to love hiking up Mt. Egmont, and I did a bit out in the Waitakere Ranges when I first came to Auckland. I really love the bush and river walks."

"Me too." Grant smiled briefly. They slowed as they found themselves sandwiched between a group of German and French tourists and a Japanese family. The air was filled with excited voices in different languages as everybody called to each other or made comments. Grant and Meredith walked on silently, absorbed in their own thoughts as the clamor allowed them to be. As the path began to climb steadily, the groups began to spread out, the youthful hikers striding ahead while the family of small children and an elderly couple lagged behind.

As they reached a large plateau, Meredith glanced around. "This is odd—a big flat area in the middle of all this rockiness."

Grant paused and pointed to their left. "They brought inmates over from the city prison to clear all this and begin the road around the island—by hand."

"Sort of like Alcatraz?" Meredith observed.

"Not exactly." Grant smiled. "From what I understand, most of them were low-security prisoners, and they actually had quite a good time here. Really took pride in creating the road for visitors."

Meredith pressed at a coral-like clump of solid red basalt with the toe of her boot, the rubber of the sole giving way to the rigid rock. "How on earth did they clear all this by hand? It's so sharp and hard."

"Determination, I guess . . . and they had plenty of time. It took over four years to finish the road."

Meredith began walking again. "Four years . . . imagine working on this for that long."

"Well, how long did you work on your degree?" Grant fell into step beside her.

"The last four years," she answered promptly. "But that was mental labor."

"It was still hard, though . . . wasn't it? I know it was for me."

"Mmm." Meredith nodded, wondering if he meant his own law studies or the last four years of his life.

They continued in silence for a while, the path becoming more rugged as they progressed, with weirdly tangled roots and rocks ingeniously combining to make steps. Often the steepness of the incline required a large step and she would feel Grant's hand under her elbow giving her the needed boost.

"Have you heard how your mother is doing?" Grant asked as they entered a wide area of pathway overhung with spindly trees whose branches intertwined to form a natural canopy.

Meredith dug her hands into the pockets of her shorts.

"She's actually doing much better than Dad expected. She went into the hospital last week and they thought they would have to do a mastectomy, but they just removed a lump and they're giving her other treatment." She shook her head. "I was so scared it was going to be worse because she kept getting breathless while I was there—but it was just worry bringing on her asthma. Probably worry about me," she finished quietly.

"Why would she worry about you?" Grant looked genuinely surprised. "Aren't you the perfect daughter? Loving, dedicated, studious . . . qualified?"

Meredith glanced at him sideways. He wasn't smiling. In fact his brows were drawn together in a slight frown. She didn't say anything, and he continued quietly.

"Sometimes I wonder what sort of daughter Emily would have been."

The statement was simple and sincere, and so unexpected that Meredith couldn't speak.

"When I let myself think about her, I try to imagine what she'd be like now . . . physically, emotionally . . . and how I would be—what sort of father I'd be to her."

There was a short silence as an enthusiastic hiker strode purposefully past them with a vaguely murmured greeting.

"I think you would be a wonderful father," Meredith assured him quietly. "I see the relationship you have with your own father, and you speak so fondly of your mother. They've obviously been great examples."

"Hannah used to tell me I was too focused . . . that I had to learn to relax to be a better father."

At Grant's reference to his wife, Meredith found her courage failing and took a moment to respond.

"She was obviously a very astute lady. My mother often tells my dad off for being too busy . . . in a loving kind of way."

"Hannah was a very loving person. I think I took her for granted in too many ways."

The shelter of the canopy suddenly ended, and Meredith blinked rapidly as bright sunlight glared in her eyes. She didn't see another twisted step on the path and tripped and fell forward, but with an instinct born of years of training, she rolled with the fall and was on her feet almost immediately.

"Are you all right?" Grant looked concerned as she quickly brushed some loose fragments of gravel off her hands and knees.

"I'm fine." She pulled a face. "Just a wee bit embarrassed."

"Well, that was quite an impressive tumble. You recovered yourself well." Grant grinned and leaned forward to pick a piece of twig off her sleeve. "Very martial-arts-ish."

She couldn't suppress a giggle at his expression and felt a warm glow as he laughed with her. She felt his hand tighten on her arm, then slide down to loosely clasp her hand. "Maybe I'd better help you over the next little bit . . . it gets a bit rough in places."

Grant kept talking as they walked up the narrow track. He stayed slightly ahead, but still held her hand lightly. On the occasional steeper step he would grasp it more tightly and pull her up easily with him. Her initial discomfort at the contact eased and she began to enjoy the pressure of his hand around hers, but when they passed an older couple resting at one of the lookout stations, she instinctively tried to pull her hand away. Just as quickly, Grant tightened his grip and returned the couple's greeting, stopping to answer their questions.

Meredith heard nothing of the conversation. She tried to stand nonchalantly, but when Grant folded his arms and pulled her hand into the crook of his elbow, she took a deep breath and fiddled with the strap of her backpack with her other hand.

"Well, thank you so much for answering our questions," the gray-haired woman drawled in a distinctively American accent. "I can see your young lady wants to move on." She smiled widely at them both. "You just have a wonderful day."

He still held onto her hand as they walked away, and Meredith felt an unreasonable surge of frustration brewing. *I'm not his young lady . . . so why does he keep holding my hand? And why do I keep enjoying it? . . . Why doesn't he just talk? I could handle that.*

A small signpost with "Summit" printed on it, and an arrow pointing ahead, appeared as they rounded the next corner. With a quick twist, she pulled her hand free and began to run ahead. "Race you to the top!"

If she had taken a moment longer to look at the smaller printing on the sign, she would have seen that it was just an indicator, and that the summit was, in fact, still quite a distance away—and steeply uphill. But she ran until her lungs felt as if they'd burst, willing herself not to look back to see if Grant had followed. She felt herself reach that point where an increase of adrenaline pushed her on, until she reached the base of a wooden stairway that seemed to wind without end farther up the hill.

Each bank of stairs had a wooden deck extending off to the side with planked seating around the edge, and tourists were gathered in small groups at each landing, resting or taking panoramic photos.

Suddenly deflated from her run, Meredith made her way slowly up to the second level, but there she was surrounded by an enthusiastic group of children, so she kept walking up to a level nearer the top, finally finding a seat that looked out over a splendid view of the Hauraki Gulf.

She sat down slowly, slipping off her backpack and leaning back against the wooden railing.

Now what do I do?. . . Just wait? . . . What do I say when he gets here? . . . Why was I so stupid to just run off like that? . . . What if he turns back? The questions kept coming, but never any answers.

* * *

Grant hadn't meant to keep holding onto Meredith's hand. It had almost been a shock to feel her fingers underneath his at first, and he'd reacted by tightening his grip. Then he liked it, and when she didn't try to pull away he found it enjoyable to walk together, talking companionably. When they'd stopped to talk to the American couple, he'd felt her hesitation and responded, almost perversely, by pretending to be a couple.

"And you accuse Charles of doing stupid things," he muttered under his breath as he continued up the path alone. "Now she probably doesn't want anything to do with you."

He stopped for a few minutes, silently contemplating the junction of two paths, one leading to the summit and the other to some lava caves. Maybe he could pretend to take the wrong path. Meredith knew to be back at the boat by five.

"Chicken," he muttered at the signpost and turned deliberately toward the summit. The rest of the climb seemed to take twice as long without Meredith beside him, and he found himself scowling as numerous groups and couples came down the track toward him, most of them laughing together. *Just apologize and start over. Don't wreck the best thing that's happened to you since . . . Hannah and Emily.*

He kept walking and his thoughts seemed to keep in time with his footsteps. He recalled standing on the patio with his father the evening Meredith had stayed for dinner. They'd stayed in the study after Stella and Meredith had left, both busy with their own thoughts until Frank had given a gruff laugh.

"We're a bit hopeless, you and I."

"Speak for yourself," Grant had answered affably.

"I will then, but I think you should take some notes," Frank had grunted. "Meredith asked me tonight, before you got here, why I was suddenly talking so much about Stella." He chuckled. "Darn girl came right out and asked me why I was telling her and not Stella, and I couldn't answer."

Grant had been surprised. "That was pretty forward of her."

"It was, and I didn't mind a bit." His father shrugged. "Then tonight, while we were all talking, I was enjoying myself, but I kept thinking about Barbara and telling myself, 'I don't need to tell Stella anything—I still love your mother.'"

He'd stood up and moved over to the desk, staring hard at the photo of his wife. "Then it came to me that I'll never forget Barbara—I'm not meant to—but I can move on." His jaw had tightened, then relaxed as he looked at his son. "Stella is probably the best friend I have, Grant—I just never realized it until now."

"So are you trying to tell me something?" Grant had asked quietly.

"Maybe I'm asking you something." Frank had shaken his head. "I don't know how Stella will react to anything different from being boss and secretary. . . but I'm going to try. I just want you to know—to ask how you feel."

Grant had taken a while to respond. *Stella? How would his mother feel?*
A distinct image came to him of both women laughing together one Christmas evening as they prepared dinner. He had watched his mother suddenly give Stella a warm hug before they'd picked up the platters to take them to the table. They had shared a lot over the years.

He stood up slowly and faced his father. "It sounds good to me, Dad. In fact, knowing Mum . . . she's probably playing matchmaker."

The tears had glistened in Frank's eyes as he moved toward his son. "She probably is . . . she never did trust me to look after myself."

As they'd embraced, Grant had felt his father's shoulders begin shaking and he'd hugged him more tightly. His father had always been there for him; now he felt like he was the comforter.

"They don't want us to forget them." Frank had finally coughed and blown his nose soundly on a handkerchief. "But we can move on."

"Is that what you and Meredith were talking about before I got home?" Grant toyed with the leather piping on the back of the couch.

"No." Frank had looked puzzled. "What makes you say that?"

"Um . . . nothing really. Just that we had a talk on Monday . . . after I left the hospital . . . and she made a comment that I shouldn't try to forget about Hannah and Emily and Mum." He drew a deep breath. "That they didn't want to be forgotten." *That there's a way we can be together again. We can see them again,* he thought to himself.

Frank had nodded. "There's something different about that young woman. I find myself saying things . . . and being told things." He'd looked straight at his son. "She's a very special young lady."

"A very special young lady," Grant now murmured as he quickened his stride on the path to the summit.

* * *

Meredith glanced at her wristwatch as she rested her head against the railing. She'd been sitting at the summit for nearly fifteen minutes. Even though the sun was shining, she felt a cold shiver run down her back.

He must have gone back. I've really blown it now. How can I talk to him on the boat . . . and what about the office?

She picked up her backpack and pulled it on while she threaded her way glumly through a large group that had just arrived on the platform. The final body didn't move.

"Excuse me, please." She tried to move past, but another group burst onto the step as they finished their race. "Excuse me."

She felt herself pulled to one side. "So you swim like a fish, kick like a ninja, and run like a deer. Anything else you excel at, Miss Winstone?"

Meredith finally looked up and found herself staring at a tiny brown pigment mark just below Grant's left ear. She'd never noticed it before, but his hair was curling damply with perspiration and she could see it clearly. *Anything else I excel at?*

"Making a fool of myself?" she offered.

"No, I think I win on that one." Grant lightly gripped her arm as another youth with an oversize backpack swung against her. "Let's move," he suggested.

He led the way up to the top level and over to the railing. Meredith gasped as she did a full turn, momentarily forgetting her embarrassment as she saw the complete view of the city and the gulf for the first time. "Oh, this is beautiful. I was only a few feet away, but I couldn't see the whole picture like this."

"Same," Grant murmured as she turned back to face him. He saw the half-frown appear, the one that meant she was about to say something that was bothering her.

"I think I ran away."

"You think?"

"Okay, I did run away—"

"And I made you. I'm sorry." Grant folded his arms and leaned against the rail, facing her. "At least . . . I'm sorry that I made you run away. But I'm not sorry I held your hand." His voice softened. "Actually, I enjoyed that. And I'm not sorry about the way we can talk about things. And I'm not sorry that you came to work for us . . . even though I was opposed to it at first. And I'm even getting used to your telling me what to do."

"I don't do that!" Meredith looked aghast.

"Yes, you do . . . in a very nice way." Grant held up his hand at her protest. "What I'm trying to say, Meredith, is that I realize things have changed between us, and I hope it's for the better."

Meredith nodded very slowly, trying to make her mind comprehend what he was saying.

He folded his arms again as if it helped him think more clearly. "After Dad's accident, you were so understanding, and yet you made me mad at you at the same time—because you were honest with me. Then the other night at home, we just relaxed and talked. That's the first time in four years that's happened to me. Afterward, Dad and I talked . . . and he said the same thing as you—that we don't have to forget. That we can move on." There was a long silence as he studied her face, then stared out at the endless expanse of ocean and islands. "Except I don't really know how to move on. I don't know what the next move is, Meredith. I thought I did today . . . but I think I blew it."

Meredith stood very still, trying to absorb the implications of what he was saying. Was he really suggesting a relationship between them? Could she handle that?

I know I want—I need—to help him find his family again and to understand that they're not gone forever. Wanting to do that has helped me regain my own testimony, so he's already helped me more than I've helped him. I really admire him professionally and how he's helping me to be a better lawyer—but how would this change our work relationship? And now that I've committed myself to the Church again, would I want to start getting serious about someone who isn't in the gospel? Because I know I couldn't stop from getting serious about him . . . I'm already well on my way.

She closed her eyes briefly as her father's voice sounded in her head. *"How important is this young man . . . to you?"* And her answer, *"Grant is a very special person . . . to me."*

"Whew . . ." She exhaled deeply and raised her eyebrows as she smiled weakly. "Am I going to wake up soon? Did I just run too fast and I am suffering from oxygen deprivation?" She poked a finger softly at his chest. "Nope . . . you are real. Darn it."

Grant's relieved laugh made the people beside them turn and stare, which made Meredith feel even more conspicuous; but he seemed oblivious as he quickly took hold of the end of her finger and held her hand firmly against his shirt.

"Thanks for that . . . it's nice to know where I stand."

"I'm glad you do," she responded quietly. "Because I can't quite grasp all of this. You're my boss," she almost moaned.

"Not technically . . . Dad is. I'm just another lawyer." Grant shrugged, then let her hand go. "Why don't we get out of here and walk down to meet Dad and Stella at Islington Bay? We've got plenty of time." The mention of Frank and Stella made Meredith's head jerk up so quickly that Grant laughed again. "Your face is a dead giveaway to what you're thinking."

"Only sometimes." She recovered herself quickly and moved forward as he stood aside. "I think walking is a good idea."

They made their way down the wooden path through all the other tourists and onto the gravelly summit road. Meredith instinctively moved briskly, keeping at least a body's width away from Grant and making random remarks about the distinctive shrubbery and landscape. He, in turn, walked silently until they saw a family group coming toward them up the hill.

The entire family was outfitted in shorts, shirts, and proper hiking boots with thick socks. A teenage girl had raced ahead and now stood looking at another small sign that marked the way to lava caves. Her younger brothers were running up to see what she was pointing at, while an older sister remained with her parents, unashamedly walking with her hand in her mother's.

As they all reached the sign, a brief family council took place. The father glanced at his watch and nodded. Within seconds the younger girl had led the way off the road and up a narrow track into the dense bush, the rest of the family following close behind. "So which one would you be?" Grant had turned his head to watch the family.

"Pardon?"

"Which one of those children would you be in your family—or which of the girls?" Grant nodded his head back toward the family.

"Oh." Meredith caught his meaning. "Um . . . I'd probably have to say the one getting into things with her brothers. My older sister, Wendy, was always the quiet one by Mum's side, learning to sew and cook. She always looked after me when we were little and I'd do everything she wanted . . . until I discovered sports and other things." She held up her hand. "Not that I ever got into any bad trouble. I just found life more of an adventure."

"So you were the risk taker?" Grant smiled and Meredith found herself trying to detect a double meaning to his words, while at the same time feeling a genuine thrill at the way he smiled at her. She shrugged as she tucked both thumbs into the straps of her backpack.

"I don't know about 'risk taker.' I'd probably say that I was just naturally inquisitive and liked a challenge."

"So would you regard me as a risk or a challenge?" Grant looked straight ahead. "Or would it just be 'definitely hard work and not at all smart'?" His voice had taken on a quality of mimicry.

Meredith's mouth dropped open as she recognized the comment she'd made to Stella about Grant after her first few days on the job.

"You were listening!"

"Not intentionally." He kept walking although she'd stopped. "You just have a very clear voice. It'll be very useful in a courtroom."

Meredith put her hands on her hips and looked at the back of his head in frustration. She had felt as if she were floating when he first held her hand, then she was running from him like a scared rabbit, then she was imagining being close to him, and now she was . . . her heart skipped a beat as he turned, and in the slightest gesture, held out a hand to her.

Very hard work and not only 'not very smart'—you're stupid, Meredith! This is crazy! She began to walk toward him. *Please, please help me do what is best . . . for both of us.*

As she reached him, she felt a brief sense of relief as he just kept walking, so she fell into step by his side. She noticed that he shortened his long strides so they were walking in step.

"So, tell me more about your family." Grant pulled a small bar of chocolate out of his pocket, unwrapped it, and broke it in half, handing her a portion. "I know you have a sister and at least one brother, a mum and a dad, and that you're pretty close to them all."

"Two brothers—both younger," Meredith corrected him as she took a bite of chocolate. "And a dog."

"Of course." Grant grinned and then glanced at her more seriously. "You've told me the worst thing about when you were growing up . . . but what about the other times? What makes your family close now?"

For the next fifteen minutes, they strolled at an easy pace down the gravel road with Meredith sharing stories of her childhood and

Grant asking questions or making comments. The conversation flowed easily and Meredith felt a complete lightening of her spirit from the frustration she had felt earlier. As they picked up speed down a slightly steeper section of the road, she adjusted the pack on her back and straightened her shoulders.

"So now you know all about my family. It's your turn to tell me about yours."

"Not much to tell." Grant shrugged. "Great parents . . . financially spoilt only child . . . one crazy cousin. You pretty much know the rest."

"Not all of it." Meredith swallowed. "What about your family?"

"My family?"

She could almost feel a wall going up between them. "Um . . . what were Hannah and Emily like?"

The only sound was the rhythmical crunching of their footsteps on the coarse gravel, their steps slowing as the road leveled out. They'd covered several yards before Grant finally spoke.

"Hannah and I practically grew up together. We were the sheltered offspring of two well-established Devonport families. We went to kindergarten together and then just stayed together all through primary school and then high school. Our mothers put us into dance classes and so we partnered each other. And then they enrolled us at the local yacht club and so we sailed together." He pursed his lips. "In retrospect, it was all very convenient."

Meredith nodded. "But you obviously enjoyed being together, and from the photo I saw at your home, she looked lovely."

"She was definitely lovely—both to look at and to be with." Grant nodded. "We were best friends," he finished simply.

Meredith felt her breath catch and she had to fight an immediate tightening in her stomach. "So," she forced herself to speak, "when did you get married?"

"Um . . ." Grant looked distracted for a moment. "Actually, we were engaged the day I finished my final exams at law school. Hannah had finished at Teacher's College and we were married just after my graduation." He smiled. "Most of my friends at university thought I was crazy getting married so soon . . . but I couldn't see the point in waiting. I was happy with Hannah."

He suddenly plunged his hands deep into his pockets, and Meredith watched the muscles work in his jaw. "I thought I was totally happy . . . until Emily was born. When I first held her I couldn't believe she was so perfect—that she was my daughter. It just blew me away."

"A whole new level of happiness?" Meredith asked quietly.

"Completely." Grant nodded and rubbed his forehead. "I loved Hannah, but what I felt when I held Emily was different. It was like she was part of my soul."

The trees ahead of them blurred as Meredith fought a surge of emotion. When she glanced at Grant she could tell he was experiencing the same thing. Instinctively she moved closer, and as his hand dropped to his side she slipped hers into it and tightened her fingers around his. For a second she felt no response, but then his hand closed firmly around hers and his chin lifted.

"She was the cutest little thing. Even when she was first born the nurses said she had perfect skin. It was almost transparent . . . and she had these soft blue eyes. I swear she used to watch me, though Hannah said she was too young to see anything properly." He gave a short laugh. "I'd always prided myself on being a fairly down-to-earth sort of person . . . but that little girl. I don't know what she did to me."

"Was she much like you?" Meredith asked quietly.

"I don't know." He shook his head. "Physically, she was very like my mother was as a baby, and they certainly had a special connection as well. Emily would just laugh and laugh when Mum came to play with her."

He tightened his grip on Meredith's hand. "You said, when we were talking . . . that day, that we weren't put here to love people just to lose them." They walked in silence until he coughed and spoke again. "Then you said that we're meant to have hope—that we just have to know where to find it."

Meredith nodded and tried to breathe calmly as her heart began beating rapidly.

"What I can't understand—" Grant hesitated. "I just can't reconcile what you're saying—that I could see Emily again . . . with what happened when she . . . died." He took a deep breath and she felt his body tremble. "I was told that because she hadn't been christened, she couldn't be saved. That she couldn't . . . go to heaven."

He stopped walking and his fist clenched so that Meredith felt her fingers crushed. Then he shook his head. "I'd always accepted the concept of God and heaven even though I hadn't really thought about it specifically, but . . . even if there is such a place . . . if there is, I can't believe that a tiny little girl like Emily . . ." He stopped and Meredith imagined the pain he must be experiencing.

Grant swallowed and finally continued, "Why couldn't she go there, when I was the one that killed her? She never did anything wrong. She couldn't do anything wrong!"

Grant let go of Meredith's hand and strode across the pathway to the metal railing. Beyond it, the ground dropped away into dense vegetation, and he stood staring out over the panorama of endless ocean, his arms folded across his body as he drew in deep breaths.

Meredith waited helplessly until she saw his shoulders slowly relax. Then she went and stood beside him.

"My mother and father lost a baby . . . another brother in between Ryan and Cam. I was very young, so I don't remember it actually happening. What I do remember is having a family night when I was a teenager, where they talked about Stephen. Mum said that she'll never forget the pain of losing him, but at least she knows she'll have the chance to be with him again." Meredith smiled. "She had a little wooden rocking chair that she'd made, and she told us that in heaven, if we were faithful, there'd be no empty chairs in our family . . . that Stephen already had his chair and it was up to the rest of us to make sure that ours wouldn't be empty."

Grant took hold of a small leaf on a bush beside him and rubbed the shiny, waxen surface. "But how does your mother know, Meredith? That's what I can't grasp."

"I can remember feeling the same way . . . asking that same question." Meredith scratched at her eyebrow. "Then Dad showed us some scriptures in the Book of Mormon that talked about how it was wicked and a mockery to suppose that God would save one child because it was baptized and another would perish because it wasn't. He said that all little children were alike to Him and that they were whole and had no need for baptism." She shook her head. "I remember Mum finishing with a verse that she'd memorized when Stephen died . . . 'Teach parents that they must repent and be baptized, and humble themselves as their little children, and they shall all be saved with their little children.'"

"So she lives in hope," Grant finished quietly.

"Absolutely." Meredith nodded and looked directly up at him. "And so do I."

Her final statement was serenely emphatic, and Meredith felt a long-forgotten burning in her chest as she uttered the words. As much as she wanted to convince Grant, it was her own testimony that was growing.

"You really are different, aren't you?" He was shaking his head, but there was no evidence of the intense pain she had seen in his face earlier.

"I want to be." She toed the ground, causing a few loose pebbles to roll down the bank. "Especially if I can help you."

"I seriously don't know if you are," Grant muttered and rubbed the back of his neck. "All I know is that I haven't spoken to anyone like this—about Hannah and Emily—and one minute I feel like I'm being tortured and next thing, you talk and I feel . . . calm. But I don't know why!"

Meredith suddenly found herself pulled against his chest in a tight hug. At first she was afraid to move, but when he didn't release her, she hesitantly wrapped her arms around his waist. As soon as she did she felt his whole body relax.

"I don't know what to do about you and your Bible stories," he whispered to the top of her head. "And I don't even want to think about hope . . . but you make me."

"I'm sorry." She could barely speak as her face was pressed against his shirt.

"No you're not." She felt the reluctant laugh in his throat as he pulled her closer again.

They stood silently, leaning into each other without reservation, and as Grant bent his head and kissed her gently on the lips she began to wish that the moment would never end.

"I think my mother would have liked you," he admitted, resting his cheek against her forehead and looking out toward the horizon. "She had the same sort of faith."

* * *

"Is that Grant and Meredith?" Frank pointed up the hill as Stella glanced up.

"Yes, but why are they coming down here to the bay? They must've been walking for hours already, and we'll all still have to walk back to the wharf."

Frank nodded as he waved. "Nothing wrong with walking." He squinted. "As long as they were talking as well."

He bent to help Stella pack up the remains of their lunch as Grant and Meredith approached, but Stella could see Frank watching them surreptitiously.

"You're just an old matchmaker," Stella chided him comfortably.

"And why not?" Frank straightened up. "I'm not going to settle for that son of mine grieving for the rest of his life—not when I know he could be happy."

"So you think Meredith is the right person for him?" Stella precisely folded a tea towel before placing it in the bag.

She waited for a response, but Frank was standing with his hands on his hips, smiling thoughtfully. She turned to see Grant help Meredith down a slight incline . . . then keep hold of her hand as they approached the beach.

"Maybe not . . . but more maybe," he answered cheerfully.

CHAPTER 15

"So, how did your day go?" Telesia held a long grass skirt at arm's length, running the woven-straw waistband decorated with brightly colored raffia flowers, beads, and shells through her hands. "You look pretty happy."

"It was a good day." Meredith smiled as Telesia placed the skirt around her and began to fasten the plaited ties so that the skirt sat snugly onto her hips. "I'm sorry I was so late getting here. We walked all over Rangitoto and it took a little longer than we thought it would. Then we had to wait to get into the marina, et cetera, et cetera. That's why Grant dropped me straight here."

"And how was it spending the day at close quarters with 'the bosses'?" Telesia rolled her eyes as she held up several floral leis for Meredith to choose from.

"Weird . . . at first." Meredith selected two leis and held them up against her cobalt-blue T-shirt. "Which one do you think?"

"I'd go with the pink and yellow. It matches the skirt." Telesia nodded approvingly as she picked up several shell bracelets and wound them around her wrists. "And a pink hibiscus over the appropriate ear. Yes, very striking attire for the young lawyer."

Both girls laughed as Meredith swung around and moved her hips so that the grass strands rustled and flicked.

"I cannot believe I'm doing this, Sia. I'll never in a million years be able to roll my hips like you do, or my hands."

Telesia responded by raising her hand and gracefully rolling and extending her fingers. "Just remember . . . you're stroking the cat using all your fingers—and twist. So why was it weird . . . at first? What happened second?"

Meredith shook her head. "In a nutshell—Grant and I went walking on our own up to the summit. Then I tripped and fell, and so he held my hand . . ." She paused as Telesia gasped. "I freaked and ran. Then we talked and walked some more and ended up talking about his wife and baby and infant baptism . . . and basically the plan of salvation."

"Wow." Telesia breathed the exclamation, her brown eyes wide with surprise. "No wonder you were late." She touched Meredith's arm lightly. "Are you all right?"

Smiling at her friend's genuine concern, Meredith nodded. "I thought my weekend at home was an emotional roller-coaster, but this definitely came close." She thought about Grant's arms around her and blushed. "If not equal to it."

"So next question . . . how's it going to be at work on Monday?"

Meredith hesitated and smoothed down the thick layers of straw on the skirt. "At first that was all I could think about. But, the more we talked, the more natural it felt just to be with him. I just had no idea he could be so . . . nice."

"And how did Mr. Bascombe react? It must have been fairly obvious something was up with you two." Telesia finished putting on her own skirt and decorations.

"That was the second weird thing." Meredith frowned. "It was almost like he'd orchestrated the whole thing—to put Grant and me alone together. In fact, I think he and Stella also wanted to be on their own."

"Stella? The secretary?" Telesia rolled her eyes. "Oh my goodness, nothing like this ever happens at our office!"

With that comment, the girls gathered their things and headed into the cultural hall. When they got there, most of the ward had turned up for the cultural evening, and the hall was filled with people resplendent in the costumes of many different nationalities. The challenge had been to teach or learn a song or dance from a different culture and perform it together so that everyone could learn more about each other. The whole ward seemed to have taken it seriously, learning in groups or couples. The girls quickly checked their place on the program, then found a seat.

They watched and applauded each of the performances: an American country line dance, a Filipino wedding dance, a Japanese fan dance, a Maori stick game, a Korean folk song, and then it was their turn to go and wait offstage.

* * *

Grant was nearly home when he saw Meredith's backpack sitting on the backseat of the car. His first impulse was just to leave it there until Monday or drop it off at her house. *But she may need something in it for tonight,* he reasoned on second thought. He slowed the car and pulled in at the side of the road. *Or maybe you just want to go back and see what she's doing.* He thought about all the activity he had seen going on at the church building when he'd dropped her off. *She said she was going to be doing a Polynesian dance with her roommate.* He turned the car around.

It was an interesting experience making his way into the church hall. People were coming and going in colorful costumes, and most of them greeted him cheerfully without knowing or asking who he was—until a sprightly, elderly woman took his hand and shook it enthusiastically.

"Hello there, I'm Lydia Crowsen. Are you looking for somebody, dear? You look a bit lost. Have you been here before?"

Grant waited until the questions finished. Then he glanced around the hall. "Actually I'm looking for Meredith Winstone." He held up the bag. "I think she may need this."

"Oh, she won't be needing that right now." Sister Crowsen took hold of his arm and led him directly into the hall. "The young sisters are just about to do their dance. You're just in time to watch them."

There weren't any nearby chairs vacant at the moment, so Grant stood beside her near the door as the steady rhythm of Polynesian music began to pulse through the sound system.

"I saw them getting ready," the older woman continued as she pulled on his arm to get his attention. Then she whispered loudly, "They're such beautiful young ladies, and their costumes are so bright. And doesn't everyone else look wonderful as well?"

Grant watched as Telesia seemed to float onto the stage in time to the music, followed closely by Meredith. *Meredith?* He slowly straightened up as she began to move in time with Telesia, the grass skirt sitting low on her hips and swinging almost in opposition to the movement of her body. He saw the concentration on her face as she watched Telesia and carefully copied her movements, her arms outstretched and swaying gracefully.

"Aren't they lovely?" He felt his hip nudged by Sister Crowsen.

"Yes . . . very lovely," he agreed without shifting his gaze. *Very lovely, Miss Winstone.*

The tempo of the music began to increase, and he saw the slight frown of concentration on Meredith's face suddenly disappear as Telesia laughed and flicked her hands. Both girls began to move more quickly and freely around the stage. Meredith began to laugh and smile and respond to the clapping of the crowd. The drumbeats came to a sudden end and both girls finished with a swift hip movement, bowed low, and then took the flowers from behind their ears to throw to the audience.

* * *

Moments before Grant had entered the room, Meredith had smoothed her T-shirt over her stomach to try to still her nervous feelings as she'd followed Telesia onto the stage. The first strains of mellow guitar music had begun to flow around the hall, and she'd watched as Telesia began to swing her hips in time with the music and roll onto the balls of her feet, creating the smooth, rounded motion of the Samoan dance. Then, in unison, they were dancing across the stage, the music building the story that their hands were telling in time with their swaying hips—a story of love between the warrior and his princess . . . of leaving . . . the journey . . . of reuniting . . . of eternity.

At first she had watched Telesia carefully to make sure she was doing the right movements, but then the music got faster and she felt herself respond to Telesia's infectious laugh, and suddenly they were both dancing as they'd done at home, just enjoying the feeling of the costumes and the intense beat of the music.

Suddenly, it was over and she'd followed Telesia in bowing low to the audience, laughing as she turned to throw her floral hair decoration to the audience. As she looked out over the rows of seats to find someone to throw to, her heart suddenly jumped.

Grant was standing near the back doorway, his arms folded as he leaned against the wall with his head bent forward, listening to Sister Crowsen. He was still watching the stage, and she saw him smile and nod as Lydia pointed toward her.

"Meredith!" She heard Telesia calling her as if from a distance. She quickly threw the flower and picked up her skirts to run offstage. *What is he doing here? What do I do now?*

She didn't have time to think anymore as she watched Sister Crowsen leading Grant by the hand through the doorway crowded with nervous performers. He was holding her backpack in his other hand, and as they stopped in front of the girls he held it up almost apologetically.

"I thought you might need this. You left it in the car."

"Isn't it lovely, dear? Your young man got here just in time for your item." Sister Crowsen clapped her hands together. "Och, and weren't you just wonderful?" She turned back to Grant. "Weren't they wonderful? Oh, you must stay and watch the other items."

Meredith felt like she was frozen in place. She saw Telesia's startled look as she glanced at Grant and then at her and back to Grant again. As if in a daze, she heard Telesia's mellow chuckle and watched her wave her braceletted hand at Grant and sweep forward in another graceful curtsy.

"And welcome to our cultural evening, Mr. Bascombe. We're so glad you could come."

They found seats and watched the rest of the items while Telesia and Sister Crowsen gave a running commentary on who was performing—Grant listening carefully. Meredith sat quietly beside him, trying to appreciate the performances and failing miserably.

Why do I feel so awkward about him being here? I'm quite happy to dance in front of two hundred people, and yet I'm embarrassed by one man watching? And what am I embarrassed about? She put her hand to her forehead and squeezed hard. *How can I want to be telling him about the gospel so much and yet feel so awkward about him actually being here at church?*

"Are you okay?" Grant spoke quietly beside her ear. "I didn't mean to upset you. When I saw your bag in the back, I thought you might need it for something. But when I came in and asked for you, they said you were on stage shortly." He smiled. "I couldn't resist watching. You were wonderful. In fact, this whole thing is amazing."

"Amazing?" Meredith looked around. With the show over, people were milling around in their costumes putting chairs away, talking and laughing, and congratulating each other on their performances. It was organized bedlam, but it was strangely comforting.

She tucked her hair behind her ears and pressed her hands to her cheeks.

"I'm sorry I wasn't very welcoming before. It was just such a shock to see you here . . . and with me looking like this." She touched the lei around her neck.

"As I said, you were great. I had no idea you could do anything like that." He sounded genuine and she shook her head.

"I had no idea either. Things have a habit of happening to you at church . . . I think it's called developing talents," she responded wryly.

The two began to move slowly toward the door as numerous people stopped to say good night and congratulate Meredith on her performance.

"Is it always like this?" Grant stopped and looked back across the recreation hall.

"Oh no." Meredith smiled shyly. "All the decorations will come down tonight. And tomorrow everyone will come back dressed in their Sunday clothes and it'll all be much, much quieter."

"Fascinating." He held the door open for her, and she shivered as the cold night air surrounded them on the walk to his car. She clasped her arms firmly around her body and turned to face him.

"Telesia asked me how my day went."

Grant turned and leaned against the front of the car, playing with the keys in his hand.

"And what did you say?"

"I told her things had changed . . . between us. That we'd had plenty of time to talk."

"What did she think of that?"

"She asked how it would be at work on Monday."

Grant spun the keys slowly around his finger. "How is it going to be, Meredith?" He watched her for a moment, resting his hands

behind his back. "I really bared my soul today . . . like I've never done
. . . ever. I felt so comfortable with you by the end of the day that I
found myself really looking forward to going to work on Monday. I
didn't even want to leave you here when I dropped you off. And when
I saw your bag, I was grateful for the excuse to bring it back." He hesitated. "Then when you saw me here tonight, you looked almost . . .
devastated. And I felt like I must have got it all wrong, that I was
intruding or something."

Was that how I'd felt? That he was the intruder? She closed her eyes
and shook her head.

"You didn't get it wrong at all." She reached out and took his
hand. "I just can't believe what has happened today . . . the things
we've shared. It doesn't seem real, even though it seems so right. Then
when I got here, it was so busy all of a sudden and I just focused on
what I had to do. Things are so different at church, and I guess I
wasn't ready to share that side of things yet. When I saw you . . . I was
embarrassed. I was dressed up and doing a Polynesian dance in front
of you for Pete's sake." She moaned at the memory and put her free
hand over her face until he took it down and held it.

"Meredith," he reminded her, "I've cried in front of you." His
voice was so soft she could hardly hear it. "I think that beats a
Polynesian dance. At least you looked beautiful."

He tugged gently on her hands so that she came closer. As a car
drove past them, she caught a glimpse of the bishop's wife and children grinning at her. Instinctively, she tried to pull back and look
casual, but he was already tightening his grip on her hands and she
fell back against him.

"Oh, Grant." She stamped her foot pathetically as her cheek
rested on his chest. "I just wanted to be a good lawyer."

CHAPTER 16

"Good morning, Stella." Meredith tried hard to keep her greeting as normal as possible as she crossed the reception area. It had been a challenge just to make the short walk up the stairs to the office, especially since she had been unable to decide exactly how to enter the office on Monday morning.

"Oh, my goodness . . . what beautiful flowers!" She stopped to admire the dramatic display of mauve roses and deep purple lisianthus offset with bronze Singapore orchids sitting on the secretary's desk. As she touched them lightly with her fingertips, she saw Stella's normally calm demeanor give way to a broad smile.

"I've been spoilt," she admitted calmly.

"As you should be." Meredith felt her spirits lift at the sight of Stella's obvious happiness and she drew a deep breath. Maybe today wouldn't be as difficult as she had thought it might be.

She busied herself with phone calls for the first part of the morning and deliberately kept her door closed so that she wouldn't be constantly waiting to hear Grant's voice in the outer office. By eleven o'clock, her determination had run out and she walked out to the reception area with a pile of folders.

"Has Grant called in at all?" She tried to keep her tone businesslike.

"No, he hasn't, Meredith, which is surprising." Stella frowned. "He usually lets me know if he's going to be detained."

"Okay." Meredith patted the folders nonchalantly. "Well, I'm supposed to go over these cases with him, but they can wait. I'll be in the back room. I've got to go back over those old Wilson files."

She walked down the hallway to the small room that housed their archived case files and switched the light on absently.

That was ridiculous. Just because he's not in the office on time, there's no need to start asking where he is. You haven't done that before, so don't start now.

She began pulling out files with a frown on her face, scowling even more as the dust from the old files irritated her nose. She finally put the folders down and rubbed her face and nose vigorously before surrendering to a sudden large sneeze followed by several small ones. The effect was quite exhausting, and she leaned against the tall metal filing cabinet, shaking her head and searching in her suit pocket for a tissue. She finally found one and blew her nose hard, making her eyes water even more.

"Oh my, who's a mess?" she muttered to herself as she blindly tried to correct the mascara that had smudged.

She pulled the files she needed and walked back out to the reception area just as Grant walked in the front door, looking once again the well-dressed, self-contained lawyer. As he turned to face her, she actually felt her pulse begin to beat faster against the folder as the memories of the weekend clamored in her mind.

"Meredith?" His immediate reaction was a question and a look of genuine concern.

"Good morning, Grant." She nodded brightly and held the folders more tightly as she walked round the desk and straight past him. *I have no idea what to say.*

"Meredith?"

She heard him close the door to her office behind him as he entered, and her heart beat crazily as she set the folders on the desk.

"Yes?" She leaned over and picked up a pad and pencil. "Do you want to go over those cases now or shall we wait a while? I've got some other things I can go over until you're ready. Did something else come up this morning?"

"Are you all right?" Grant stood with his back to the closed door, a slight frown on his face.

"I'm fine." She tapped the pencil on the pad.

"Then why have you been crying?"

"Crying?" She opened her eyes wide, then put her hand to her face and rubbed a finger under her eye. A smear of mascara came off.

"Oh! I haven't been crying—just some huge sneezes in the file room. Same effect." She shrugged and grimaced. "Not good."

She stood awkwardly as Grant began to laugh quietly by the door and shake his head.

"Oh, Meredith . . . I had the hardest time coming to work this morning." He folded his arms and stared at the floor. "I wanted to call you yesterday. Then I thought about how you said that your church meetings went for three hours. But you never said which three hours, so I walked Takapuna Beach . . . quite a few times."

"I finished at twelve," she offered uselessly.

Grant frowned as he looked up. "After the sixth lap I figured it would be better to just wait until today. Get everything off on a businesslike footing." He cleared his throat. "Which was fine in theory . . . until I saw your car parked outside and just kept driving. Then I got really annoyed with myself for acting like a pathetic teenager and finally came upstairs—only to see you walk out with your eyes all red like you'd been crying!"

He stood up and ran his hand through his hair in exasperation. "I'm a competent lawyer and I'm acting like a kid!"

"Same." Meredith pulled a face. "And I have absolutely no idea what to do about it."

There was a long silence until Grant straightened his tie and coughed.

"Miss Winstone, can you bring me those Haeata files, please?"

Meredith looked at him quizzically. Then she slowly picked up a file behind her.

"Bring them here, please," Grant held out his hand and she moved forward until she was standing in front of him. As he reached for the file he took hold of her hand as well and pulled her slightly closer, but the file remained between them. Then, very gently, he leaned forward and kissed her lightly on the forehead before taking the file.

"Thank you," he said. "I really needed that." He half turned, then looked back. "And Miss Winstone . . . confine your social activities to outside office hours in the future, please."

Meredith found herself grinning as the door closed behind him. "Yes sir, Mr. Bascombe."

CHAPTER 17

The next two weeks passed in an almost surreal bubble for Meredith. Going to work was a delight, as everybody seemed happy, and Grant was extra diligent in tutoring her through the intricacies of the legal process, often taking her with him to court appearances. Her appreciation of his legal prowess grew each day she spent watching him in court, where his astuteness often left his opponents floundering. During working hours they maintained a strictly businesslike relationship, but there was always the underlying anticipation of dinner or an activity together in the evening. Several times they just stayed at Meredith's flat and played board games or watched a game of rugby on television with Telesia and Tavita.

At the end of two weeks, Telesia sat down on the end of Meredith's bed just after her friend had come in from a late evening walk along the beach with Grant.

"Another successful evening out?" She watched as Meredith slipped off her shoes.

"Mm hmm . . . we went down to Cheltenham Beach. It was dark and the moon was just reflecting perfectly across the water. It was magic."

Telesia smiled and toyed with the tufted wool ties on Meredith's bed quilt. "We must have just missed you then. Tavita and I were down there earlier." She pulled her legs up to sit cross-legged and rested her chin on her hands. "It is magic there. It'll certainly always be a special place for me."

Something in the tone of her voice made Meredith turn around from hanging up her jacket and look at her. Neither girl spoke, and then Telesia wiggled her fingers slightly. "With very special memories."

"Sia! You're engaged!" Meredith leapt onto the bed and grabbed her friend's hand. The tiny diamond nestled on top of a fine gold band. "Again!" She giggled and hugged her friend tightly. "I am so happy for you! Tell me what happened!"

Telesia laughed happily and held out her hand to look at the ring again. "We arranged to take a picnic dinner down to the beach and Tavita said he'd organize it. He brought down a proper picnic basket with all sorts of lovely goodies . . . all my favorite things like sushi and samosa . . . and chocolate mousse." She laughed. "It was quite a combination."

"So what happened then?" Meredith also sat cross-legged on the bed.

"We finished dinner and he put the basket away. Then we walked along the beach toward Mount Victoria." Telesia smiled. "We walked out around the rocks and just watched the water and the stars coming out, and then he told me to sit down . . . and then he got down on his knees."

"A proper proposal!"

Telesia nodded. "It was so lovely . . . and then he asked me to marry him in the temple."

Her chin quivered and tears began to flow slowly down her cheeks. She did nothing to stop them as she looked at Meredith and shook her head. "I said yes, Mele, and I meant it with all my heart."

Neither girl spoke for some time. Telesia finally wiped her eyes and gave a small laugh. "I think I liked getting engaged better the second time around."

"And you're okay with everything this time?"

"We know it won't be all plain sailing, but we're determined to just have a small reception after the temple ceremony. I guess I had to grow up enough to realize that it was Tavita that I was marrying and not my family." She sighed. "I love my culture very much . . . just doing the dancing with you made me realize that, but it also helped me realize that I don't have to do anything that conflicts with Heavenly Father's plan for me just because my family is set on their favorite wedding custom."

"Oh, Sia." Meredith leaned forward and hugged her friend tightly. "You are such an inspiration to me. I just know you and Tavita are going to be so happy . . . and such a good example."

Telesia hugged her back, and then she said, "Tavita and I thought we would like to have a little celebration dinner . . . with you and Grant. Do you think we could? Maybe Friday night?"

Meredith looked surprised, then she shrugged. "I guess so . . . I . . . I just haven't answered an invite for both of us before. I'll talk to Grant about it tomorrow. Though I'm sure it'll be fine."

Telesia studied her friend's face and put her head to one side. "Mele . . . how are things going? After you first went to Rangitoto Island, you were so excited about how you'd talked to Grant about his wife and baby and the plan of salvation . . . but you haven't mentioned anything since." She frowned almost apologetically. "I know you are very happy, but where is it going?"

Meredith sat without moving for a few seconds, and then clasped her hands in front of her and stretched. "Everything is going fine— honestly. Grant is so good to work with and he treats me so well. We spend our time together talking about everything under the sun. It's wonderful."

"Do you talk about the Church?" Telesia asked simply.

"A little bit." Meredith hesitated. "He enjoyed the cultural evening."

"But have you talked any more about his family—about any doctrine?"

"No, not really. We've just been enjoying being together. Besides, there doesn't seem to have been a right time since Rangitoto."

"And you don't really want to talk about his first wife now?" Telesia squeezed Meredith's hand gently. "Mele, I want you to be happy. But I don't want to lose you again, my friend."

* * *

They had booked a small restaurant along the King Edward Parade, and the harbor put on a spectacular display of crystalline lights reflecting on an almost motionless ocean as they sat down to dinner. They took their time to decide on what to eat, and then Tavita ordered some sparkling grape juice. When it arrived and the waiter had filled their glasses, he solemnly raised his glass and put his other arm around Telesia.

"I'd like to propose a toast to my beautiful fiancée, Telesia, and thank her for accepting my proposal to be her husband for time and all eternity."

The words were softly spoken, and Meredith and Grant raised their glasses as the couple shared a quick, shy kiss.

"So when are you planning to get married?" Grant took a tentative sip of the grape juice and nodded after his taste. "That's quite nice."

Telesia smiled as she also took a drink. "Not quite the hard stuff, but you're guaranteed a safe ride home." She swallowed, then took Tavita's hand under the table. "We've decided on the fourteenth of October."

"But that's only . . ." Grant calculated quickly, ". . . seven weeks away! Why the rush?" He stopped suddenly and toyed with the stem of his glass. "I'm sorry . . . that's none of my business."

There was a moment's silence. Then Tavita chuckled. "It's okay, Grant . . . we don't *have* to get married." Then he added more seriously, "It's just not recommended to have long engagements, so we can avoid . . . temptation. We want to be morally and spiritually worthy to be married in the temple of our Lord."

Meredith looked at Grant as he nodded slowly and set his glass down.

"But why is it so important that you get married there . . . in the temple? What's wrong with the chapel you go to on Sunday?"

Telesia and Tavita glanced at each other, and Telesia smiled. "We could be married anywhere we want to, but it's our understanding that the temple is the very best place—the only place where we can be not just married, but sealed together for this time on earth and also for eternity."

Tavita rested his arm along the back of her chair. "I couldn't bear to think that I would have to leave Telesia when I die. I know that when we marry in the temple it's forever and that our children will be sealed to us as well."

Grant didn't respond immediately, and Meredith found herself beginning to talk about the wedding preparations with an enthusiasm that she suddenly wasn't feeling. As they finished their meal and walked to the front door, Grant stopped beside Tavita and held out his hand.

"I'm glad you two are so happy . . . and I really do wish you all the best."

"I know you do, Grant." Tavita shook his hand firmly. "Sometimes it's hard to understand things if you're not quite sure of the full story . . . maybe someday . . . ?"

"Mmm . . . maybe." Grant nodded as he held the door open. "But that's one huge brief to consider."

They didn't go directly to the car parked across the road, but kept walking along the parade past the trees which stood thickly stolid on the wide, grassy verge. The breeze was slightly cool but it was more the anticipation that created the shiver down Meredith's spine.

"Cold?" Grant finally spoke as he walked with his hands in his pockets.

"A little." Meredith rolled her shoulders. "The restaurant was quite warm."

"It was," he responded absently. "Lovely meal."

"Yes. I've never been there. I never ate out much—until I met you."

Grant glanced at her, then stared ahead. "Interesting how things change—how your life changes—when new people come on the scene."

They walked on in silence. As they reached a particular tree they both turned back.

"Have you ever watched people running or walking," Grant said thoughtfully, "and wondered what makes them turn around and run back? Whether they decide on a certain place to turn at or maybe a set time . . . or do they just run till it feels like they should turn?"

"I think it depends on the circumstances," Meredith answered, grateful for something to talk about. "When I'm exercising I usually plan to go to a certain place, but if I've got a set time, I run faster and just turn back halfway."

"But what if you have no plan . . . no idea where you're going or how long it will take?" Grant looked up at the sky. "What if you only feel like you're getting lost . . . ?"

They finished their walk in silence and drove back to Meredith's apartment. Grant switched the engine off after they arrived, but instead of jumping out to help Meredith out of the car, he sat back in his seat, his hands resting on the steering wheel. For several minutes, neither of them said anything. Grant slowly ran one hand back and forth over the top of the steering wheel while Meredith sat quietly.

"They seem very happy." He stared straight ahead. "Telesia and Tavita."

"They are." Meredith nodded, fighting a growing feeling of bleakness. "They're very happy."

"Are you looking forward to being a bridesmaid?"

"Of course. Isn't that every little girl's dream?" She tried to laugh lightly.

"I thought every girl's dream was to be the bride." Grant glanced at her. "Isn't that yours?"

Meredith shrugged. "I'm pretty good at being a bridesmaid. I've done it twice before."

"You're being evasive."

"You're being a lawyer."

Grant laughed. He reached for her hand and held it against his knee. "Is it your dream to be married in the temple, Meredith?"

She almost didn't want to answer, but then she lifted her chin and looked straight ahead. "A few months ago I probably wouldn't have been able to answer that immediately. But now . . . I'd have to say yes, that's my dream."

"Why only now?" Grant sounded genuinely curious. "What's changed?"

Meredith hesitated, then she leaned her head against the window. "You."

"Me? What have I got to do with it?"

She gave a short laugh and turned so she could look at him. "You've got everything to do with it, Grant, even though you haven't been aware of any of it."

"I'll say," he agreed. "So, tell me exactly what I've done."

Meredith took a deep breath. "Before I came to Auckland to study law, I used to go to church regularly. I was a bit of a rebel, but I enjoyed church and it was always my—dream, I thought . . . that when I grew up, I would marry a fine young man—a Latter-day Saint—in the temple. Except that when I got to the big city, going to church was different. The programs and doctrine were all the same, but I felt like a stranger. I missed my family and friends . . . and I found it hard to fit in. Instead, I got really involved with my studies, a job, and doing lifeguard service."

"That sounds realistic." Grant frowned. "I don't see anything wrong with that if you didn't feel comfortable there. It doesn't change your beliefs."

Meredith smiled. "That's exactly how I justified it. And it worked—so much so that I stopped going to church entirely, and after a while I didn't really even miss it. I sort of had it in the back of my mind that I'd maybe go try again after I graduated, but it never happened. Until I met you."

"Now there's where you lose me."

"The thing is," she said, spreading her hands, "I had absolutely no intention of working in Auckland . . . until I heard from Charles and it seemed like a good idea to apply. He was so enthusiastic about the firm and that he thought it would be the perfect job for me."

"Sounds like Charles . . . get you the job so he doesn't have a bothered conscience about taking off overseas."

"Well, whatever his motives, it sounded good, so I applied, and then when I had my interview, I really liked your father . . ." She hesitated.

"But you weren't so keen on the son?" Grant laughed dryly.

"Not particularly." Meredith's voice slowed. "In fact, I was sure he wouldn't even allow me to work there, and I resolved to leave then and there because I just couldn't imagine working amicably with him. But then his father offered me the job on the spot, and next thing I knew, I was saying yes. I couldn't believe it, but it just felt . . . right."

"Gut instinct?"

"I guess you could call it that. Anyway, as I got to know the son—"

"Why are you calling me that?"

"Because it's easier to tell the story," she said, her voice shaking. "So . . . as I got to know him, I found out he'd lost his family, very tragically. I began to wonder what it must feel like—how I would feel if I lost everybody I loved. And then I realized that, in my own way, I was losing them."

"Just by not going to church?" There was a trace of disbelief in Grant's voice.

"No . . . it was much more than that." Meredith rubbed her face with her hands, then laid them in her lap. "My parents were married in the temple and I have been sealed to them as their daughter for eternity—as have all my siblings. That bond remains intact for each of us as long as we live faithfully . . . keeping the commandments and honoring the laws that we believe Heavenly Father has given us."

"But you're a good person, Meredith. I can't see that you wouldn't . . . qualify."

Meredith smiled at his attempts to reassure her, and then sighed at her own inability to explain properly.

"I never did anything horribly wrong, Grant . . . but I didn't do everything I could that was right, either. Things I knew I should do—things that the rest of the world doesn't even regard as important."

"Like going to church?"

"Like going to church, and keeping the Sabbath day holy, and honoring my parents. I mean I didn't break any 'big' commandments like murdering or adultery or anything, but . . . it's like when you're trying a case in court. You've spent all those years gaining all the right knowledge and you research everything, but what would happen if you only used a tiny portion of what you knew to help someone—especially if you knew you could do more? You wouldn't be doing your client justice. You wouldn't be giving the best you were capable of. And both of you would lose in the process."

"Okay . . . I can see that." Grant tapped his fingers on the wheel. "But I'm still not sure where I fit into all this."

She glanced sideways at his profile. "When I found out about Hannah and Emily . . . and your mum . . . I could see the pain that you were in because you thought you'd lost them forever. But I knew that you hadn't, that it is possible to be sealed to your family—forever. I knew it all, but because I wasn't living the principles I wanted to tell you about, I felt you would think me a hypocrite . . . so I didn't say anything at all." She clenched her fist. "Then when I went to visit my family and Mum was sick and Ryan was leaving . . . and all of a sudden it was so, so obvious exactly what I was letting myself slide away from. And what was so important for you and your family."

"You were different when you came back." Grant nodded. "When I came back to the office that day, I just knew I wanted to see you, but when you started talking . . . it was different."

They sat in silence for a long time. Then Grant began tracing a pattern slowly in the frosted residue on the window. After a while

Meredith noticed that he'd written the words "So what now?" and she shook her head.

"I'm really not sure."

"Well, what if this was a court case and you were trying to save my life . . . even though the evidence seems really far-fetched, how would you present it?"

"You mean about the temple and being sealed?" Meredith asked quietly.

"I think so." Grant shook his head in some confusion. "From what I understand so far, you're saying that to be with my family again, that it would need to be done through the temple. Like your parents have done and like Telesia and Tavita are going to do. But I don't even go to church, let alone your church. I don't even really know that I believe in God anymore, so I don't see how—"

"No, no, you're going way ahead." Meredith put her hand to her head and closed her eyes to offer another swift, silent prayer before facing him again. "Grant, while we were on Rangitoto Island we talked about God and Jesus Christ, and I told you how I believed that we're here on earth to find happiness with, and through, our families and our faithfulness. I've grown up with that knowledge, while some people come to an understanding at other times in their lives. We're also told that we can demonstrate our understanding by being baptized."

"You're saying I have to get baptized?" Grant shook his head. "Meredith, I'm thirty years old . . . this is crazy."

Meredith felt her courage failing her, but she resolved to try.

"You remember how you said your mother would tell you Bible stories? Well, do you remember about how John the Baptist baptized the Savior? How old was Jesus? He was about thirty years old," she answered her own question then continued breathlessly. "Age is not even relevant except that it makes people more skeptical. The question is whether you can believe in these things and are prepared to show it—and move on."

She finished almost in a whisper, then watched in despair as Grant leaned forward and rested his arms and forehead on the steering wheel. He didn't say anything for several minutes, then he spoke to the front of the car.

"I'm really fond of you, Meredith . . . and I am beginning to understand what you're saying. As weird as it all sounds, I can even appreciate the concept of temples and being married for eternity. I just . . . I can't reconcile the concept of this happening with Hannah—or Emily—and quite frankly . . . it hurts to even try to think about it. Besides," his voice became harsh, "I have loved being with you the last few weeks and I was beginning to think that we could even have a future together, that I wouldn't have to forget Hannah and Emily—just build a new life with you. But I just can't see that anymore at all. I just feel like the runner with no plan . . . like I'm only getting lost faster. I just think I need more time to think about it all—without the pressure of trying to believe just because you want me to."

There weren't any tears left, only a hollowness that drained any resistance or protest from her. Meredith watched his hands tense and release on the wheel, and the way the veins moved in his hands as she'd noticed so many times when he was writing. Closing her eyes, she could visualize the way his hair was trimmed cleanly against his neck, the slight wave of black hair above his ears, the way his jaw moved when he was concentrating, and the way his eyes could soften and actually light up when he laughed. But the images blurred as she realized she didn't have a choice. If she really wanted what was best for her—and for Grant—she knew what she needed to do. With difficulty, she swallowed the solid lump in her throat.

"I had a friend once—when I first came to Auckland. He asked me if I was prepared to date someone who wasn't a member of the Church." She felt an almost physical weight compressing her chest. "I really liked him, but at first I told him I wouldn't. Then I said yes— and that's when my problems really started."

"Meaning?"

"Meaning that I don't want to make the same mistake twice." She barely breathed the statement but it was emphatic. "I do feel the same about you, Grant. But I'm not prepared to lose again."

CHAPTER 18

"Dad?"

"Hello, love. How come you're calling so late? Is there anything wrong?"

"No, I just wanted to hear your voice again." Meredith tried to laugh. "Actually, Telesia just got engaged to Tavita."

"Well, that's wonderful to hear. They've resolved their problems then?"

"Mmhm. They're going to have a small reception after their temple wedding. Telesia said she just had to get far enough away from everyone to see that it was Tavita she wanted to marry and the Lord she wanted to please. They're so happy now."

"And is my girl happy?" There was a long pause. "Meredith?"

"Not very, at the moment." Her voice sounded muffled.

"Is this anything to do with that special young man?"

"Just a bit . . . a very big bit." She tried to laugh. "We had a celebration dinner with Telesia and Tavita and they talked about temple marriage, and after . . . well, Grant couldn't exactly understand how he could be sealed to his family or why there were such strict rules for the temple and why you had to be baptized . . . and I basically failed dismally trying to explain it all to him."

"It's hard when you're very close to someone. You tend to see the big picture at the end—that's what gives you hope for them—but it's hard trying to fill in all the little bits in a way that will really help them understand."

"That's it exactly!" Meredith shook her head. "I really think I made things much worse."

"Not necessarily. You've planted the seeds."

"Yes, but I've never been any good at actually getting things to grow," she tried to joke, but her voice broke.

"Meredith, just how close have you gotten to Grant?"

"Not too close, Dad. I promise. Not this time."

"I wasn't really meaning that, love. I was thinking more about your heart."

Meredith brought her hand up to her chest and patted it. "Ooh, I'd say he's probably got possession of a good eighty percent right now."

"That much?"

"Probably more if I hadn't talked to you guys and sorted out my life before I got too involved."

"So where's the relationship heading?"

"Definitely not to the temple right now, if that's what you mean."

"I already got that impression."

At the sudden dryness in her father's tone, she sat forward in the chair. "Dad, I understand the whole scenario of dating a nonmember and I don't want to go there, but at the same time . . ."

"But?"

"I told you that when I came to work here I felt strongly about being needed, and I recognized that need as helping Grant to be with his family. At that point I wasn't even thinking of a relationship with him. That sort of developed the more I tried to help him."

"And now you're in love with him?"

"Yes."

She heard her father's muffled laugh. "Honey, you're meant to deny it at least once or twice."

"Oh, believe me, I've tried that. It doesn't work anymore."

"So . . . what now?"

Meredith rested her head against the phone. "Dad, I don't know if I have the courage . . . but I want to try and see this through."

"The relationship? Isn't that being a bit hopeful?"

"I was thinking more about helping him understand better. I just couldn't walk away from this knowing I could have done more to help him and his father understand about eternal families."

"Are you sure that's not just an excuse to stay with him?"

Meredith shook her head. "I'm trying not to think that way. Tonight I said that I couldn't carry on our relationship." She hesitated and her voice faltered. "I've been working so hard on getting my testimony back, and I was really thinking I was helping Grant, and then it seemed like our relationship was like . . . my reward for coming back."

"And now?"

"Now, I'm sure where I want to end up—for the time being," she finished hastily.

"Meredith . . ." She detected the tone of loving warning in his voice. "I don't want to see you getting hurt."

"Me neither, Dad, but you know how I love a project."

"Honey, this is a bit different from rescuing pets and building tree houses."

"But I always saw them through, Dad. I have to this time as well."

She heard her father's laugh and could almost see him shaking his head the way he always did when she was determined to succeed against all odds.

"Dad, I know you'll talk to Mum about this and I know she'll worry. Can you tell her that I promise there'll be no empty chair—whatever the outcome with Grant."

* * *

"Meredith, can I talk to you for a moment?"

"Certainly, Mr. Bascombe." Meredith stood up and walked around her desk. "Do you want me to come to your office?"

"No, no." Frank pointed at the chairs in front of her desk. "This'll do fine."

They sat down, and Meredith waited while he made himself comfortable.

"I'll come straight to the point." He wagged his finger. "A couple of weeks ago, my son was on cloud nine when you were around, and you looked the same, if I'm not mistaken?"

Meredith rolled her eyes. "That's straight to the point, all right."

"Am I wrong?"

"No."

"So, what happened? I mean, I see you working together, but . . ." He clenched his fists. "I don't see the spark anymore."

Meredith smiled. She had really come to love this man, and his outburst just reinforced the feeling. She put her head to one side. "We agreed to extinguish the spark before we both got hurt."

"You agreed . . . ? What sort of nonsense is that?"

"Not nonsense. Just common sense. We couldn't agree on . . . religious issues, so we're just maintaining a businesslike relationship."

She felt herself begin to squirm as Frank studied her intently, and he almost barked the question, "What sort of religious issues?"

CHAPTER 19

"Meredith, you're getting so thin. We can't keep taking that bridesmaid's dress in." Telesia frowned as Meredith zipped up the dark blue satin skirt. It fell well down on her hips instead of at the waistline—where it was meant to sit.

"Well it won't matter after tomorrow, will it? You'll be Sister Tavita and you won't have to worry about it anymore."

"I'll always worry about you . . . until you're happy."

"I'm happy, Sia." She shrugged her jacket over her shoulders. "My job is great. Grant and I have a good working relationship. I love my calling at church with the Young Women, and—"

"And you're wasting away. You run and swim every day, you're doing fitness classes nearly every night, and Brother Edwards said you'd volunteered to help organize the ball."

"So? He needs help and I've got plenty of time, especially once you leave."

Telesia sat on the bed and stared at her wedding dress hanging on the door. The two girls had spent the last several weeks sewing the satin, princess-line dress. They'd appliquéd delicate lace flowers around the neckline to form a v-shaped design in the front, and repeated the trim on the sleeves.

"We'll just be living up the road." She stood up and stroked the dress lovingly. "You'll come and visit all the time."

"Sia . . . we're best friends, but you're going to have a husband. He is your priority—not a spinster friend." Meredith pulled a face as she said the last sentence. "Everything is fine."

* * *

"So, how did the wedding go?" Grant looked up from the papers he was reading as Meredith walked into his office. Their practice of going through cases first thing in the morning had become a habit that was a mixture of pleasure and pain. Sometimes she found herself dreading it—like this morning.

"It was lovely." She sat down in the chair in front of his desk and tucked her hair behind both ears. She'd combed it back quite severely in a sleeker style, but it only served to accentuate the almost gaunt contours of her cheekbones. "Telesia looked beautiful and Tavita couldn't take his eyes off her. They were really happy."

"And did the bridesmaid catch the wedding bouquet?" He flicked a pen between his fingers and tried to ignore the fact that she wouldn't look at him.

"Oh, no . . . I dodged that one. Telesia's sister caught it."

"Does that mean you've given up wanting to get married?" Grant raised his eyebrow and Meredith felt a wrenching feeling in her stomach. They had both played out their agreement to a platonic relationship to a fault, but in the last few weeks she'd noticed their remarks had become more cynical—almost cutting—toward each other. Although her heart still beat unsteadily when she heard his voice or footstep, it was now accompanied by a feeling of apprehension, and more recently, of failure.

"I wouldn't say I've given it up, just put it on hold . . ."

The silence lengthened, and Meredith was just about to stand up and excuse herself when the buzzer sounded on Grant's phone. He picked it up and listened, then nodded to Meredith. "You have a visitor at the front desk."

"Me?" She glanced at her watch. "I'm not expecting anyone until two."

"Well, you'd better go see." He looked down at his desk. "We weren't getting anywhere, anyhow."

His last remark seemed to cut into her like a knife as she stood up quickly and left the room. *That had a harsh mark of finality to it,* she thought sadly.

"Meredith?"

She stopped in her tracks as a man turned from studying a magazine in the waiting area. He seemed enormous, with a very full ginger moustache and beard just a shade darker than his thick mass of curly hair. The breadth of his ample upper torso was emphasized by a sturdy sheepskin leather jacket and plaid shirt, and he wore thick denim jeans and heavy tan leather boots.

"I'm sorry?" Meredith frowned. "I'm not sure . . ."

The man took a few steps across the room. "Don't tell me you've forgotten an old buddy?"

As soon as he said the word "buddy," Meredith's hand flew to her mouth. "No . . . Mitch? It can't be!"

In a second she was across the room and swallowed up in a huge hug as Mitch lifted her right off the floor. Stella watched from her desk with one eyebrow arching even higher than normal—then both eyebrows as she noticed Grant appear at his office door.

"Oh, my goodness . . . Mitch! Is it really you?" Meredith leaned back as Mitch lowered her to the ground. "Underneath all that?" She put up a hand to touch the bushy beard.

Mitch's once-familiar laugh rumbled in his chest as he gave her another, more subdued hug. "Yep, all of me," he chuckled again and held her at arm's length. "I've been so looking forward to seeing you. I was wondering if you'd recognize me."

"Hardly . . . but how did you find me?" She clapped her hands. "Hang on, let's go through to my office. I've got so much to ask you."

"Miss Winstone." She stopped as Grant spoke behind her. "Perhaps you'd like to conduct your reunion outside the office. Why don't you take a couple hours off?"

Meredith turned slowly. "That would be nice, thank you. This is quite a shock for me." She gestured politely toward Mitch and then back toward Grant. "Mitch Savage . . . my boss, Grant Bascombe."

She stood aside as both men approached each other with a hand outstretched. As they shook hands she noticed the look on Mitch's face change swiftly from pleasant formality to stunned surprise. He recovered quickly, but Meredith watched the way he stared as Grant turned back to his office. She took Mitch's hand and pulled him the other way.

"I'll just get my handbag and then we can go to the café downstairs. Have you eaten yet?"

"Not yet." He laughed and patted his stomach, but she saw him look thoughtfully back at Grant's door again as she went to get her bag.

"So, tell me how you found me." Meredith pulled out a chair in the café and sat down. "I don't even have a phone listing."

"Ah, you can't cover your tracks that easily," Mitch chuckled as he sat down opposite her. "I went straight to the bakery where you used to work, and Vee said that you had given her your work details in case she got sick again. She said you'd helped her out a few weeks ago."

"Oh my goodness, fancy you even thinking of the bakery." Meredith nodded. "I went in one day and she looked dreadful, so I helped a couple of early mornings. She's been diagnosed with a heart murmur, so I told her to call me if she needed help again."

"Still leaving your options open in case the law thing doesn't work out?"

"Let's not go into that again." She pretended to scowl. "I'm a regular lawyer now, so if you ever need any help, you know where to come. But tell me, where have you been and what brings you back?"

"Well, I went to England via South Africa to begin with. Got rid of the wanderlust, and then made my way over to Canada where I've been working for the last three years."

"Wrestling bears by the look of you." Meredith reached out and flicked his thick mane of hair.

"Actually, this is just the last few months' growth. I've just finished a contract right up the far north and it got pretty cold up there. It was just warmer to let everything grow. And then I thought it would be fun to surprise the family, so I kept it all on."

"Well, it certainly surprised me." She laughed. "I had no idea who you were until you said 'buddy.'"

"Meredith's surf patrol buddy." Mitch shook his head. "I've often thought about that over the last few years. We did have some good times, didn't we?"

"Yes, we did." Meredith nodded and clasped her hands in her lap as she recalled some of their activities. "You're a good man, Mitch. I'll always appreciate how you were such a good friend when I came to Auckland."

They sat quietly, then Mitch took a drink of water and cleared his throat. "You know, when I was flying in, all I could think about was finding you again, but I had no idea where to start. Do you know what I did?"

"You went to the bakery?" Meredith looked faintly puzzled.

"Before I went there." Mitch shook his head, "Why do you think I thought of the bakery?"

"I have no idea."

Mitch took a deep breath, then he looked straight at her. "I prayed about it . . . and I felt prompted to go there."

Meredith stared, then she frowned. "Excuse me?"

"I prayed about it, Meredith. To know where to find you." Mitch spoke more confidently and deliberately. "And I felt the promptings of the Spirit."

"Mitch?" Meredith's voice was barely a whisper as she began to recognize what he was saying. "How do you know . . . I mean . . . you just . . ."

"Talked like a Mormon?" He nodded. "I'm really used to it all now."

Meredith held up her hand. "Hold on . . . What am I missing here?"

"You aren't missing anything. You're thinking I sound like a Mormon, and I'm saying that I am."

Meredith was speechless. She opened and shut her mouth several times, then just giggled helplessly. "I don't believe this."

"Heck, it's not that funny, Meredith." Mitch pretended to look offended. "I thought you'd be pleased."

"Pleased! Shocked! Happy! You name it . . . I just can't comprehend it. How?"

Mitch reached out and took hold of her hand. "Actually, it's all your fault. You know how when we were . . . dating . . . you had such high standards for yourself, and therefore me. And you'd talk about church things and your family and everything, and we went to that luau—well, I enjoyed it, even though I didn't really appreciate it."

"So what happened . . . ?"

"What happened?" He smiled. "When I got to Canada I worked in the French-speaking part for a while, and then I got the opportunity to go on contract to a place called Cardston. It was really nice and I settled in there, and then I met this girl. She worked at an office where I used to go to get plans copied. I went quite a few times."

He smiled shyly and took another drink. "Anyway, I asked her out and we went bowling with a group of people from the job I was on. Afterward, they all wanted to go to the hotel for a drink, but she asked me to take her home." He smiled again. "I guess I was a bit slow to pick up the vibes, but we talked when I took her home and it turned out—"

"She was a Latter-day Saint," Meredith finished for him.

"Exactly . . . and so I immediately said that one of my best friends back in New Zealand was one too." He smiled a bit sheepishly. "I'll admit that I kind of elaborated on that dance you took me to, but it was enough to reassure her, and we went out again."

"And again?"

"And again . . . only we started going to more of her activities . . . at her church." He shook his head. "And pretty soon I stopped drinking. And then she invited me to church on Sunday . . . and I went."

"I can't believe this." Meredith patted her cheek. "I'm going to wake up soon."

"That's what I kept telling myself . . . for three months. Then one Sunday, we were walking home from church—her family lives near the chapel—and she said that I needed to make a decision."

"About her?"

"About everything. She said that she didn't want a serious relationship with anybody outside the Church, but she was getting too fond of me . . . so I either had to make a commitment to finding out as much about the Church as I could and whether I could make that my way of life—or we had to finish the relationship."

"The lady has guts," Meredith murmured. *Guts that I didn't have . . . until it was too late.*

"I'll say." Mitch nodded. "She's amazing. Anyway . . . we got back to her home and they just happened to have the missionaries visiting for dinner, so I started having the discussions that evening."

"How convenient," Meredith commented wryly. "Did you feel like it was a setup?"

"Sort of . . . but I also realized how important it was to Sharon."

"Ah, the lady has a name."

"Of course, sorry, I forgot . . . Sharon Arquette. Her family is French-Canadian."

"So what happened after that?"

"The usual, I gather. I had the discussions and it all seemed so right. I was baptized about eighteen months ago."

"Oh, wow!" Meredith raised her eyebrows. "You're an old hand."

"Pretty much." Mitch shrugged. "Certainly can't think of life without the Church anymore."

"And what happened to Sharon?"

Mitch grinned. "Actually Sharon Arquette Savage is waiting for me to find a home down here so she can join me as soon as possible. She's four months pregnant and having pretty bad morning sickness, so I came ahead to get things ready."

"Oh, Mitch . . . I'm so happy for you." Meredith felt genuine tears of happiness welling in her eyes. "This is like a fairy tale."

"That's what it feels like . . . and it's largely due to you, Meredith." Mitch's voice dropped. "If you hadn't sewn the seeds when we were friends here, I don't think I would have recognized how special Sharon is . . . or the gospel."

"Gosh . . . I don't know what to say." She fanned her cheeks. "At least there's one success story."

Mitch picked up on the tone of her voice. "So, how has it been with you?"

"Oh . . . I think we were developing in opposite directions for a few years." Meredith tried to act nonchalant. "After you left, I sort of lost the plot completely with church . . . I couldn't seem to figure out exactly what Heavenly Father wanted for me, and my legal studies seemed to present a logical alternative, and the surf club and my job provided the service aspect. By the time I graduated I wasn't attending church at all."

"So where are you at now?" Mitch looked genuinely concerned. Then he attempted a grin. "Should I be talking to your bishop?"

"Oh, Mitch . . . that sounds so good coming from you!" Meredith laughed, then she nodded. "Actually, I had a few incidents happen recently that made me realize what I was losing . . . and I've been back at church for about four months now."

"For good?"

"For good." She smiled. "I have such great examples now to keep me on track."

They ate lunch silently for a few minutes until Mitch suddenly tapped the table. "Oh, I nearly forgot . . . your boss!"

"My boss? Oh, you mean Grant."

"The guy I met upstairs." He paused. "Meredith, I've met him before."

"Grant? Really? Where?"

Mitch shook his head. "I wasn't sure at first, but then he said something and the way he looked—sort of right past me—Meredith, he's the guy I pulled from the surf at Muriwai that time. You know . . . the day you weren't there and we rescued the little boy and the man."

Meredith slowly lowered her sandwich onto her plate. "The one you said was trying to . . . ?"

Mitch coughed. "To stop me from saving him. It's definitely him."

"That would have been nearly four years ago," she calculated slowly. "He would have just lost his wife and baby in a car accident."

"Then no wonder he didn't want to live." Mitch played with the napkin on his plate. "I could never figure why a guy like that would want to end his life, but now I think about Sharon and our child—I don't know what I'd do if I lost them."

"But at least you understand about eternal families now." She hesitated. "Were you married in the temple?"

"Oh, yes." Mitch grinned. "I had to cool my heels and prove myself for a year, but, Meredith, it's seriously been the best time of my life. I can't believe what I've learned and what I know I have to look forward to—especially once our baby is here."

Meredith sat quietly. Part of her was overwhelmed with happiness for Mitch, but the rest of her ached for what Grant couldn't see— wouldn't see—and what that meant for her.

"Hey . . . do I detect some undercurrents?" Mitch asked softly. "Is the boss more than just the boss?"

Meredith looked up sadly. "No."

"That was a 'no' with an awful lot of meaning behind it. Do you want to tell your buddy?"

She toyed with the straw in her glass, holding it up then watching the water drain out.

"It's funny to think I can talk to you straight up now . . . about gospel principles." She hesitated. "The thing is, when I began work here and found out about Grant's situation, I just wanted to tell him about how he could be with his family again. Then it made me realize how important the whole concept was to me, but . . . I've found it really difficult to explain anything to him."

"And in the process you've fallen in love with him." It was a statement rather than a question.

"Is it that obvious?" she sighed.

"Not at first, but the more you talk about him, it is." Mitch bent forward to get her attention. "I'm going to take a leaf out of my wife's book and be brutal here. Is there any future in it, Meredith, or would it be better to move on?"

The waitress had come and taken their plates and brought the bill before she finally got back to his question. "I wanted there to be a future . . . and I've tried to be platonic because I thought I had a mission to teach him."

Mitch reached over and patted her hand. "You said that meeting Grant helped you realize what you were losing by not being at church. Maybe the reason you met him was to help you get back on track . . . rather than the other way 'round."

Meredith frowned. "I never thought of it that way."

"Well, it's worth thinking about if it's going to help you move on." Mitch stood up. "I don't want to see my buddy wasting her life."

They walked across the road to where Mitch had parked his rental car, and he turned to face her as she wrote down her number and address for him. "Meredith . . . you've helped give me a life I'd never dreamed was possible. I owe you, buddy, and if there's anything under the sun you ever need, I'll be there for you. We'll be there for you," he corrected himself with a wide grin before he wrapped his arms around her and gave her a brotherly hug.

"Why do I suddenly feel jealous of your wife?" She thumped him underneath his thick jacket.

"Hey . . . it's to be expected. I'm a great guy!" Mitch laughed and put the key in the lock. "Keep me posted . . . promise?"

"I promise." Meredith waved as the car pulled out from the curb, then turned to face the ocean. The sea was a dull green color, reflecting the gray, clouded sky. Only a couple of large cargo ships were out on the water, one waiting to dock as the other moved slowly out of the channel toward the open ocean. She rested her hands on her hips and took a deep breath.

Time to move on.

Grant stood at the window of his office as Meredith and Mitch crossed the road to the parked car. He watched as they laughed together and then as Mitch wrapped his arms round her. He saw Meredith rest her head against his chest and they laughed again.

"Just friends," he said to himself. But he felt an unreasonable surge of resentment followed swiftly by a feeling of dejection. "Best friends, by the look of it."

He turned back to his desk and slumped down in his chair. The last few weeks had been nothing short of painful as he'd tried to maintain a professional relationship with Meredith. He would find himself anxious to share something with her but then as soon as she got close, he'd say or do something harsh or intimidating in order to stay aloof.

Every evening he tried to find other activities to occupy the time they'd been spending together, but most places just brought back memories . . . good memories that only hurt.

He was even wary of sitting still for too long because snatches of their conversations would play out in his mind . . . conversations about God and eternity and his family and things about her church. He closed his eyes and the image of Meredith's face floated in front of him, the way her eyes shone when she was excited or her slight frown and the way she used her hands to explain something that she was trying to make him understand . . . the emptiness in her eyes when he was abrupt with her.

He dropped his hands down onto the arms of his chair and stared at the ceiling. How long were these images going to play out in his mind?

"Um . . . I've finished the briefs you wanted for tomorrow's hearings." Meredith stood in the doorway, the expression on her face shadowed and tentative, as opposed to the happy smile she'd shared with Mitch earlier. "Shall I leave them with you or at reception?"

Grant didn't appear to hear her although he was staring straight at her. As she opened her mouth to ask again, he dismissed her with one hand.

"Miss Winstone, I really don't care what you do."

CHAPTER 20

"You know what? I think it needs more garlic and oregano." Telesia licked her lips as she savored the mix on the wooden spoon. "It's not quite spicy enough."

"I can't believe how you know what to add or subtract." Meredith handed over two bottles of herbs from the rack on the wall. "I just put the can of flavoring into the meat."

"I know." Telesia grinned. "You use more sachet mixes and canned sauces than anyone I know."

"Hey . . . it works." Meredith shrugged. "If it wasn't for people like me, there would be thousands of others out of jobs. I don't just cook dinner . . . I actually contribute to the economy."

They laughed together as Telesia stirred the meat in the pot and Meredith drained off some pasta. Within minutes they were eating their meal, sitting out on the wooden veranda.

"So how is married life?" Meredith finished a mouthful and thoughtfully twisted her fork in the long noodles.

Telesia didn't hesitate. "Absolutely wonderful. I am so glad we're married. It makes everything so different . . . so much nicer . . . more wonderful than I thought possible."

"Okay . . . I get the idea." Meredith rolled her eyes. "And I appreciate how privileged I am to have your company this evening. Is Wednesday night going to be a regular late night for Tavita?"

"I think so." Telesia nodded. "And I'm so glad you're here. I always thought I was pretty independent, but when he said he had to work late I felt instantly lonely. Can you believe how pathetic that sounds?"

"I think it sounds like it should be that way," Meredith responded quietly. "And I'm glad you've come over, because I wanted to talk to you about something."

Telesia paused with her fork halfway to her mouth. "Is it serious? Has something happened between you and Grant?"

Meredith shook her head and pushed her plate aside.

"Nothing has happened with Grant since I told you he didn't want to discuss anything religious anymore . . . except that our professional relationship has deteriorated as well. We have very brief contacts and only when absolutely necessary." She shrugged. "So there's nothing there, but . . . I had something quite amazing happen yesterday. Do you remember the guy I dated the second year at university?"

"You mean Mitch the lifeguard?" Telesia nodded immediately. "The only guy you dated, despite all my efforts at matchmaking you with the young adults."

"That's him." Meredith ignored her last comment. "He turned up yesterday at the office. Fresh from the Canadian wilds . . . big beard, longish hair . . . I didn't even recognize him at first."

"So did he come back to steal you away?"

"Not exactly . . . although he had come to find me." She hesitated. "He wanted to tell me that he'd joined the Church and married in the temple."

She couldn't have gotten a better reaction.

"You're not serious?"

"I'm absolutely serious—and I was as shocked as you are." Meredith shrugged. "But it's for real, and he's bringing his Canadian wife out here to live. He's going back into property development with his father."

"Oh my goodness," Telesia breathed the words slowly. "Who ever would have thought . . . I mean . . . you two went completely opposite ways."

"Okay . . . rub it in." Meredith frowned. "I've already been over and over that fact in my mind a hundred times . . . but you won't believe the next part."

"There's more?"

"Mitch recognized Grant as the man he pulled from the surf that time . . . the one that tried to . . .'"

"The same weekend as the little boy that nearly drowned?" Telesia's eyes were wide with surprise. "That's an amazing coincidence."

Meredith nodded. "I can't quite believe any of it. But it's all true, and . . . I think it's all come at an important time for me." She absently picked up the fork and began to toy with the cold pasta. "After Mitch told me about his conversion, he asked me where I was at and I told him I was making a comeback at church. Anyway, all this time I've been thinking that I was at work here to help Grant. But Mitch made a comment—he said that maybe it was the other way 'round. That maybe I wasn't there just to help Grant—that the reason I met him was to help me get back on track because it helped me realize what I was losing."

She waited as Telesia pursed her lips thoughtfully, then began to nod. "Could be . . . the Lord does work in mysterious ways."

Meredith placed her fork aside decisively. "That's exactly the idea that has been going through my mind the last twenty-four hours— that, and the thought that I should serve a mission."

Telesia bent her head forward in an instant reaction, her eyes even wider.

"My goodness. I should come to dinner more often!" She held up both hands. "Are you serious, Mele? A mission? Really?"

"I'm very serious." Meredith folded her hands in her lap. "And it feels very . . . right."

"So this wouldn't just be the easiest way to get out of the Grant situation right now?"

"No." She shook her head slowly. "I've thought about that, too. It's more like there's nothing to hold me here rather than that he's sending me away."

"But it's still only been twenty-four hours." Telesia leaned forward. "You do have an excellent job."

Meredith took her time answering as she stood up and went to lean against the wooden balustrade that ran the length of the veranda.

"The whole time that I've been trying to explain my beliefs to Grant I've just felt frustrated at my inability to say the right thing in the right way. When I asked Dad and Mum to clarify the answers for me, I just had an overwhelming feeling about how true everything was. I could literally feel the Spirit coming back to me, and everything I heard was like a confirmation for me—but I still couldn't get Grant to accept it."

"Maybe he's not ready yet," Telesia offered quietly.

"Whether he's ready or not . . . I *do* understand. And now I have a testimony back and I want to be able to teach others who need to understand the same gospel principles." She ran the toe of her sandal along a crack between the wooden boards. "If I serve a mission it might repay Heavenly Father for a lot of time I've wasted over the last few years."

"I'm sure He doesn't need repayment," Telesia answered softly. "Just your being back is enough."

"But it's not enough for me, Telesia." Meredith looked up at the ceiling. "I really feel strongly about this."

Telesia sat quietly, and Meredith knew she was absorbing the news. She would shortly present her objections or thoughts in a carefully considered way. It was the sort of approach that made her an excellent lawyer.

"So . . . you want to go on a mission—and probably right away, knowing you." She smiled as Meredith nodded. "A mission isn't just a short-term project, you know."

"I know that," Meredith acknowledged. "And I'm not just thinking of it as a project . . . really."

"So . . ." Telesia began to count the fingers on her hand. "You've made the decision . . . you feel confident about the decision . . . now the practical elements: Ryan is also out on his mission. Have you got enough money to fund yours?"

Meredith frowned, then nodded. "I have been saving most of my pay since I started working—apart from what we spend here at the flat—and I've been thinking about that, too. Now that you're gone, the rent is too much for me. So if I finish work and go live at home before I go, I can work there and save the rest."

"Finish work." Telesia nodded. "That does sound very final."

"It has to be." Meredith turned and looked out across the deep blue harbor. "It's time to move on."

* * *

"You're doing what?" Frank's voice shot up an entire octave. He paced around the desk with his hands clasped behind his back. "Run that by me again, please?"

"I . . . want to tender my resignation." Meredith clenched her hands together on her lap and pressed her ankles together to stop her legs shaking. "I've made a decision to . . . go on a mission . . . for my church."

"And where did that idea come from?"

"I've been thinking about it for a while." She cleared her throat. "I really want to do this."

"But what about your career? You're a brilliant lawyer, Meredith. It would be such a waste."

"That's very flattering, Mr. Bascombe . . . and I realize how ungrateful it must seem when you've helped me so much getting my career started."

Meredith stopped and bit at her bottom lip to stop it from quivering. It had taken five days after talking with Telesia to finally build the resolve to speak to Frank, and she could feel her courage slipping away as he expressed his genuine concern for her.

"Have you told Grant yet?"

"No. I wanted to speak to you first."

"Well, what do you think he's going to say?"

She rubbed the cuticle on her thumb, then looked straight at Frank. "To quote him exactly, it would probably be, 'Miss Winstone, I really don't care what you do.'"

"Oh, I see . . . that's how it is, is it?" Frank nodded and continued his pacing. "I know he's been a pain at home lately, but I thought you two had an 'amicable agreement' here at the office."

"We tried, but it's just disintegrated." Meredith coughed. "Anyway, that's not the reason I want to leave—"

"Baloney!" Frank swung around. "Tell me how you really feel, Meredith. And I want the truth."

His outburst made her look up quickly, and she didn't hesitate. "The truth. The truth is I thought I could help him, but I only hurt him—and myself in the process. I love working here, but every day is misery, because it just can't work. When I tried to tell him about . . . spiritual things . . . I failed. But in the process, I discovered how much they meant to me." She faltered. "If I go on a mission I'll learn how to better communicate those things, and maybe even teach someone who wants to hear."

"I see." Frank was very quiet. "Then I guess I can only wish you well."

Meredith nodded, surprised at his quick acquiescence. "Um . . . how long a notice do I need to give?"

"I suggest you just notify your clients that we will be looking after them and . . . in light of your current . . . situation . . . you can finish at the end of the week."

"This week?"

"No point in prolonging the agony."

She stood up slowly. "No, I guess not. And it would mean I can spend some more time at home with my family."

As she reached the door, he turned around. "I was going to suggest a staff luncheon as a farewell, but I think I'll just add the amount to your final paycheck. It should help your funds a bit."

* * *

The rest of the week passed in a blur . . . a physical haze where tears kept threatening. A super-human effort kept them at bay but created a constant headache and perpetual frown. Even informing her clients was difficult, as each one seemed to have made an indelible impression on her life in such a short time.

Frank had obviously told Stella, and the older woman seemed to shift into overdrive to make the transition easier, often casting concerned looks in Meredith's direction. On Thursday afternoon, she quietly walked into Meredith's office and closed the door. Meredith glanced up from the file she was organizing.

"Stella . . . have I left something out?"

"No . . . this is more of a social visit." The secretary sat down in one of the padded seats and crossed her legs, then uncrossed them and leaned forward. "Can you please tell me exactly why you're leaving? Frank says you've decided to go on a mission or something . . . but . . . I want to hear it from you."

"Frank is right." Meredith looked down at the pile of papers. "Circumstances have changed here, and it's precipitated my decision to go on a mission for my church."

"But you're such a good lawyer!" Stella frowned. "Isn't that a waste?"

Meredith looked up and smiled. "I can still be a good lawyer when I come back. In fact, I'll probably be a much better lawyer because I'll have learned a bit more compassion and humility."

"But how long are you going for?"

"About eighteen months." She shook her head. "Not very long at all, really . . . but long enough to—"

"Long enough to get Grant out of your system?" Stella pressed her fingertips together. "Is that a good reason to give up your career?"

"I'm not giving up my career, Stella!" Meredith protested, leaning back in her chair. "And my going on a mission is definitely not to just get Grant out of my system."

"Then what is it?" Stella persisted. "I'm sorry, but I don't want to see you make a rash decision." Her voice dropped. "I've become very fond of you, Meredith, and I only want to see that you've explored all the options."

Meredith found the tears welling up again at Stella's unexpected display of concern, and she began to draw tight circles on the desk pad with her pen.

"I've always had the Church in my life, Stella . . . and I've always accepted the things I was taught about the Savior and God and families. And I guess I took it for granted that it would always be the same. I never doubted my beliefs—until I came to Auckland—and when it came to adjusting to life on my own up here . . . it was sort of . . . easier to find other things to do. I think I was so determined to prove to everyone that I could be the best lawyer that I lost the bigger picture."

"Which is?"

"Which is that my family and the gospel are the most important things to me—they go hand in hand."

"And Grant won't buy into that?" Stella asked quietly.

Meredith stared at her graduation certificate hanging on the wall.

"He tried to, and we had some good talks, but he seemed to relate more to the practical aspects of the Church. When it came to the more spiritual things—he found it harder." She shrugged. "Actually, he found it impossible."

There was a long silence. Then Stella leaned forward.

"I can't begin to understand the religious side of things, Meredith. I just know that since you came to the office, you've changed a lot of things here—and not just in the legal sense. Frank keeps talking about how you seem to radiate something. And whatever it is has changed my—our—lives." She smiled hesitantly. "Changed them a great deal."

Meredith watched the delicate color touch Stella's cheeks and her heart felt full. She smiled. "Are you telling me . . . ?"

"I'm not telling you anything that you don't know already." Stella studied her fingertips. "Since you seemed to have instigated it in the first place." She hesitated. "I'll always be grateful for that."

"So—so you and Mr. Bascombe . . . ?" Meredith stammered, then smiled again as Stella nodded.

"Yes . . . me and Mr. Bascombe." She shrugged. "I don't know how you do it, but I think you do seem to have the power to change people's lives, Meredith. And if that's what a mission is all about . . . then maybe you are making the right choice."

"You do seem to have the power to change people's lives" . . . *except Grant's.* The frame on the wall became a blur. *There are others. Maybe you are making the right choice.* "Thank you, Stella . . . I needed to hear that." She stood up and walked around the desk. "And as for you two . . ." She grinned and gave Stella a hug. "I'm just so glad I could help, and I'm so happy for you."

Stella stood back, then gave her another quick hug. "And I hope things work out for you as well." She smiled hopefully. "Maybe Grant just needs time."

"Maybe . . ." Meredith nodded. "But I think that is one project I'll just have to say I didn't get right. You can't win them all."

* * *

Frank had diplomatically taken control of most of her clients, but on Friday she was forced to meet with Grant to hand over one last file. She stood in her office for a long time with the folder in her hand before walking briskly across the reception area and knocking firmly on his door.

"This is the last one, Grant." She tried to sound businesslike. "I've left everything else organized with your dad, and this one just needs your signature and then it's all done—and I'll be away."

Grant looked up slowly as if he were preoccupied with his work. Then he flicked the pen between his fingers.

"I see. Well, I guess that's it, then." He stood up. "You've done some very good work in your time here. Thank you for that."

His formality was almost more than she could bear, and she had to fix her gaze on the window behind him.

"It's been a pleasure," she responded just as formally. "And thank you—for all that you've taught me. It's been a very . . . it's been a great learning curve."

She finally looked straight at him, her heart willing a sudden miracle, but there was nothing in his eyes except a dull blankness. He began to hold out his hand as if to shake hers, then let it drop to his side as she stared at it without moving.

"Then I wish you well, Miss Winstone." He sat down again. "I'm sure you'll have a most successful mission."

* * *

"Sweetheart, I think it's lovely that you've come home. I'm just surprised, that's all." Nan hugged her daughter as she climbed out of her car. "I thought you were really happy at your job in Auckland."

"I was, Mum." Meredith pulled her bag out of the trunk of the car. "But things change."

"So how long are you staying? Are you planning to get work down here? That would be so lovely."

"Actually, Mum, I'm not planning to do legal work for a while." She grasped the bag handle with two hands in front of her. "I've decided to go on a mission."

"A mission?" Nan looked startled. "When did you decide to do that? You've never mentioned it before."

Meredith walked toward the house with her mother close beside.

"Does your father know?" Nan held the door open. "He never mentioned it to me."

"Dad doesn't know yet. In fact, you're the first person I've told, apart from at work and Telesia."

"And how did they take it? Did they understand at work what you meant about a mission?"

"Mr. Bascombe, Sr. was surprised, to say the least, but when he realized I was serious, he said that I could leave straightaway."

"But what about Grant? I thought . . . well, I thought there was something—"

"Something between us?" Meredith didn't even manage a smile. "We thought there could be for a while, but he wasn't really prepared to change, and neither was I. When I told him I was leaving . . . well, he didn't really have much to say at all."

"Oh dear, that's such a pity. After all our talks last time, I was quite hoping you'd have good news."

Meredith put her bag down and wrapped her arms around her mother. "Mum . . . you are the eternal romantic. I'm sorry, but you may have to wait a while for something to happen to this particular daughter. It's a good thing you have Wendy and the children to keep you occupied in the grandparent stakes."

"Well, it certainly seems that way, if you're determined to go on a mission." Nan hugged her, then stood back. "Darling, I'm really sorry things didn't work out for you . . . but deep down I'm so grateful you didn't compromise yourself. I know it sounds trite, but it's better to have the pain pass now than live with it forever."

"You're right, Mum—it does sound trite and it's really no comfort right now. But I do see what you mean." Meredith attempted a laugh. "Now where's that father of mine so I can get all the explanations finished in one day?"

* * *

Grant checked through his planner to see what appointments were arranged for the next day. Since Meredith had left, his workload had increased, and although his father had initially taken some of the cases back, the extra work was almost a relief since he could absorb himself in it.

He pulled out the necessary files, then picked up the correspondence from the morning mail. The top letter was addressed to Meredith, and he took it from the envelope to read it again.

Dear Miss Winstone, I know that it's usual to just pay a fee and leave it at that when dealing with a lawyer, but I just wanted to personally express my appreciation for the way you handled my case. I confess I was dubious about someone so young handling the work, but I was happily impressed with the competence and insight that you demonstrated. You're an asset to your company, and I look forward to working with you in the future.

"You're an asset to your company." Grant slipped the letter slowly back into the envelope. "Not anymore."

He glanced again at the pages in his planner and the date at the top. She'd been gone two weeks. He rested his elbows on the desk. What had he done in the last two weeks? After a few seconds he raised one eyebrow. "Not a whole lot."

"Grant . . . I've decided to get in touch with Charles and see if he wants to come back to work here." Frank walked into the office with his hands in his pockets. "His mother said that he e-mailed from France to say he was running out of money fast and may come back soon, anyway."

"Are we that desperate?" Grant pushed himself back from his desk and stretched. "Sorry, I shouldn't say things like that. I know Charles will do just fine—with a bit of strict parental control. Trouble is . . . who gets to be the parent?"

Frank walked over to the window. "I think we can share the responsibility, just like with Meredith." He paused and nodded his head toward the window. "It's funny how you get used to things. I still look outside and expect to see that beaten-up little Volkswagen sitting there."

"Mmm." Grant stood up and began putting papers into his briefcase. "I guess I've been too busy to notice."

"Rot!" His father didn't turn around. "You've noticed. You just won't admit it."

"What would be the point?" Grant snapped the lock shut. "It just didn't work. Case closed."

"The case shouldn't be closed, Grant," Frank responded stubbornly. "And we should still have an excellent young lawyer working for us, and you should be enjoying yourself with her and getting on with your life."

"I can get on with my life with any number of other women."

"And what sort of women would they be? Would they be women who can share your interests and your profession and who can make you look forward to each day?" Frank turned around. "How many of those are there really, Grant? Or have you just driven the only one away?"

"I didn't drive her away." Grant tightened his grip on the brief-case. "It just didn't work once we discussed . . . marriage."

"So it did actually get that far?"

"Sort of." He shook his head. "Meredith has a rosy picture of being married in their temple and families being forever . . . I just can't feel right about that."

"Why not—your mother did." Frank spoke quietly. "I asked Meredith to explain a few things to me before she left, and when she talked about families being reunited after death . . . I felt like I was listening to your mother all over again just before she died. I don't know if she had some sort of—insight—to help her through those last few months . . . but she was convinced we'd be together as a family."

"Mum always had more faith." Grant smiled grimly. "But it wasn't very practical and it ultimately didn't help her."

"Then maybe it's a possibility that your mother had faith . . . but Meredith has the knowledge."

"Faith is not to have a perfect knowledge of things, but to have hope for things which are not seen . . . which are true," Grant whis-pered, suddenly remembering the discussion at the beach where Meredith had recited that scripture. He had changed the subject at the time, but her words had played themselves over in his mind as he'd driven home, until they were etched into his memory.

"What's true?" Frank frowned.

"I don't know, Dad," his son answered wearily, then braced his shoulders. "But at the moment I'm not sure that I really care. And now I have to go and meet one of those women who dosen't share my interests or profession and who I don't care if I see the next day."

CHAPTER 21

Life in Taranki settled into a steady rhythm very quickly. Meredith stayed in her old room and reorganized her belongings. There wasn't much, as she'd left furniture and books back in Auckland with Telesia, who had moved back into the apartment with Tavita as soon as Meredith left.

For the first few days she rested in bed a lot or just pottered around the house, watching television or baking. It wasn't until her father had asked her about how she was going to fund her mission that reality had taken hold.

Her parents were already partially supporting Ryan on his mission, and although Stewart Winstone's job was steady, it was not highly paid. Since being sick, her mother couldn't even do the part-time job she'd taken up as a teacher's aide. The family resources were stretched to their fullest. Suddenly the notion of serving a mission was more than just a desire to serve—Meredith had to face the practical issues as well.

She set herself a rigid routine of exercise, spiritual feasting, and looking for a job. Every day she would get up early, study the scriptures, then go for an hour's run around the neighborhood. During the day she helped her mother with housework, then went looking for a job. Most evenings she spent with Cam, either at the local martial arts studio or playing basketball at the church hall.

The morning of the tenth day she lay in bed, watching the early morning sun making stealthy tracks across the duvet cover, creating two completely different shades of the same deep violet blue. For the first time she felt a weakening of her resolve to get up and study.

Despite a steady effort to find work—any work—she'd failed to even get a supermarket job. With the thought in mind that she would only want temporary employment before leaving on a mission, she had honestly approached would-be employers, offering to work any hours but for a period of only three or four months. The response had been consistent as they perused the CV.

"You're a lawyer! . . . Why aren't you practicing law? Why would you want to work here? Oh, I'm sorry . . . I really need someone on a more permanent basis . . . but I appreciate your telling me up front . . . best of luck, I hope you find something soon."

"Me too," Meredith muttered and rolled over to stare at her scriptures sitting on the bedside cabinet. She'd been reading the Book of Mormon from cover to cover in order to understand the sequence of events better, but this morning, as she reached for the book, she placed her hand on the cover and slipped her thumb into a random page. "Maybe just a quick read this morning . . . see what Alma has to say to Meredith."

Turning back over, she propped another pillow behind her head and began reading at the top of the page. She only made it to the second verse. ". . . for I do know that whosoever shall put their trust in God shall be supported in their trials, and their troubles, and their afflictions, and shall be lifted up at the last day."

Somehow the words seemed to strike a chord and she felt the tears welling in her eyes.

She had come back to Taranaki feeling a failure, but her family had refused to let her stay in that frame of mind. Each one of them, in their own way, had supported her and somehow managed to lift her self-esteem and encourage her to have more confidence, both mentally and spiritually.

"I just have to have more faith." She stretched her arms up behind her and rested her head in her hands. "I have to trust in God that things will work out all right for me . . . and for Grant."

Even the sound of his name brought familiar images to mind, and for the first time since she'd left the Bascombe office, she let her thoughts just wander through the memories of her time with Grant: Rangitoto Island, long walks, and intense discussions about work, then the laughter and shared impressions.

She deliberately erased the harsher, more frustrating images from her thoughts, stubbornly replacing them with happier things until the smile on her face was a genuine reflection of her recollections.

The sunlight was well across her room and creating shadows on the wall when she climbed out of bed and sank down on her knees.

"Heavenly Father . . . I thank Thee for the opportunity to know Grant. It has made my life so much better, knowing him . . . and even though I wasn't able to teach him what he needed to know, I just pray that I may have planted a seed . . . that one day he might recognize the truth."

It was nearly ten o'clock when she finally walked into the kitchen to find her mother talking on the phone. She busied herself getting some toast and her dog Milo something to eat, then sat down at the table as her mother finished the phone call.

"Was that Uncle Rob?"

Nan stood tapping the phone. "Yes . . . yes, it was."

"Is something wrong?"

"Well, they're certainly having their share of ups and downs. Grandma Harvey has been causing a bit of concern. She's really been forgetting more, and doing strange things, and the other day she just didn't come back from a walk, so Aunt Sheryl has been trying to spend more time over with her and Grandpa. Now they're thinking of having them move into their downstairs rooms."

Meredith frowned. "I can't imagine Grandma being . . . unstable. She's always been so busy and capable."

"That's what makes this hard. Most of the time she's fine, then she's . . . not." Nan sighed. "Then on top of that, Rob said they've just heard from Charise. She and Carl are doing a stint for his company down in Hokitika and the good news is that she's pregnant, but unfortunately she had a bad fall the other day and there's a possibility she'll lose the baby if she doesn't have complete bed rest for the next few weeks."

Nan paused to take a deep breath. "Rob was wondering if I could go down and help out at all, but I just don't know that I can at the moment."

Meredith frowned. "Mum, you need to take care of yourself, and Cam needs you here right now." She popped the last piece of toast into her mouth and stood up. "I'll go."

"Pardon?"

"I'll go and look after Charise," Meredith stated simply as she cleared her plate and mug off the table. "I'm in limbo at the moment, and although I'd like to have a job, that isn't happening, so I'll go and help Charise for a few weeks."

"Are you sure?" Nan folded her fingers together and rested her chin against them. "It would really solve their problems."

"And I'd like to solve some problems instead of creating them for a change." Meredith gave a wry smile. "Besides . . . it's been too long since I saw Charise. I was too shy to go to their wedding because I wasn't going to church, so . . . we have a lot to catch up on. It'll be perfect."

Meredith left early the next morning after a quick series of phone calls between Christchurch and Hokitika. She decided to drive so that she'd have a car to use while she stayed with Charise and Carl, even though it meant a long drive and the ferry crossing between the North and South Island.

Cam sauntered out to the car as she was stacking the last few items of food that her mother had insisted on sending with her.

"How long do you think you'll stay down there?" He leaned against the side of the car.

"I'm really not sure." Meredith pulled a blanket up over the boxes in the backseat. "As long as Charise needs help, I guess."

"But that could be for another five months if she has to sit tight till the baby's born." He grimaced. "Who'd be a mother?"

Meredith laughed as she gave him a hug. "It won't be that long. Carl is only on temporary assignment in Hokitika. They're heading back to Christchurch in about six weeks and then Auntie Sheryl will be able to help. Anyway, you know Charise, she'll be up and about as soon as she can."

"Yeah, I guess. She must have taken a pretty nasty tumble to even admit she needed help."

"That's what concerns me, so . . . the sooner I leave the sooner I can help."

"Will you come back here afterwards?" Cam kicked at an innocent weed with his boot.

"I'm not sure yet. I may go and visit Grandma and Grandpa in Christchurch first, and then I'll see what happens after that."

"What about your mission?"

Meredith cupped her hands in the back pockets of her jeans. "The papers are all filled out and Dad's going to send them in when I'm ready. I still need to earn a bit more money so I don't put any more burdens on Mum and Dad."

Cam nodded as he folded his arms. "I'm going to get another job—and stick with it this time. I figured out that if I can save about two and a half thousand a year while I'm at school, then work full-time another six months, I can have most of my mission paid for by my nineteenth birthday."

She was speechless for a moment. "Cam . . . you haven't mentioned . . . at least . . ."

"I know, I haven't really been missionary material for a while." He actually began to blush. "But Ryan keeps sending these letters, and he's so excited that you're planning to go. I just got to thinking about how I was mucking up . . . and then it kind of hit me the other day that . . . I really do want to serve a mission."

His voice broke and Meredith immediately hugged him tightly, the tears brimming in her own eyes.

"Oh, Cam, I'm so proud of you." She sniffed and wiped her eyes. "Seems like the family rebels are growing up at last . . . we may as well do it together."

She drove straight through from Taranaki to Wellington with only a few brief stops. Even the novelty of traveling the road for the first time in eight years didn't stop her feeling of urgency to reach Wellington in plenty of time to board the Interislander Ferry.

The first cars were just beginning to pull onto the ferry when she arrived at the wharf and quickly joined the line. An hour later she was standing at the rails of the large boat as it pulled out and began its three-hour journey across the Cook Strait.

Meredith watched, fascinated, as a continual stream of passengers made their way up onto the deck, took photos, then quickly returned to the warmer enclosed decks. She'd noticed that a number of the comfortably padded seats inside were already occupied by seasoned travelers, who had made themselves comfortable with a book or their laptop, or had just gone to sleep.

She stayed longer out on the deck, feeling an almost rejuvenating sensation as the wind teased at her clothes and hair.

The last time she was on a boat she had stood up at the front with Grant's arms around her while he pointed out all the places at North Head that he'd played at as a child. She wrapped her arms around her body. That had been a good day.

As soon as she left the ferry at the Picton dock, she followed the road to the larger town of Nelson. It was already five thirty in the evening and she glanced at the road map on the seat beside her. It was at least another six-hour drive down to Hokitika, which meant she'd arrive around midnight. She stifled a yawn and then she heard Grant's voice. *"I'm just ensuring it's not your funeral from driving back on those winding roads in the middle of the night."*

She pulled into the next motel and took a room.

* * *

It was chilly when she started out the next morning, but she felt fresh and ready for the drive. There was only a moment's hesitation as she reached the junction in the road at Inangahua before she turned the little car toward the coast road. Within the hour she had passed through Westport with its treasure trove of beaches, rivers, and streams and had reached the fascinating composition of layered rocks at Punakaiki.

"Look, Mum . . . they're pancakes." She smiled as she repeated the description from childhood vacations, when a night's stay at the motel beside the rocks was a must.

She paused briefly at one bay to stretch her legs and watch a group of fur seals sunning themselves on some rocks. There seemed to be a family, as several little ones were playing in and out of the water while the larger seals rolled laboriously along a rocky shelf. Occasionally they would slither into the water and swim beneath it with stunning swiftness, then resurface and nudge the younger ones back toward the safer confines of the rocks.

The signposts on the outskirts of Graymouth suggested a plethora of activities for tourists, from kayaking and horse riding to gold mining at an authentic shantytown. She knew Carl was involved in promoting some of these activities with the travel business he was working for, so she quickly noted some of them and kept driving.

"Might even have time for a bit of adventure," she mused, then began humming hymns as the last few miles passed quickly, and she was soon pulling into the driveway of a small, pale-pink weatherboard cottage with white-painted wooden joinery.

A car was already parked in the driveway, and as she turned off the engine a tall blond man in a denim shirt and jeans came out the front door and loped down the three concrete steps in one stride.

"Meredith . . . I'm Carl. I'm so glad you could come down. Charise is so excited to see you." The distinctive accent and the enthusiastic way he shook her hand took Meredith briefly by surprise. She'd forgotten Charise had married an American. Carl nodded toward the car. "I'll get your bags in a minute. Charise said to bring you straight in."

They walked straight into a tiny lounge with one chair and a two-seater couch, and Carl opened the door to an even smaller bedroom and motioned her in.

"Meredith! You are an angel! Come here and give me a hug!"

Charise struggled to raise herself off the mass of pillows that was supporting her, then fell back awkwardly as the heavy plaster cast on her leg caught on the sheets.

"Stay still!" Meredith rushed around and gave her cousin a tight hug before standing up with a frown on her face. "Nobody mentioned a broken leg."

"That's because it's only my leg." Charise grinned and patted the slight mound of her tummy beneath the bed covers. "Junior here is the one causing all the problems. He can't decide if he likes his new home or not and he keeps threatening to leave."

Her tone was deliberately lighthearted, but Meredith could detect the anxiety in her voice and the slight frown on Carl's face as he watched his wife.

"Well, if I know you and the speed you operate at, he's probably been holding on for dear life since he was conceived." Meredith sat down cautiously on the edge of the bed. "And do you know for sure if he's a 'he'?"

Charise nodded and she was suddenly serious. "I had to have a scan to see if everything was all right after I fell and there was a bit of telltale evidence. He's definitely a 'he.'"

"So, is he settling down? What does the doctor say?"

Carl sat down on the other side of the bed and took hold of Charise's hand. "The placenta tore away a bit when Charise fell, so they're concerned he's not getting fed properly. They've told her to get total bed rest, but she keeps wanting to 'just hop up and do things' as soon as I've left the house."

Meredith stood up and crossed her arms. "Well, she won't be doing much 'hopping' now. Give me a quick tour of the house and I'll be your resident sergeant major from now on."

Charise glanced at her husband and gripped his hand dramatically. "Please, don't leave me, Carl. She's scary when she gets a project."

"Good." Her husband grinned and gave her a quick kiss on the forehead. "I'll show Meredith around, which should take at least ninety seconds, and bring her gear in. And then I have to be at the office within half an hour."

"That'll be fine." Meredith was already walking out the door. "I so need something to do."

* * *

"I feel such a dummy," Charise said as she eased herself out of bed later that afternoon. She reached for the crutches leaning against the wall, and suddenly held onto her stomach, grimacing. "Yep, he's there all right."

"Are you okay?" Meredith was immediately by her side.

"Oh, yes. That was one of the good twinges." Charise grinned. "Those are the movements I like to feel because at least he's moving."

"You're going to have to get me up-to-date with all these baby things, because I have absolutely no idea." Meredith held Charise's elbow to help her to her feet. "I haven't even been part of Wendy's pregnancies because I've been away at school, so this is all foreign territory."

"Great," Charise giggled. "Good job on not sending references to get this one."

They laughed as they made their way slowly to the bathroom and back again. Then as Meredith settled her back into bed, Charise looked suddenly serious.

"I really do appreciate your coming so quickly, Meredith. Poor Carl was at his wit's end trying to be nursemaid and run the office." She ran her hands down the bed covers. "He's such a good person."

"I got that impression already." Meredith nodded. "But who'd have thought my cousin would end up marrying an American?"

"Not me, for certain." Charise smiled. "I was always going to marry a high-country farmer and raise sheep and heaps of children."

"And you got an American businessman with a taste for adventure." Meredith thought about the work that Carl had brought home the night before and left scattered on the kitchen table, showing all the tourist adventures his company was initiating around the South Island.

"Funny that." Charise pointed at a group of photo frames on the dresser. "Carl's brother is going to marry the high-country farmer instead. The picture on the end is his brother Wade, and Wade's fiancée, Mackenzie."

Meredith picked up the photo. "Oh, my goodness—he's so like Carl! Are they twins?"

"No, just very close. Wade works for the family woolens business back in America."

"But his fiancée is from here?" Meredith peered more closely at the photo. "She looks lovely."

"She is. From a beautician's point of view she's a dream, but she's really down-to-earth."

"Is she a member?"

"She is now." Charise pointed at a wedding photo of her and Carl. "Did Auntie Nan not mention that Wade baptized her the morning of our wedding?"

"Oh, I do remember." Meredith laid the photo frame in her lap. "I'm really sorry I never came to your wedding, Charise. It's one of those decisions I'll always regret."

Neither girl spoke for a moment. Charise laid her head back against the pillows. "I did really miss you, but I figured you had a good reason."

Meredith shook her head. "No, there wasn't a good reason—more like a bad reason. I just didn't feel worthy to be down there . . . at the temple . . . even on the temple grounds. And I knew all the relatives would be looking at me and wondering when I was going to get back to church. So, I just worked longer hours that weekend and justified my absence that way."

"But Dad says you're planning to go on a mission now." Charise frowned, then she folded her arms over her rounded belly. "I am so glad you're here for a few weeks. It's going to take us that long to catch up."

CHAPTER 22

Meredith stood for a long time in front of the shop window, as she had several times before in the last three weeks. The shop front was not ostentatious. In fact, there were just a few glass shelves running the length of the window, with rectangular pieces of board covered in cream velvet propped on each shelf. It was the exquisite jewelry hanging on the boards that provided the eye-catching display.

She had discovered the little shop in a side street on one of her frequent walks to the beach. The slightly weathered appearance of the shop's exterior had not warranted a second look, but on her third walk past, Meredith had noticed the very large rock in variegated shades of green and gray in the corner of the window display.

It was a piece of natural greenstone found on the riverbed just out of town, but the interesting part for Meredith was the way the display detailed the cutting and carving of the rock to produce the rows of finely crafted green jewelry that were beautifully accentuated on the cream boards.

"Pounamu . . . New Zealand greenstone or jade." She read the handwritten display cards, then moved along to the board that had kept her attention over several visits. It held four pendants, each hanging from a fine length of black, waxed cord. One was shaped like a hook, the next a uniquely twisted shape, and the third a more ornately carved rounded hook.

"Hei matau . . . strength, determination and peace—two lives becoming one. Manaia . . . sky, earth, and sea." She whispered the Maori names, enjoying the sound. Then she nodded as she looked at the last pendant. "Koru . . . new beginnings."

The pendant was a beautifully carved spiral, the highly polished greenstone forming a smooth, flat disc with perfectly rounded curves that diminished from the outside to a tightly curved point in the center. There were no finely detailed Maori designs as on the other pieces, as the stone itself provided a contrast of light to dark in its spiral.

"New beginnings," Meredith repeated, and with a nod of resolve, she pushed open the door of the shop.

* * *

Grant rested his head on his hand and tried to concentrate as another burst of laughter sounded in the reception area, followed by Charles's deep tones elaborating on yet another issue that he obviously had an opinion on. Since he had begun work less than a week before, he'd managed to turn the normally subdued atmosphere of Bascombe and Bascombe into more of a vaudeville show. Even Stella had succumbed to his charm.

"Well, let him discover that he can't just make people happy in a court of law," Grant muttered as he stood up to close the door. "He might actually have to practice being a lawyer sometime."

Just as he reached for the doorknob, Charles swung past him and dropped his expensively dressed length into one of the lounge chairs beside Grant's desk. Somehow, despite returning from Europe in a penniless state, he'd still managed to turn up at the office looking as sophisticated as ever.

"Can I help you?" Grant remained standing by the door.

"Actually . . . I think I need to help you." Charles eased himself farther down the couch and crossed his legs at the ankles. "What exactly happened between you and Meredith?"

For a split second Grant looked taken aback. Then he folded his arms.

"Truthfully . . . nothing. Not that it's any of your business."

"Of course it's my business. I recommended her," Charles responded easily, unperturbed by Grant's abrupt reply. "The thing is . . . Uncle Frank says that you two were going out but that you decided on an amicable business relationship, and then she left."

"That's about it." Grant nodded. "And as I told Dad—case closed."

"I'm afraid that's not good enough." Charles was unexpectedly serious as he stared at his cousin. "What actually happened, Grant? What's your side of the story? And don't beat about the bush."

"My side? My side is that basically . . . Meredith was a very good lawyer and we enjoyed a good working relationship. There was some personal attraction, and we took it a bit farther but . . ." He paused, suddenly beset by a very distinct image of Meredith running along the beach, laughing and reaching for his hand, her hair lifting off her shoulders in the wind.

"But?" Charles asked abruptly. "But what? Why did it stop?"

"I . . . we . . ." Grant tapped his fingers against his arm. "We just couldn't see eye to eye on some things . . . like religion. Legally speaking—conflicting beliefs creating irreconcilable differences."

Charles was silent for a long time. Then he slowly stood up and shook his head.

"I've always admired you, Grant. You've always been the sensible older cousin, and even though I probably don't show it, I've really appreciated how you've watched out for me since we were little. I've sometimes felt like you always helped me, and what could I ever do for you?" He pointed a long finger directly at Grant's chest, his tone firm and determined. "Now I've got the opportunity to stop you from making a very, very big mistake."

He paused, but when there was no response, he held up the fingers of one hand and began to systematically count them off with the other.

"First, Meredith Winstone is a great person. She's honest, reliable, smart to the point of ludicrous, gorgeous-looking, and completely immune to my sort of charm." He chuckled dryly. "I just thought that would be an added benefit from your point of view."

When Grant didn't even smile, he shook his head and continued to count off again. "Second, from what I understand from Uncle Frank and Stella, she's been pretty up-front about her religious beliefs and she's only ever tried to help you—especially concerning Hannah and Emily. I mean, seriously, Grant. Most women who might be interested in you would be trying to make you forget your first wife."

"It's nice to hear that you've been discussing my affairs behind my back." Grant clenched his jaw, but his anger was lost on Charles.

"You know, Grant, I may be leaping to the wrong conclusions here, but I really think you've mucked this up. You're meant to be the big-gun investigative lawyer, and yet I don't think you've really tried to find out what Meredith believes. Whatever happened to researching the evidence properly? What sort of lawyer are you, anyway?"

"Obviously a pretty pathetic one, from your point of view," Grant responded quickly, stung by his cousin's comments.

"Then maybe I should rephrase the question. What sort of man are you—to just give up on this sort of opportunity?" Charles's voice dropped. "I know you've been hurt, Grant—beyond what I can even begin to comprehend. But I really think that if there's a glimmer of hope here, then you should pursue Meredith as if your life depended on it."

* * *

"I'm thinking I'll just stay in bed and pretend to be sick—then you'll stay longer." Charise stood up without any assistance. "But it's so good to be actually moving again."

"Both of you." Meredith pointed at Charise's stomach. "I swear that child has doubled in size in six weeks."

"It certainly feels like it." Charise puffed out her cheeks and glanced at her husband. "What's it like to be married to a whale?"

Carl stood behind and put his arms around her, holding her much-larger belly lightly. "I always liked whales." He grinned as she punched him on the arm. "Especially beautiful ones."

Meredith watched as her cousin smiled at her husband. She had come to enjoy their bantering and the obvious love they shared, even though at times it spurred a pain in her heart that was almost physical.

She glanced around the room. "Well, everything is cleaned up, so . . . I guess I'm past my use-by date. I told Grandpa that I'd be leaving before nine, so they're probably waiting for me right now."

Charise frowned as she walked over and gave Meredith a warm hug. "I'm really going to miss you. But I understand that you need to go back to Auckland. Do you think Grant will see you?"

Meredith shrugged her shoulders. "I'm really not sure, but talking to you two and just having the time to think has made me realize that

I left a lot of things unresolved between us." She touched the spiral pendant hanging around her neck. "If I'm going to get serious about these new beginnings, then I have to clear up the past first. I don't want to go on a mission thinking about what I might have said but didn't because I was too personally involved."

"You don't think there's a chance you may get personally involved again?" Carl asked quietly.

Meredith shook her head. "I really don't think so. I've been praying about it a lot and I feel like I've reached that point of . . . inner peace. I know I want to serve a mission more than anything. But I also know that I need to explain as best I can to Grant before I do. If I can do that, I'll feel so much better prepared to serve."

* * *

Grant pulled up across the road from the house. It was a pleasant, well-kept home with gardens that obviously had intermittent care, although perennials flowered regardless of attention around the base of several fruit trees. The driveway led up to a wider concrete area where a tall, lanky teenager dressed in an oversized T-shirt, basketball jersey, and shorts was shooting a basketball into the hoop attached to a homemade backboard.

"And that must be Cam." Grant drew a deep breath and gripped the steering wheel more tightly as he put the car into drive and turned into the driveway.

Cam was rebounding the ball at the same time the bronze BMW drove up behind him, and in the split second he was distracted, the ball ricocheted off the hoop and bounced toward the hood of the car. With a look of horror, he lunged forward to retrieve it, only to knock it forward harder onto the car and up against the window. He caught it as it bounced off again and stood twisting it in his hands as Grant got out of the car.

"I'm sorry about that." Cam peered around Grant. "It didn't do anything, did it?"

"No, it's fine." Grant smiled, feeling almost grateful for the loose ball as a means of breaking the ice. "You've got a good shot."

"Just a lousy rebounder." Cam grinned and held out his hand. "I'm Cam Winstone. Have you come to see Dad?"

Grant felt a brief sense of surprise as Cam pumped his hand in a firm handshake.

"Uh . . . yes, I have." He glanced toward the house then back to Cam. "My name is Grant Bascombe. Your sister used to work with me in Auckland."

Cam began to palm the ball quickly from hand to hand as he looked Grant up and down, then looked at the car. "Used to work with you . . . so why are you here?"

The abrupt question had an accusing undertone and Grant nodded slowly. "Um . . . I take it you've heard of me, then?"

"Meredith did mention you." Cam bounced the ball and caught it again. "She was pretty upset when she came home."

There was a long silence as he bounced the ball a couple more times, then rested it on his hip. "If you're looking for her, you're too late. She's been gone for weeks."

"Gone?" Grant felt his mouth go dry and he cleared his throat. "Where has she gone to?"

"Down south," Cam answered briefly, then nodded toward the house. "Maybe you'd better talk to Mum and Dad . . . although I'm not sure they'll be that happy to see you either."

* * *

Meredith ended up spending the next week in Christchurch visiting her grandparents. Her initial resolve to just say hello and move on was completely undermined when she saw how much her grandmother had changed since she'd seen her nearly a year before. The vibrant yet stoical woman had dimmed to a mere shadow of her former self, both in physical stature and personality, and Meredith found it difficult to reconcile her childhood memories of Grandma Harvey with the frail woman who now clung to her husband's hand and looked blankly alarmed if he left her for very long.

She spent long hours over the next few days sitting with her grandmother in the bright sunroom in her uncle's home, reading to her and going through photo albums. At times, Grandma's memory was excellent, and then within minutes, it was if she were talking to a stranger.

On the fifth morning, Meredith carried a breakfast tray into the sunroom and set it down on the table between them.

"Would you like some toast and orange juice, Grandma? I squeezed the juice just now from the oranges on Uncle Rob's trees, so it's as fresh as you can get."

Grandma Harvey stared at the tray. Then she smiled brightly and immediately folded her hands in her lap and quietly blessed the food even before Meredith had sat down.

"Thank you, dear. I get so spoilt these days." She grinned impishly. "Maybe getting old isn't so bad after all. Your grandfather keeps telling me that being looked after is my reward for doing it for everyone else for years."

She bit delicately into the marmalade toast and chewed happily for a moment before picking up the glass of juice. Suddenly she set the glass down again and peered past Meredith toward the doorway. "But where's your husband, dear? Isn't he coming?"

Meredith stopped chewing and looked back over her shoulder, unsure what to say.

"We'd better leave him some toast, hadn't we? Men get so much hungrier than we ladies." Grandma deliberately set aside two pieces of toast, then pointed to Meredith. "You need to look after him well and he'll treat you well."

"Um . . . Grandma . . . I'm not married." Meredith swallowed her mouthful. "You're thinking of Charise. She's married to Carl."

Her grandmother frowned slightly, then she put one finger to her lips. "Whoops, how silly of me. So where's your young man, dear? Is he coming later?"

"Actually, I don't have a young man, Grandma." She stared at the tray of food and muttered, "At least . . . not anymore."

"What's that, dear? Please don't mumble. Old ears can't hear as well as they should." Grandma Harvey patted her ear. "So . . . where is he?"

Meredith sighed and smiled. "I don't have a young man anymore, Grandma."

"But why not?" Grandma looked puzzled. "You're a beautiful, smart young woman."

"Sometimes that isn't enough." Meredith shrugged sadly, unsure how much her grandmother would comprehend if she tried to elaborate.

"Did you love him, Meredith?" Grandma's voice was surprisingly soft and knowing as she reached out and laid her wrinkled hand over Meredith's.

"Yes . . . yes I did, Grandma . . . very much."

"Do you still love him, child?"

Meredith stared at the myriad lines and creases on her grandmother's hand. The darkened sun spots had blended together in places to form large shadowy patches. She finally looked up with tears in her eyes.

"Yes, Grandma . . . I do love him, but it's too late now."

"It's never too late, my dear." Grandma gave her hand a very firm squeeze. "Why, if I'd had that attitude, none of you children would have existed. Sometimes a good woman needs to let a good man know how good she is—for him."

"You mean Grandpa—"

"Needed a little encouragement." Grandma nodded and smiled coyly again. "A few times. But it was worth it. At the time I could've just walked away because I didn't think I was worthy of him. But then I look at all you beautiful children . . . I'm so glad I got over that feeling."

"Oh, Grandma. Thank you so much." Meredith leaned over and hugged her grandmother tightly for a long time, suddenly aware of the bony shoulders and thin, wispy white hair. For just a few minutes she had been talking to the old Grandma, the one who had been fun, strong-willed, forthright, and cuddly all at the same time when she'd been growing up. "You are such an angel."

"Angel? What angel? I'd like to see an angel." Grandma stared blankly past Meredith. "Have you brought your baby to see me?"

Meredith sighed and smiled as she stood up. If only for the briefest moment, her grandmother had provided an insight that made many things clearer in her mind. She reached out and stroked the soft, white hair. Grandmothers were such a blessing . . . even if they didn't know it.

* * *

Grant stood in front of the piano and gently tipped the tiny rocking chair with his finger. It rocked back and forth, then stopped, so he touched it again.

"No empty chairs." He could hear Meredith's voice as he recalled their conversation, and he smiled. It was so easy to imagine her here in her own home, where her mannerisms were duplicated by her parents and brother. None of them were exactly alike, but sometimes when one of them laughed or frowned or quickly interrupted with their opinion, it was almost like she was in the room.

"Do you want some dessert, Grant?" Nan spoke quietly behind him, and when he turned she was holding out a dessert bowl full of steaming fruit sponge and ice cream. "Stewart and I thought we'd just have some here in the lounge tonight."

Grant took the bowl and patted his stomach. "It's probably a good thing I have to leave tomorrow. Your cooking is really bad for my resolve."

"Time enough for resolve when you're back at work." Stewart settled himself onto the couch with a bowl in either hand. "Here you are, love."

Nan sat down beside him and glanced at his full plate. "Did you leave any for Cam? He's always so hungry when he gets home from Young Men's."

"There's plenty." Stewart took a mouthful, then motioned to Grant to sit in the chair opposite him. "So, Grant . . . any more questions?" He chuckled. "I must confess I've been enjoying the last few weeks. First Meredith came home and began to ask me all sorts of gospel questions, and then you arrive and want to know even more. It's just a wonderful feeling to be able to share all the knowledge that I've been accumulating all these years. I feel like I'm on a mission."

Grant nodded. "You've surely helped me understand a lot. I guess Telesia knew what she was talking about when she told me to come and visit you instead of just phoning to find out where Meredith was."

"I think it was very brave of you, dear." Nan smiled. "First of all to come, and then to have to break down the family defenses—especially Cam's."

Grant grinned. "I didn't think he was even going to let me in the door. As soon as I said my name the BMW didn't mean a thing."

"But he's fine now . . . just as we are." Stewart played with the dessert spoon in the bowl. "Is there anything else we need to clear up, though?"

Grant nodded as he carefully placed the empty bowl on the floor and rested his elbows on the arms of the chair. "There is maybe just one more thing. I was thinking last night about the temple." He shook his head. "It still feels strange to be talking like this . . . but, I was wondering . . . I mean, I understand about marriage in the temple being for eternity. The way you've explained it really makes sense."

"I think the problem was that, before, you were looking at the end result before you understood the first steps," Stewart interjected quietly. "You needed to understand about Joseph Smith and how that truth was restored first . . . and why it is so necessary for families to be sealed together so they can progress."

"It certainly helped to get the whole picture." Grant shook his head. "I'm afraid Meredith did try to explain, but I just cut her off. I really felt that I didn't need to hear all those things at my age."

"And how do you feel now?" Nan rested her hand against her husband's knee. "Does it feel right knowing what we understand about Jesus Christ and Heavenly Father and the Atonement?"

Grant took a deep breath and clasped his hands together, looking straight at them.

"A week ago I came down here knowing about the Church and the beliefs but . . . after all our talks I can say that I feel that I under-stand—really understand—what Meredith was trying to tell me." He pulled a face. "When you asked me to say prayers with you all that first night . . . I admit I did it because I wanted to impress you that I was serious about being here."

"I got that impression." Stewart nodded as Nan glanced at him. "I even said as much to Nan when we went to bed."

"He did . . . but we were so pleased that you would." Nan spoke quickly. "Do you feel more comfortable now?"

Grant nodded slowly. "I can't believe I'm saying it, but I even said my own prayers the other night. I compromised a bit at first . . . just down on one knee, but by the time I finished I really felt like I was talking to someone." He shook his head as tears began to well up. "I've pled before . . . when my daughter was dying in my arms . . ."

"And you're still bitter about that?" Stewart leaned forward. "Sometimes it's difficult to think about praying to a God whom you think has deserted you before."

Grant looked surprised. "That's exactly what I was thinking when I went to pray. It was all right when you two were saying the prayers, but when it came down to one-on-one . . . I just couldn't stop feeling that He'd let me down before, so what good was it going to do me now?"

"Do you still feel like that?" Nan rolled her fist into a ball as she waited for Grant to reply.

Grant sat for a long time. When he finally shook his head, she leaned back against her husband and rested her head against his shoulder.

"It took a long time to get onto both knees." Grant wiped his eyes with the palm of his hand. "And for ages I couldn't think of anything to say. It was like if I began, then it was all over—everything I've ever known as normal."

"But you did begin," Stewart stated flatly.

"As soon as I got past saying 'Heavenly Father'. . ." Grant cupped his head in his hands and took a while to continue. "As soon as I did that, I had the most unreal feeling of peace, and then it was like I could see . . . like I could see Emily—only she was older." His shoulders shook. "She was so beautiful."

Nan moved forward, but her husband restrained her with a slight pressure on her arm.

"Was that all you saw, Grant?" Stewart spoke softly and waited as Grant shook his head.

"No . . . I thought I could see Hannah . . . and Mum." He smiled and nodded. "They looked happy—really happy—and then they were gone."

"And was it easier to pray after that?"

Grant gave a short laugh and wiped his eyes. "I couldn't stop. It was like I was talking to them and God and everybody . . . ." He looked up with a slight frown. "Do you think I really did see them, or was I just fantasizing?"

"I think you saw exactly what you were meant to see." Stewart smiled. "When we talked about impressions of the Spirit the other night, I could sense you were a bit skeptical. Maybe you believe me now?"

Grant drew a deep breath and exhaled very slowly.

As he watched Grant visibly relax, Stewart lowered one eyebrow. "I said before that I've had some very good doctrinal talks with Meredith lately. She may have lost her way for a bit, but she's certainly making up for lost time. She kept asking me questions until I felt like I was in a courtroom." He hesitated and squeezed his wife's shoulder. "I think she's going to make an excellent missionary."

He deliberately avoided Nan's quick look as Grant stared at his hands, then looked up, staring straight at both of them.

"Mr. and Mrs. Winstone . . ." He licked the side of his mouth. "I've got to tell you . . . I've been thinking about it a lot and . . . I really don't want Meredith to go on a mission."

* * *

Meredith traveled at a leisurely pace back up the east coast of the South Island, stopping briefly in Wellington before the final, long drive back to Auckland, only pausing a few times for refreshments.

Passing through one town in the center of the North Island, she slowed as a pair of young missionaries rode past on their bikes, their white shirts and dark ties and trousers a distinctive contrast to the green trees and hills behind them. They smiled and waved to acknowledge her slowing for them, and she quickly raised a hand in response.

That could be me in a few weeks. She swallowed hard with firmer resolve. *That WILL be me in a few weeks. After I've spoken to Grant and told him exactly what he needs to know—what I didn't explain properly before.*

As the first outlines of Auckland city appeared over the crest of the Bombay Hills, her hands tightened on the steering wheel.

"Okay . . . Heavenly Father . . . I have faith that I'm doing the right thing. I know I don't have the perfect knowledge, but I know enough now to help Grant and his family, and I can only hope that I can say it in such a way that they'll be able to understand." She relaxed. "Then it's Thy will be done."

CHAPTER 23

The black sand seemed to catch hold of the skin on Meredith's feet and inject a wave of heat directly into her soles; it lingered until she made a quick run down onto the wet sand that was even blacker.

"Youch." She wriggled her toes and legs so that her feet sank into the dampness, then stood still, letting her feet sink farther until the sand and water closed around her ankles. It was a very soothing feeling until a large wave crashed high on the beach and the water raced up the sand, engulfing her legs in a foaming froth of white bubbles and thin strings of seaweed.

She watched the water ease back down the beach, then slowly pulled each foot from its sandy trap. Farther along the beach, a man and a woman were holding the hands of a young child and letting her experience the same thing. The child was squealing with a mixture of fear and delight as she watched another wave rush up the beach toward her.

Meredith smiled as she began to walk along the water's edge, feeling a sense of freedom as the wind and sun played with her sensations. She'd been working at the bakery since the early hours of the morning, and the trip out to Muriwai Beach had suddenly seemed a far more appealing prospect than going back to the small room she was staying at in the city.

She opened the zipper of her nylon jacket, pulled her beach towel from around her neck, and adjusted her nylon bathing suit beneath her shorts. The safety flags weren't up, but she estimated where they would be and stopped to drop her jacket, towel, and shorts onto the dry sand near the sand dunes. Then she walked slowly into the tide until it swirled around her thighs.

The exhilaration of the icy water soon settled into a soothing, swelling motion as her body rose and fell with the movement of the waves. Usually the water was far more turbulent and brutal to swimmers, but today a light wind created only rounded swells that broke close to the beach.

She struck out with firm strokes for several minutes, then turned over to float on her back with her arms outstretched. Her body rocked to and fro as the sun warmed her face and shoulders.

Heavenly Father . . . I did try. Grandma said not to give up, and I really felt I should come back to Auckland to try once more with Grant. But he's gone . . . so maybe I wasn't meant to. She thought about the phone call she'd made to the Bascombe office and the high-pitched voice of a youthful receptionist.

"I'm sorry, but Mr. Grant Bascombe is away on extended leave. I can put you through to Mr. Unsworth."

Charles. She had hesitated briefly, then decided against talking to him. *Charles must have come and taken my place. I wonder how he reacted to that . . . and how Grant is handling it.*

The water lapped around her face as she spoke emphatically to the sky.

"I know I've done what I could and now I just need to focus on my mission. I feel like Mum is going to be all right, that she will still be here when I get back, and I know that things will work out for Grant. I've planted the seed . . . and it's up to someone else to help it grow."

The salt of her tears mingled with the salt of the sea.

"I just know it will happen . . . it has to happen," she murmured softly to the sky, then turned and began to swim back to shore, letting the waves propel her forward. As she stood up from the final surf into the beach she swung her head down and shook the water from her hair then brushed the wet strands back with her hands.

Her arms froze behind her head as she suddenly noticed a man sitting beside her clothes on the beach, his cap pulled down over his eyes. She glanced around, but there was nobody nearby and she began to feel an irrepressible fear. Even after fifteen years, the memory of her childhood attack returned vividly, and she turned to walk quickly toward the familiar shape of the surf-patrol tower at the southern end of the beach. There was bound to be someone in the tower . . . and if there wasn't . . . she began to break into a run. The car was parked by the clubhouse—she could reach that—but the key was in her jacket pocket back by the man. A feeling of terror began to rise in her throat and she fought for control while her legs pumped faster.

"Meredith!" She heard her name dimly but it didn't make sense and she kept running. "Wait! Meredith!"

Her breath came in gulps as she stopped, but found herself unable to turn around.

"Meredith?" Grant spoke quietly behind her and she felt her whole body shudder as, in a flood of relief, the tension released only to build again at the prospect of the imminent conversation with Grant.

"Here, put this around you before you get cold." She felt her towel placed around her and the warm pressure of his hands on her shoulders. "Were you planning to just run away and leave everything there?"

"If I had to." She finally turned. "I may still do that."

Grant stood with his hands in the pockets of his jeans, her jacket and shorts draped over one arm, his shoulders slightly hunched forward. His hair was tousled and his chin sported a layer of dark stubble, yet he didn't look tired. On the contrary, his eyes glistened as he stared at her.

"Please, don't run away—not before we talk." He spoke slowly and deliberately and she felt her heart quicken its pace.

"Um . . . I'm not sure we have anything to talk about." *Except all the things that I've been planning to say to you.* She looked down at the sand and blinked fiercely. Why was it so easy to think she could talk to him objectively . . . when he wasn't standing in front of her holding her clothes, and she hadn't just felt his hands on her shoulders?

"Well, I am sure . . . so you can just listen if you like." Grant held out her clothes. "You should probably put these on. This could take a while."

They walked back along the beach for a few minutes after she slipped her jacket and shorts on. Then Grant pointed toward a sheltered spot close to the bank of black sand and beach grass, and they sat down. Meredith waited as he stared out at the rolling surf.

"This feels a whole lot different than the last time I was here." He rested his arms on his bent knees and linked his hands together. "Still tormented . . . but a whole lot different."

Meredith nodded but couldn't speak. Tormented was a good word to describe how she felt too.

"I've never been back to Muriwai since . . . since I thought life wasn't worth living." He cleared his throat. "I can't believe I've been chasing all over New Zealand and finally find you here, of all places."

"Chasing?" Meredith looked at him quickly, then she frowned. "I'm really not following this. How did you find me here, anyway?"

Grant opened his mouth, then shut it again and scratched his head. "I've rehearsed this so many times in my head, and now that it's finally come, I don't know where to start."

Meredith felt a warmth beginning to creep from her belly to somewhere around her heart. She took a handful of soft, black sand and let it run through her fingertips to form a tiny, symmetrical pyramid. "Well, you know the old cliché . . . the beginning is always a good place to start."

Grant glanced at her sideways. "Okay . . . the beginning . . . which technically was the end. When you walked out of the office to go away on a mission."

Meredith nodded, remembering her last day at the office. "Not one of my better exits."

"But still memorable in its brevity." Grant frowned. "In fact, I've been trying to keep it out of my mind ever since you drove off down the road in that crazy little car of yours."

"It's not crazy—it's been great." She looked offended. "It's taken me all over New Zealand in the last couple of months."

"As I said . . . I'm well aware of that," Grant remarked dryly. "Anyway, after you left, we heard that Charles was coming back, so we offered him your job."

"I know," Meredith rolled her eyes. "The secretary with the very high voice informed me when I called."

Grant shuddered. "That voice has about shattered my nerves. She's taken Stella's place for a while. Between her and Charles, I've nearly gone crazy."

"So that's why you were trying to find me." Meredith smiled more confidently. "You needed my mature influence."

"Actually, no." Grant looked out at the water. "As frustrating as the two of them were, it was you who was driving me crazy. Dad had dressed me down about being responsible for your leaving and then, after a week or so, Charles turns up in my office one day and comes right out and asks what I'd done to you."

"Charles did?"

"Oh, yes. Apparently Dad had given him a rundown of his interpretation of our . . . relationship—and Charles wanted my side of the story." He smiled. "I actually think Charles might make a good litigator after all. I was pretty intimidated—so I confessed all."

"All of what?" Meredith tried to swallow but her mouth was suddenly dry.

Grant took a breath. "Oh . . . all about how you turned out to be a great lawyer and how much I'd enjoyed working with you."

"Oh." She tried not to sound disappointed.

"At which point Charles told me to stop beating around the bush and to tell him exactly what I had done to upset you."

"I think I like Charles," Meredith murmured as she picked up another handful of sand.

"Well, he's certainly been your champion. I ended up trying to describe how you'd helped me with dealing with . . . the past . . . and how we started spending time together. And then he asked me why it had stopped."

The only sound was a seagull crying somewhere over their heads.

"And what did you say?" Meredith finally spoke.

"I couldn't tell him," Grant shrugged. "I just couldn't explain. I muttered something about religion and not being able to reconcile different beliefs."

She felt the warm feeling begin to turn cold as if he were pouring icy water right over her heart.

"At which point Charles swore, then told me that I was a stupid fool—which was a bit rich coming from Charles—but he then qualified it by listing everything I was throwing away, all because I didn't bother to investigate the whole situation properly."

"Investigate?"

"He basically said that you'd tried to tell me something that was really important to you and that I hadn't really listened or studied it out properly because I'd jumped to the wrong conclusions . . . and what sort of lawyer did that make me?"

Meredith couldn't suppress a short laugh as she conjured up an image of Charles lecturing his cousin. "I wish I could have been there." She spoke to the ground, but Grant heard her.

"I wish you could have too—it would have saved me lots of miles and anguish." He flashed a grim smile. "But that's not all . . . it gets better."

"Better?"

He nodded. "After listening to Charles, I then had to hear the same lecture from my father again. Both of them made me feel like a total idiot but didn't give me any idea on how to resolve the situation. I thought about calling Telesia or just turning up at church . . . but I was too chicken, basically." He made a half-circle in the sand with his hand. "Then one morning this new client turns up. Very well-dressed guy . . . white shirt, tie . . . nice suit . . . hair short in the back and on the sides. He asks for you, so Stella sends him in to me. He was obviously a bit put out that you weren't there, but we discussed a few things and then he came back a few days later with his wife. Really pretty Canadian girl . . . quite pregnant."

Meredith turned her head slowly to look at him . . . her mouth dropping open.

"Mitch?"

"Mitch," Grant nodded. "He tells me that we've met before, that he's a friend of yours. And suddenly I realize it was the big, red-haired yeti that was hugging you in the middle of Devonport."

She felt the blush reaching up her cheeks. "He's a good friend."

Grant's voice softened. "He's a very, very good friend . . . to both of us. He insisted that I go out to lunch with them and then proceeded to tell me his story . . . about joining the Church and how you'd helped him so much when you were friends back at the surf club."

"He was the one who helped me, and I couldn't believe it when he told me that he's a member now," Meredith responded quietly. "It was amazing."

"The upshot of it was that they invited me to their home a few times. The second time he let the real bomb drop . . ." He paused for a moment until Meredith realized what he meant.

"Oh . . ." She slowly made a fist in the sand. "He was the lifeguard."

"He was THE lifeguard." Grant let out a low whistle. "Nothing could have prepared me for that one . . . and it knocked me for six. I won't go into any details, but it seemed like everything—Hannah, Emily, you, Mum—it all just came and hit me between the eyes." He shook his head. "I was a mess . . . but Mitch and Sharon were great. We ended up talking till about three in the morning. And then they invited me to church the next day."

Meredith's hands went completely motionless by her sides. The only movement was the tear that began to run down her cheek. If Grant noticed, he didn't say anything, but she felt his hand gently cover hers in the sand.

"They kept asking me 'round and we'd talk . . . about all the things you'd been trying to tell me."

"Which I didn't explain very well," she commented hoarsely.

"Which I didn't listen to very well," Grant amended. "I guess I just got confused. I was trying to forget and move on, and you were telling me to remember and move on . . . but I didn't know why—or how. I just wanted to be with you, but you were somehow putting all these conditions on everything. I just got really defensive."

"Do you understand now?" She was almost reluctant to ask.

"Much more . . . although I still have to stop and wonder at it all sometimes." He smiled. "You probably don't realize how huge the concept is when you've lived with it all your life."

Meredith nodded. "I think I do now. When I was staying with my cousin I told her how frustrating it was . . . that I could see so clearly what I wanted you to know and yet I found it so difficult to explain. She made the comment that her brother-in-law, Wade, had the same problem when he fell in love with his fiancée . . . he'd just get tongue-tied because he wanted so much for Mackenzie to under- stand." She smiled. "Charise and their families had to help him out as well. They were the ones that ended up teaching Mackenzie."

Grant tightened his grip on her hand. "Well, it does make a difference when other people reinforce what you're saying. Your dad really helped a lot."

"My dad?" Meredith's head jerked up and she frowned at him. "What has my father got to do with this?"

Grant didn't answer immediately. He stood up and brushed the sand off his trousers, then held his hand out to her. "Let's walk . . . there's still quite a bit more to tell."

As he helped her to her feet he noticed the greenstone pendant hanging around her neck and touched it with his finger. "This is beautiful. I don't remember seeing it before."

Meredith immediately reached up and unconsciously rubbed her finger over the smooth jade spiral. "I . . . didn't have it before. I just got it in Hokitika. It's a koru." She hesitated. "It stands for . . . for new beginnings."

She bent her head as she clenched her hand around the pendant and took a deep breath, unable to look straight at Grant.

She barely heard him murmur, "Good choice," as they walked down the slight rise from the sand dune and headed toward the northern end of the beach. Neither spoke for a while, and Grant reached for her hand again. She didn't pull away, but the other hand played absently with the greenstone.

"Anyway . . . I told you I've done a few miles. After a few weeks up here being chastised by my family, I decided—with a bit of encouragement from them—to come and find you. Telesia said you were with your family in Taranaki."

"Telesia?"

Grant nodded. "Um . . . I saw her at church. I was going to phone you until she told me, very bluntly, that I needed to go and visit your family."

"Oh, my goodness." Meredith rubbed her forehead. "I think I'm definitely dreaming."

She felt her hand squeezed tightly as if in assurance that she wasn't. Then Grant laughed. "Anyway, I think I know where you get your litigating abilities from. Your father and your mother—and Cam—gave me some serious grilling when I turned up on their doorstep."

"Oh, dear." She closed her eyes.

"No . . . it was fine . . . honestly." He laughed again. "Each one of them—Cam especially—gave me a little insight into the pain and grief that I'd caused you. In the nicest possible way, they let me know that unless I was serious about the gospel, I'd better just leave you alone."

Meredith stopped and hung her head. "Oh . . . boy."

Grant swung her arm playfully. "Your parents and I had some really good discussions about lots of different things. It's interesting . . .

Mitch and Sharon shared a lot of great information, but with your father there's a confidence—a sureness—about everything he says about the Church. It just compels you to listen. Oh, by the way, some good news. Your mum got an 'all-clear' on the lump biopsy, and she's just concentrating on getting her iron levels back up. She's feeling much better."

Meredith stopped. "Oh, this is getting embarrassing. I mean, I'm thrilled about Mum's news, but you . . . them . . . I'm so glad I wasn't there."

"So anyway, back to your Dad's words being pretty powerful."

Meredith sighed as she composed herself. "Well, he just loves the gospel," she stated simply. "He has such a testimony of the Savior. He just can't help himself—he loves to share it."

Grant let go of her hand and tentatively put his arm around her shoulders. When she didn't resist, he kept walking with her close to his side.

"He really gave me some interesting insights . . . especially about eternal families." He put his other hand in his pocket and looked up to the sky. "Even after talking with Mitch, I was still a bit defensive about everything, but . . . after spending time with your dad and mum . . . well, it was then that I finally began to understand what you were trying to tell me about being with my family again. It took them a few days to really convince me, but . . ."

"A few days? How long were you down there?"

"Ooh, about six days."

"Six days!" She came to a complete standstill. "Six days with my family?"

"I'm a slow learner." He grinned.

She loved the way his eyes crinkled at the sides.

"Your mother wanted me to stay longer but I said I needed to find you, so she let me go. And that was when I met your grandparents."

"My grandparents!"

"And your aunt and uncle . . . and Charise and Carl. They arrived just before I left Christchurch. It was like a reunion."

Meredith covered her entire face with both hands and shook her head. "This is insane."

"You're telling me?" Grant acknowledged. "I'd be driving along for hours on my own, in pursuit of this woman who hated me, with no idea whether she'd be pleased to see me or not, and facing a grilling by every family member who loves her to bits."

"I never hated you." Meredith spoke quietly. "Ever . . . although it would have been a lot easier if I had."

"I know." Grant stopped and gently lifted a few strands of hair off her face to tuck them behind her ear. "In fact, the more I got to know your family, and about your beliefs . . . the more I hated myself for hurting you."

Meredith shook her head. "You did hurt me . . . but you also helped me realize what I wanted most. You gave me back my belief . . . and my family."

She didn't make any attempt to stop the tears that began to flow freely down her cheeks, and there was no resistance as Grant gathered her into his arms and held her tightly.

A small dog ran past and investigated them closely until its owner discreetly called it.

An elderly couple walked by with indulgent smiles, holding hands as they passed. The sun moved from behind a cloud and created a shimmering haze around them. For a while they stood in their own world until they felt inclined to move again.

They continued in silence, content just to hold each other closely as they walked. Farther along the beach, Grant slowed as they approached the twisted gray skeleton of a long-dead tree. He pulled Meredith gently toward it, then turned her to face the tide, standing behind with his arms around her.

"Last time I was here I watched those waves until I thought I could hear Hannah and Emily calling to me. It was such an easy solution to just go to them." He was barely whispering in her ear. "I hated Mitch when he pulled me out."

Meredith felt her pulse quicken, and she brought both her hands up to cover his. "The next day, when Mitch told me what had happened . . . I walked along here and I saw your footprints in the sand." She swallowed, remembering her feelings that day. "I actually stood in them and wondered how I could be so happy and yet you could have been so—"

"Devastated," Grant finished quietly, his voice rough.

"Isn't it amazing that I stood in your footprints?"

"Isn't it amazing that the same man has saved my life twice?"

"Twice?" Meredith turned her head slightly against his shoulder, and looked up at him quizzically.

"Mmm . . . the first time was physical." Grant rested his chin on the top of her head. "The second time was spiritual. And now he's my friend . . . our friend."

"I think I like the sound of that," Meredith murmured, reveling in the secure warmth of his body behind her. "Our friend."

"Our friends," Grant corrected her as he gently turned her round to face him. "Mitch . . . Telesia . . . Tavita . . . Charles . . . and family." He pulled her closer. "I think it was a conspiracy."

"You mean Heavenly Father gathered the troops." Meredith smiled happily. "He must have known you'd take a lot of convincing."

"Not anymore," Grant murmured as he kissed her lightly on the cheek, then on the lips.

"You never finished the story," Meredith finally murmured.

"I hope the story never finishes." He spoke softly against her forehead. "But . . . just to prove to you how serious I am about you—about everything—I arrived back in Auckland and Telesia told me you were helping at the bakery, so I went over."

He stopped as she giggled. "Poor Vee . . . she must wonder about my life. Everybody asks for me at the bakery."

"Mmm . . . it's a sad indictment on your legal standing," he grunted. She poked him in the ribs playfully.

"Anyway, Vee said you were coming for a swim . . . at Muriwai." He hesitated and smiled. "So then I had to face another tough decision—of all the beaches you could've picked. I had to face a few more demons driving down here."

"Oh, Grant." She leaned back and touched his face gently, as if touching him made him more real. "I'm so sorry I've put you through all this."

"No, you're not," he responded tenderly. "And neither am I."

Meredith smiled and shook her head. "I never expected all this to happen. I really only wanted to be a good lawyer."

"And you are . . . a great lawyer—and you'll be a great wife . . . and mother." Grant feigned surprise as she looked up quickly. "Whoops . . . did I say that? I promised your father I wouldn't mention that for another six months after the baptism."

"The baptism? Yours?"

"No, Charles's, actually." Grant rolled his eyes in mock frustration at the disbelief on her face. "Of course it's mine . . . and you don't have to look that surprised."

"But . . . I mean, I know you've been learning, but . . ."

"But it still doesn't compute?" he asked gently. "It is a bit hard to comprehend, isn't it? I still wake up wondering what I've gotten myself into."

Meredith watched the frown lines deepen momentarily on his forehead and saw in an instant the enormity of what he had gone through . . . losing his family . . . loving and losing again . . . trying to understand the gospel.

"You've been through so much," she whispered softly. "So much more than me."

"So much because of you," he corrected. "You're the reason for most of this . . . and I'll always be grateful."

Grateful. But conversion must be more than gratitude.

"Grant?" She swallowed hard. "What if you change your mind in a week or in a month?"

Grant frowned as he detected the change in her tone.

"Meredith . . . I'm not likely to change my mind. I've been through too much to back out now. I need you."

A lone seagull made a raucous screech directly over their heads, then lifted itself up into the sky and swooped back over the sea, lifting and falling with the current of air. It rose and plummeted several times before it leveled out and flew away gracefully.

I've been through too much to back out now. I need you. Meredith studied Grant's face and felt an immense surge of love for him that filled her from top to toe. She loved this man . . . loved him more completely than she could ever have thought possible, and wanted his happiness more than her own. Without him she would probably never have rediscovered the fullness of the gospel, but in searching for answers for him, she had found her own answers . . . and much more.

"I needed you too." She placed both hands against his chest. "I needed you to help me realize what I was losing. You say Mitch saved you, but in your own way . . . you rescued me."

"If you're trying to make me feel better about myself, you're succeeding." Grant tightened his arms around her, but she kept her hands braced against his chest.

"I'm succeeding because that's the way Heavenly Father wants it," she commented quietly. "You're a very, very special person, Grant, and He wanted you to know the truth. I was just the vehicle to bring it to you."

"And a very attractive vehicle you are." He kissed her lightly on the forehead and rested his chin on her head, staring out at the ocean. "A very attractive, down-to-earth, spiritual vehicle, who, I get the impression, is about to send me on my way."

She could feel his heart pounding beneath her palms and it matched her own pulse as his words settled into her mind. At that moment she felt as if they were one.

"I have to go, Grant." She whispered the words and felt his arms tighten. "When you talk about gratitude . . . I feel the same way."

"Then couldn't we be grateful together?"

She could hear the attempt at a joke in his voice and her heart warmed with love for him. How could she ever contemplate life without him?

"When I was trying to find the words to teach you . . . at first I tried to do it on my own." She hesitated, trying to find the right words now. "It wasn't until I started praying for help that I began to understand what I was trying to say . . . but I still couldn't get you to understand."

"But that wasn't your fault," Grant objected. "I didn't want to listen."

"I know." She thumped his chest with her fist. "But it made me pray more, and that made me appreciate how much I'd missed having the Spirit in my life. I've been really noticing the difference . . . appreciating the difference. And that's why—"

"That's why you're sending me on my way," he finished quietly.

"Not 'sending you on your way'." She took a deep breath. "Sending me on my way."

They stood in silence until Grant dropped his arms to his sides and tapped his legs.

"Wow . . . this is quite a beach for memorable moments. Remind me to stay away from it in the future."

"Grant, I'm sorry . . ." Meredith took a step toward him, but he put one hand gently on her shoulder and held her at arm's length.

"It's okay, Meredith. I think I understand." He shook his head. "I don't want to . . . but I think I do."

"I hope you do, Grant. And given time, I think you'll come to appreciate the feelings that I have right now. I prayed hard to know whether to go on a mission. And . . . even though you're here and everything is wonderful . . . I still feel that it's the right thing to do." She bit her lip. "I can only trust that you have the faith to keep learning without me by your side."

"You mean I have to prove myself." He put his hands in his pockets, in his characteristic contemplative gesture.

"Not to me. To Heavenly Father—and to yourself," she chided softly.

There was another long pause as he stared past her at the ocean.

"When I stood here—the first time . . . I couldn't imagine being without Hannah and Emily. Now I can't imagine being without you. Why does He keep taking the people I love away from me?"

She sensed the sincerity of his question but she knew it held no more bitterness, and it filled her with hope.

"Maybe they leave so that you'll be closer in the end." She put her hands to her cheeks. "I may be going away, but you'll be in my prayers constantly."

"And what if I don't measure up, Meredith? What if I don't stay the distance?"

"Then I've definitely made the right decision for both of us." She smiled and reached for his hand. "But one thing I've discovered lately is how strong our faith can be—and I have faith in you."

Of one accord they began to walk back along the beach, and although the breeze was cooling, Meredith felt warm. They didn't speak for a while. Then Grant moaned and shook his head. "When your dad said we'd have to wait a year to get married in the temple, I thought I was being sent to purgatory . . . now we're talking two years."

"Oh, no—only eighteen months," she amended quickly. "Sisters only go for eighteen months."

"Eighteen months . . . oh, that's better." Grant raised his eyebrows sarcastically, but he was smiling. "You know, I just thought about Charles—all this is really his fault. If he hadn't recommended you for the job . . ."

"I'd never have gotten to know you." Meredith nodded. "Do you think he realizes just what the implications have been?"

"Mmm . . . I don't think so." Grant rubbed his chin. "But I've got eighteen months to explain it all to him. If I'm going to learn, then he is too. That's what caring cousins are for."

"That has a malicious edge to it." Meredith grinned. "Should I warn him now?"

"Oh, no," Grant laughed and took her hand lightly. "Between Dad and I, we should be able to convince him of the error of his ways."

"Your dad?" Meredith stopped. "What do you mean?"

"Oh . . . nothing really," Grant said casually. "Except that Dad was the one who said I should pay attention to what you were saying. He thinks you're wonderful—and he also thinks that, to quote his exact words, you're 'onto something.'"

Meredith laughed, suddenly delighting in just being with him and in knowing that there was so much to look forward to.

"Mr. Bascombe . . . I foresee some exciting times ahead."

Grant nodded as he watched the wind whip the hair off her face and saw the pure delight in her smile. "I think you're right, Miss Winstone." He lifted her hand to his lips and kissed it gently. "I think we *are* onto something really good."

ABOUT THE AUTHOR

Pamela Carrington Reid loves writing romantic fiction and children's stories set in her native New Zealand and the Pacific area. Professionally, she combines writing with a bridal-design business and is currently working on her master's degree in the area of family-history creative writing and research.

Pamela and her husband Paul are the parents of five children and currently reside in the Harbor Stake, Auckland, New Zealand.